HEAVEN HELP US!

A Novel by
HERBERT TARR

BANTAM BOOKS · LONDON · TORONTO · NEW YORK

A NATIONAL GENERAL COMPANY

*This low-priced Bantam Book
has been completely reset in a type face
designed for easy reading, and was printed
from new plates. It contains the complete
text of the original hard-cover edition.*
NOT ONE WORD HAS BEEN OMITTED.

HEAVEN HELP US!
*A Bantam Book / published by arrangement with
Random House, Inc.*

PRINTING HISTORY
Random House edition published February 1968
2nd printing .... July 1968
3rd printing ... September 1968

Bantam edition published March 1969

2nd printing ...... March 1969	5th printing ..... October 1969
3rd printing ...... March 1969	6th printing ...... August 1970
4th printing .... May 1969	7th printing .... June 1971
8th printing .... November 1972	

Published simultaneously in the United States and Canada

*Bantam Books are published by Bantam Books, Inc., a National
General company. Its trade-mark, consisting of the words "Bantam
Books" and the portrayal of a bantam, is registered in the United
States Patent Office and in other countries. Marca Registrada.
Bantam Books, Inc., 666 Fifth Avenue, New York, N.Y. 10019.*

PRINTED IN THE UNITED STATES OF AMERICA

FOR FLORRIE AND ERNIE

who wanted me to be an uncle

AUTHOR'S NOTE

Since this novel's leading character and I are both rabbis, some readers may be tempted to conclude that *Heaven Help Us!* is autobiographical. Resist this temptation, please, because all the characters depicted herein are strictly fictitious. Happily, moreover, I have never served a congregation that did not enlighten me; I can only hope that the reverse is also true.

H.T.

JULY

CLERGYMAN RUNS AMUCK, FUSTIGATES 18 TEMPLE TRUSTEES! "I'M SORRY," RABBI ABEL SAYS, "BUT YOU CAN'T LOVE THEM ALL."

Y ES, I know it wrinkles the man-of-the-cloth image to fantasy neglecting the Golden Rule eighteen times in one swoop, but what the hell? Allowances must be made for ministers, especially those whom a board of trustees has just treated to a way-off-Broadway revival of the Spanish Inquisition. Like me, for example, brooding back here to the Rabbinical Seminary dorm from the Hillendale Temple, which will be notifying me later tonight whether I've been chosen its "spiritual leader." Now, after five years of divinity school, I'm wondering whether the rabbinate is, after all, a likely profession for a nice young Jew in possession of all his marbles.

I became a rabbi, as near as one can figure without that Rorschach test administered nowadays to candi-

1

dates for theological seminaries (heaven forbid an Ezekiel or Paul should slip in!), out of passion to devote myself to learning and to teaching others, as the man said, without fear of being called square, to do justly, to love mercy and walk humbly with God. The synagogue seemed the logical base for this kind of life—the synagogue, where for thousands of years Jews have come to open their souls to the Divine, their minds to the Torah and their hearts to their fellowmen. But after flunking so many congregational interviews—two in New York hostelries were so shattering that it's with fear and trembling I register at any hotel now, even when I'm alone and carrying luggage—and after tonight's fiasco, I suspect that Somebody up there may be trying to tell me something.

Happily, this last grilling enabled me to see a whole board instead of representatives thereof. The only trouble is the trustees got to see me too. One person I can outstare (just fix your eyes on his hairline; it'll drive him crazy), but how do you look eighteen people in the eye at once, while they're raking you up and down like it's a police line-up?

They let me stand in the doorway so long I expected someone to whoop, "That's the man, Officer; he's the one who done it!" And I was readying a statement when a man said, "Won't you have a seat, Rabbi Abel?"

There was only one eyeless chair present—at the far end of the table long enough to be the last mile in fruitwood. Around it in gauntlet fashion sat the trustees, who scrutinized my every detail as I bravely worked my way up the room, churning ripples of whispers in my wake.

"He doesn't look Jewish."

"So *blond.*"

"Hmmm, nice and tall, and with shoulders."

"He's sat in something. There's a big stain on his—"

"I like the way he walks."

"God! He looks just like Harry Belafonte bleached."

After what felt like a four-day journey through the Jewish bush, I reached table's end. There a mouth stood up to bark, "I'm Barney Singer, president of the temple." A massive man of about forty who looked like a pillar of the congregation, literally, he held out a loglike arm. "Welcome, Rabbi."

"Thank you." We shook hands.

I sat down, facing the board. Yes, they were still there, all those matched sets of irises; only one person interviews candidates for Secretary of State or Supreme Court Justice, but here for a rabbi eighteen people had to be in on the kill. Swiftly I turned back to Mr. Singer's horn-rimmed two eyes, which—not to press the analogy, but one brown one was slightly larger than the other—resembled knots in pinewood.

"How was your trip here?" he asked.

"Oh, fine. Just fine."

"How long did it take you to drive out from Manhattan?"

"About an hour and a half."

"An hour and a half?"

"Yes, I think it was an hour and a half."

"Strange. It takes no more than sixty minutes after the rush hour. Seventy minutes tops."

"Well, I guess it must have taken longer this time."

"Yes."

"There was a strong headwind." (A charming try, you understand, at breaking the ice.)

The room remained so quiet you could have heard a smile.

Mr. Singer said, "Really?"

Our conversation dropped dead right there. Gevalt! Had the interview been terminated because my car took too long to drive out to Hillendale? You think that's silly. Well, did I ever tell you about the other interviews?

On my first one the rabbinical placement commission sends me to a Waldorf-Astoria suite to see the vice-president of a Southern congregation. After I say how pleased I am to meet him, which retroactively turns out to be my biggest lie of the day, the man confides he's come to New York to help secure the Presidential nomination of that great statesman so needed in this perilous hour of creeping communism, graduated income taxes, mounting sex fiends, crime in the streets and/or the Negro Insubordination—the only one who can maintain freedom for America and stability for the dollar while paring welfare rolls and scaring the pants off the commies and the University of Berkeley, because he's fearless, high-minded and not one of those Eastern smart-asses. And the V.P. was speaking of none other than, as if I had not already guessed, Ronald Reagan.

Is it my fault an inadvertent guffaw transferred a sip of Scotch from my mouth to my host's face? Ronald Reagan was never even nominated for an Oscar, for crying out loud! Well, next thing I know, the veep is wiping himself off and concluding the interview (he was his state's chairman of the GOP, it turns out; yes, there are Jewish Republicans—why didn't anyone ever tell me?).

On my second interview I get a break: the pulpit committee is anxious to settle on a rabbi because they're all leaving for Honolulu that week. About to give me the call, the chairman remarks, "I don't imagine you'd object to our having a detective bureau run a routine check on you before signing contracts, Rabbi, would you?"

Benignly I reply, "Not if I can run a routine check on *you*, Mr. Ribalov." Fair is fair, right?

Mr. Ribalov, alas, didn't think so.

No grass grows in *my* head, so I go to my next interview resolved to volunteer naught but my name, profession and, if pressed real hard, religious persuasion. What happens? I hardly make it through the door. A second vice-president takes one look at my hair and asks, "Say, aren't you Whitey Abel? Weren't you a camper at Camp Cheyenne Judea?" That ends that, for as the man explains, "How could I accept as my rabbi somebody I remember as a bed-wetter?" My convincing him that Bud Schinler was the one, not I, cuts no ice; neither can my former counselor see himself following spiritually after somebody he used to wrest *Playboy* from after lights out.

Where was I?

Oh, yes—Mr. Singer and I had just finished comparing travel time from New York; now we were mulling over the results, I looking at him, and he, not to be outdone, looking at me. Perhaps I should have said, "I can even things up by driving back to the city in forty minutes flat"—but this time I was taking no chances.

Finally the president spoke up, hesitantly. "Rabbi, how about starting things off with an invocation?"

Who can deny the reality of today's religious revival? This year alone I've been invited to deliver invocations at a Little League game, the openings of two new delicatessens and the cornerstone-laying of a Turkish bath. It's a good thing God doesn't have to acknowledge each fall-up from the invocation explosion, else He'd never have time to mind the world. Yet if I declined to invoke here, the trustees were liable to think me a goy or something, maybe even the anti-Christ. "Well," I said, impulsively risking the truth, "I like to save invocations for more appropriate occasions."

Surprise, surprise! That wasn't a goof at all. Everyone looked relieved, as a matter of fact. Apparently nothing pleases people so much as not doing what they never wanted to do in the first place.

"Now that that's over with," Mr. Singer said, "let me tell you about our temple, Rabbi. We're only four years old, though this beautiful estate must have made you think we're established a good ten years, didn't it? Like most congregations, we organized primarily for the sake of our children. It was a terrible thing; come Sunday morning all the gentile neighbors' children would be asking ours, 'Where do you go? Don't you have any Sunday School? Didn't anybody ever die for you?' It was really anxiety-provoking. Or take what happened to friends of mine: their son came home one day, crying because somebody called him a dirty Jew, which his parents had never told him he was. So some of us families got together and started a Sunday School—that was four years ago. Two years later we raised enough money to hire a rabbi, and last month we bought this elegant property. It's the old Beardsley estate; he was the famous banker, you know. Well, that's how it all started. You might say our little children have led us. Don't you think that's a wonderful thing?"

"No," I said. (Using the same rationale, Mr. Singer and company could have founded a poolroom. It would have given their kids somewhere to go Sunday mornings where they would have enjoyed themselves, and you can imagine how anxiety-provoking it would have been for gentiles to hear *their* children gripe that every Sunday Sammy from next door goes to this joint down the street, shoots pool, drinks beer, smokes cigarettes, curses, so why the hell make them attend some crummy school?)

Happily, the president never heard me, he being the type who assumes everyone agrees with him, even when you say you don't, unless, to get your disagreement across, you knee him in the groin. While I marveled at my narrow escape, he went on: "In four years our membership has zoomed to a hundred and forty families. We have over two hundred children in our religious school; also a sisterhood, men's club, youth group, some twenty committees and an expansion fund. We are, you see, a very active temple."

"Your sisterhood, men's club, youth group—what have they been doing?"

"Oh, a lot. Once a month sisterhood has a luncheon, and men's club a stag dinner, catered; and every Sunday night the youth group throws a rock-'n'-roll pizza party. They sure can pack away that pizza, our young people."

"Yes . . . ?"

Mr. Singer matched me. "Yes?"

"Don't the sisterhood, men's club and youth group do anything? I mean, anything more. I mean, do they have programs? projects?"

"Certainly," the president said, and listed in book-keeper fashion sisterhood's bowling league and play reviews, men's club's World Series baseball pool and Turkish Bath Night, youth group's weenie roasts and socials, the shul's gala affairs and original shows, like this year's *My Fair Sadie*. "And then on the first Sunday of every other month—we can do this because we're still a modest-sized temple—the whole congregation gets together for a nice intimate lox-and-bagel brunch."

Could anything be more *gemütlich?* It was like Lindy's had opened a suburban branch.

Mr. Singer continued: "As for what we want in a spiritual leader, we have very high standards. You see, our former rabbi, Dr. Terman, was wonderful, very popular with the Christian community too, not only with us. Irv was a fine speaker, a thirty-second-degree Mason, a member of Rotary, and he never missed a single temple function. It was a perfect match between spiritual leader and congregation, also between his wife and sisterhood, and their four small children and—but then—" He paused, took off his glasses and wiped his eyes.

What a tragedy such a fine rabbi had died, orphaning four children. I felt bad.

Mr. Singer put his glasses back on. "Dr. Terman got a wonderful offer from this big temple in California. We were all so proud," he said.

"Wha—?"

"The second or third largest temple in Los Angeles. Naturally we hated to see him leave, but nobody expected Irv to stay here for long; he was too good. Rabbi Jacobson of Hillendale's other temple, of course, has remained ten years; he'll *never* leave. Well, to sum up—what we want in a rabbi is an all-around man who has vigor, vitality, personality, a go-getter who can sell our temple to unaffiliated Jews and earn the respect of the gentile community too."

Could the Fuller Brush Company have put it any better to their salesmen?

"Now, Rabbi Abel, suppose you tell us about yourself—your age, secular education, previous experience and such."

Welcoming the chance to speak, I listed a few statistics: twenty-eight years of age, a B.A., M.A. and Ph.D. in English, a bachelor's and master's degree in Hebrew Letters, no congregational experience, since I had been ordained the month before, a hitch in the Marines—

"Marines!"

"I told you I liked the way he walked."

One man addressed me. "Rabbi, I didn't know the Marines drafted anybody."

"I enlisted."

"He enlisted! In the Marines!" two women exclaimed, as if in comparison with that feat, walking on water were a snap.

(Was it unethical of me not to explain that I had enlisted in the Marines five years before because at that time they alone still offered the six-month escape hatch from the two-year draft? Probably. But had David conceded his knocking off Goliath with a rock had been a lucky shot? He had not, and I did not.)

Everyone wasn't won over, however. "Rabbi," one woman asked, "you're only twenty-eight?"

"Yes." That was my opportunity to say I was going on twenty-nine, and I would have seized it if I weren't twenty-six—almost.

"Only twenty-eight," she repeated, then muttered in a whisper that could have been heard by Helen Keller, "My *problems* are older than him."

Another trustee sympathized. "So's my Scotch."

A long pause. The people just sat there, becalmed, their eyes rolling ever so slightly from side to side of me.

I broke silence. "What else would you like to know?"

My query seemed to capsize them. They listed, turning to neighbors and pointing with chins. When nobody spoke up, they began to nudge one another. "Ask him something."

Finally it came. "Tell us, Rabbi, what do you think of Russia?"

My inclination was to endorse the John Birchers' contention that the Russian government was infested from top to bottom with Communists, but I forced a pleasantry instead. "Well, I prefer the United States myself."

The trustee announced to the board, "I'm satisfied." To me he explained, "You see, there was a Protestant minister here in town who was a terrible agitator." He looked me straight in the eye, man to rabbi. "You haven't, have you? Signed the wrong petitions, I mean."

"Frankly," I said, risking being taken for a wall-flower, "nobody's ever asked me to sign any petition."

"Would you have, Rabbi? Signed, say, the Stock-holm peace petition?"

"That's an iffy—which is what Franklin Delano Roosevelt used to call questions that can't be an-swered except through the benefit of hindsight (and hindsight, of course, is always twenty-twenty)." Hastily I added, "I think Roosevelt was quoting Her-bert Hoover."

"Mmmm." The man nudged a neighbor. "You ask something."

Came the next question. "Since you have a Ph.D., shouldn't we be addressing you as Doctor?"

"Rabbi means more to me."

"Dr. Terman preferred to be called Doctor."

"Well, my Ph.D is in the drama. No doubt Dr. Terman took his doctorate in a Jewish field of study, which I hope to do too—"

"His Ph.D. was in Spanish."

"Spanish? Oh. Well, Maimonides spoke Spanish. And he was a great rabbi. Also."

A longer silence this time, only now I welcomed it as a respite from questions. These were my people here, so tell me, why were they persecuting me?

"Rabbi? How do you feel about the State of Israel?"

This was like my first date all over again, with the girl asking anything that came to mind and my chattering away because we both fearfully regarded silence as something that existed only to be clogged, like a sewer. "Well, even before reading *Exodus*—"

I hadn't said anything, had I? Yet all of a sudden the trustees began to chant, "*Exodus! Exodus! Exodus!*" It was so soul-warming, eliciting a response at last, that when the roar abated, I couldn't resist starting it up again. "Yes, even before *Exodus*—"

They were off. "*Exodus! Exodus! Exodus!*" they exclaimed, as in "Two-four-six-eight, who do we appreciate?" Above the clamor rose the voice of the "only twenty-eight" woman: ". . . so I really didn't want to go to Miami all by myself, but that first morning at the Fontainebleau, walking out to the pool, with *Exodus* my sole companion, what do I see but everyone swimming was also reading *Exodus!* I'm telling you, it felt like I was home . . ." And then she asked me to bear witness. "Rabbi Abel, tell us what you think of *Exodus*."

Caught off-guard, the truth slipped out. "I never could finish the book. Since I majored in English—"

"You didn't finish *Exodus!*"

"Oh, I'm pleased it's so popular—because I share Uris's passion for the land where our forefathers lived, and my own grandfather—"

"*You didn't like* Exodus?"

"I love *Israel*." I'm not proud of what I added, but what would you have said with people regarding you like an unsmitten Egyptian first-born? "You see, I think the characters in the Biblical Exodus are better developed, more appealing, and it's better written too, the Bible is—in *some* parts—"

Mr. Singer turned from me, announcing to the board, "He didn't like *Exodus*."

Nu, nu, don't ask what happened then. Nothing. Whereas before, the trustee had struggled to fill the silence, now silence filled them: silence so deep and dead it felt like a group entombment. Believe me, at this point I'd have welcomed questions on flying saucers, the frug, the possibility of Jewish life on the moon—anything.

But nobody questioned, nobody spoke, nobody so much as spit on me. Damn! Why wasn't anybody asking about what I'd been studying for five years?

"Mr. Singer, would you like me to give the board my views on God?"

"God?" he repeated, as if waiting for me to add His surname.

"How about the function of the synagogue?"

The president stared at me blankly; he couldn't seem to place my face.

"Jewish education? social action? civil rights? how to *live* our Judaism?"

Mr. Singer shook his head. "Thank you, Rabbi. I think you've told us enough." He stood up. "If you'll please excuse us. We'll phone you later tonight with our decision."

Rising to my feet, I sank down the deep room for what felt like the third time. Now no whispers accompanied me, and all eyes were averted, like from a traffic accident that hadn't produced enough gore to make gawking worthwhile.

"Oh, Rabbi—"

Had I heard aright? Was someone addressing the pariah? "Yes?" I paused at the door and turned around. "Yes? Yes?"

A sweet motherly man inquired, "You didn't need this position, did you? I mean, do you have a large family, like Dr. Terman?"

(Some days you're ahead if you died the night before.) "I'm single."

"Single?"

"Not married?"

"A *boy!*"

(My grandfather used to dismiss his neighbors, two satyrs who lived with a succession of assorted women, as "the boys," simply because they were bachelors— and each of their beards was two inches longer than his. To devout Jews, you see, James Bond is a boy.)

I fled. I'm willing to die for my religion, of course, but who wants to be oppressed? The door behind me was thin, however, the voices inside loud, and as I tarried—not eavesdropping, just tarrying—I let myself be inundated by sound waves. Barney Singer spoke first. "Nu?" he said.

"A bachelor rabbi?" was the first response, a male one. "What could he know about our troubles?"

"Oh, poo. Rabbi Abel is right for us"—this from the "only twenty-eight" woman. "Yes, I think he's just right."

The Russia man: "But you said before, he was too young."

"Only twenty-eight" woman: "So I can't change my mind? You didn't fight on the same side as Russia during the Second World War?"

"What's the Second World War got to do with Rabbi Abel, for crissakes!"

Another lady: "I agree with Maurine Levenson. Rabbi Abel is perfect for us."

A male trustee: "By 'us', you don't mean your unmarried sister, do you?"

Some other woman: "What a nasty thing to say even if it *is* true."

Hubbub!

Mr. Singer: "Ladies, ladies, gentlemen, please . . ."

Eventually things quieted down. Things did, not I. Well, how would you like being just right for exactly the wrong reasons?

Mr. Singer: "May I make a suggestion? May I? As an accountant I always try to be scientific. Let's try that here. Suppose we make two columns on the blackboard, call one Rabbi Abel's debits and the other Rabbi Abel's credits, and then simply compare . . ."

If you think I've been exaggerating tonight's pogrom up till now—certainly I have, but within proportion—here is a list of my credits and debits, which I memorized verbatim, because how many people have been personally audited, like General Motors?

DEBITS	CREDITS
"Too young."	"He doesn't look Jewish."
"He doesn't *look* like a rabbi."	"I'm *sure* Rabbi Jacobson from the other temple is a four-F."
"Five degrees—he must be a bookworm."	
"So intense, no sense of humor."	"He looks like an albino Belafonte, doesn't he?"
"A *boy*."	"He's single!"
"Maybe we can do better?"	

"For God sake, how could
    any Jew not like *Exodus!*"
"What was he doing in the
    Marines?"
"I loved Dr. Terman."
"Where did he get that tie?"
"He doesn't seem to have
    inner strength, you know
    what I mean?"

And that's when this fantasy came to me of smiting
eighteen trustees, male and female alike. Yet con-
ditioning is an insidious thing; one can't suddenly
transform twenty-five years' indoctrination of Love
Your Neighbor as Yourself into Chop the Board Up
with Karate. (Besides, what would the gentiles have
said? Or those fretting about the Vanishing American
Jew?)

So it was back to the Rabbinical Seminary dorm
for me with clean hands, though I may yet run
amuck tonight after two shots of Jewish booze—a
double feature at the movies. Come to brood on it,
maybe that's what's missing now in organized religion:
amuck-runners—to explode this chummy coziness of
churches and synagogues, with their food-fetishistic,
social-swirling, edifice-complexed kaffee-klatschness.
This is a religious revival?

It's occupational therapy.

The phone rang as I opened my door, but I was in
no hurry to hear "We wish to inform you, Rabbi Abel,
you're lucky indeed to have escaped Hillendale with
neither tar nor feather." Nothing if not courageous,
however, I picked up the phone three hundred seconds later, when it rang again.

It was Mr. Singer. "You made excellent time getting
back, exactly sixty-five minutes. Well, congratulations,
Rabbi Abel—"

"Oh, it was nothing."

"Nothing? Oh, you mean your return trip. Rabbi, my congratulations were in reference to"—he cleared his throat—"to the board's choosing, by majority vote, to award you a year's contract as our spiritual leader . . ."

I zoomed into shock.

Mr. Singer continued, but I heard nothing until ". . . and to celebrate your election, I'd like you to join my family for dinner tomorrow night. If you would pick up my sister, Millicent, in front of the Americana at five-thirty, she can direct you to our home with a minimum of . . ."

Out of shock I catapulted. So this engagement was the prerequisite of another kind of engagement. Oh, you think I'm jumping to conclusions? You think this humble rabbi is a conceited ass? Well, let me tell you something, friend: you don't know my people. What Mount Everest is to mountain climbers, bachelors are to Jews. Because we're there: affronts. And unless I miss my guess by a light-year, the trustees elected this boy their rabbi only because a majority have girls for him.

". . . a superb gourmet cook. Millicent works as food editor at . . ."

Naturally I had to decline the position. For this I attended five years of rabbinical school? For this I studied Bible, Talmud, Midrash, theology, philosophy, education, homiletics, history, archeology, comparative religion, Hebrew literature, the Code of Laws, pastoral psychiatry? Just to get in shape for a honeymoon? "Thank you," I said, "but perhaps you should get somebody else."

"For dinner tomorrow night?"

"For your temple. You see, I've been thinking of going into chaplaincy work. In prisons or—"

There was a commotion at the other end of the phone—evidently several trustees were auditing the conversation—and I heard:

"He wants more money."

"They're very independent nowadays."

"So offer him seventy-five more dollars a year—and settle for three hundred."

"Maybe we can do better elsewhere."

"But did you ever see a *blonder* rabbi?"

"Sign him for a year. If he doesn't work out, next June we simply drop him."

Know what? Barney Singer did offer me more money, rather "a more substantial honorarium." (Divinity students of the world: forget your Hebrew, Greek, Aramaic, Cuneiform, and learn Euphemism; it's the only language. Without Euphemism in the ministry—where clergymen are "spiritual leaders," hired is "called," and "called" means either your predecessor got himself a better deal or was fired—you're dead. Or, as we say in Euphemism, you've "passed on," as if life were something you were merely touring.)

"Who's asking for an increase?" I said. "You see, Mr. Singer"—and that's when I told this great big fat lie—"I'm engaged to this girl from Westchester." Not a hundred percent great big fat lie; I was simply loose with my tenses. I *had* been engaged to a girl from Westchester, until we broke off.

The trustees reacted in echo-chamber fashion:

"He's engaged!"

"Engaged?"

"*Engaged!*"

"Sonofabitch."

Mr. Singer's response shall long live in glory, for it demonstrates how high the human spirit can soar when it doesn't want to look like an Indian giver. "Rabbi Abel," the president said, "we want you, starting August twenty-eighth, anyway." (Covering the mouthpiece inadequately, he muttered something to the board about a letter from the placement commission.)

"Well, in that case, I accept."

You're shocked? Let me explain. I am answering the call of the Hillendale Temple for one reason alone: revenge.

Perhaps also because sweet too is the injunction of *Ethics of the Fathers:* "The day is short, the work much, the laborers laggard, the reward high, and the Master urgent. You are not obliged to complete the work, but neither are you free to abstain from it." So consider this my bit to help convert the religious revival into something more than a Pax Grossinger's.

Charge!

א

——Hello, Rabbi? This is Barney Singer.

——Hello! How are——?

——Rabbi, there's been some mistake. I just got your letter about coming to Hillendale next week. Don't you remember? You're due on August twenty-eighth, not August first.

——I know. But I'm anxious to get started.

——Started? On what?

——Why, my work . . . the congregation . . .

——We agreed you'd start four weeks later. It's in our contract: August twenty-eighth.

——Yes, but——

——*Rabbi, the temple doesn't have the money to pay you for all of August. It's not in our budget, and we're so strapped for funds we may have to run two bazaars this year.*

——Oh, I don't care about the money. Let's say August is on the house, not on the temple.

——*That's really decent of you, Rabbi.*

——Not at all, Mr. Singer.

——*Very decent. I mean it. Only——*

——Yes?

——*What would you do here August? I mean, during August everybody is busy. Rabbi, you can't expect people to attend meetings in this heat.*

——Well, I can get to know the congregation, conduct Sabbath services——

——*In August?*

——August isn't a good month for Sabbath services?

——*Well, you see, Rabbi, well——*

——Who's conducting them now?

——*Who's conducting what?*

——Sabbath services.

——*Oh.*

——Who's conducting them?

——*Well, the truth is——well, nobody. I mean, there are no Sabbath services to conduct. We canceled them last June fifteenth.*

——You *canceled* them?

——*Well, look, the temple isn't air-conditioned. Besides, the children are away at camp, the women hang out at the club, the men golf. You know how it is during the summer, Rabbi.*

——I see.

——*Of course, I appreciate your offer. I'm glad to*

see you're not money-mad; too many people are
these days. But I really think you should report
on August twenty-eighth, as scheduled. You want
to start off in the temple with a real bang. Isn't
that so, Rabbi?

א

AUGUST

A T precisely the twenty-eighth of August, I arrived in Hillendale, a grassy, well-fertilized sub-
urb which looked like any other community that had
won its war on poverty by pricing it's homes upwards
of forty thousand dollars. This, local real estate agents
informed me, prohibited my living in town; on my
salary I couldn't afford it. Yet when Barney Singer
learned of my plan to live in the city and commute
to the temple, he reacted as if I were turning to
Christianity instead of to Manhattan.

"You *can't* do that!" he exclaimed. "We need you in
Hillendale for people to see." Immediately he formed
an apartment committee that combed the area block
by block—methodically efficient, Barney Singer could
systematize chaos; all he needs is to be programmed

—until they found me a local pad, former servants' quarters on a small estate, which enabled me to become a sleep-in rabbi.

It was only after moving into my cramped quarters that I learned my predecessor's contract had stipulated that the temple had to provide him with a Hillendale home rent-free. Why hadn't the same been done for me?

Barney Singer explained. "Dr. Terman was a family man, you see, and a better bargainer."

Now that there were no more interviews to render me paranoid, I found the congregation consisted of genial people—friendly, attractive, very maid-oriented, liberal, keen on golf and children's summer camps, good-humored—except for dapper Rick Adler, who dresses as if the prom were still in progress. After remarking that my sixteen-year-old green Ford looked like something extruded by a sick Mack truck, he volunteered to introduce me to the Buick dealer in town because—the well-vehicled trustee told me, very much disturbed—his own maid drove a brand-new Chevrolet.

"Ah," I shot right back, "but is she fluent in Hebrew?" That stopped him; he could figure out my *non sequitur* no better than I.

Other trustees took an even greater interest in me. Pete Schuster, for one, a muscular gipsy type, who has the self-satisfied, cruel good looks of somebody who loves 'em in *order* to leave 'em; with a sunnier disposition he'd be perfect casting for Heathcliff. I had hardly unpacked when Pete Schuster came to visit. "You have no idea how anxiously I've been awaiting your arrival," he said, and then lavished me with advice on what to say at my installation and how long to say it in; which congregants were worth cultivating for their donations; how to make ours the biggest temple in the county. "If you listen to me, Rabbi," he guaranteed, "there's no telling how far you can go."

(Did that mean that if I did not harken unto Pete Schuster, I would also go far—away?) "I'd appreciate your help."

"Good boy." He whipped out a piece of paper. "Now, Rabbi, here's a list of things you have to do—to *begin* with ..."

At the first opportunity—it arose during a meeting, when Barney Singer asked about my wedding plans; he didn't want me inadvertently to choose the evening of an important temple function, he said, like the President's Ball—I announced that my engagement had been broken. So what if it happened fourteen months before? To these people it was fresh news.

"Why did you two break up?" somebody wanted to know.

"I'm sure they had good reason," said Maurine Levenson, the temple's executive vice-president. "Didn't you, Rabbi?"

Could I explain that my fiancée and I had discovered in time that what we had most in common was a difference in sex? "No," I said, and everyone chuckled.

Laughing loudest was Dore Redmont, an easy name to remember because I'm sure it used to be Isadore Rosenberg. "I like a rabbi with a sense of humor."

"I don't," Pete Schuster said. "Watch it."

Curt Langer scowled. "Dr. Terman didn't have a sense of humor."

Early the following morning Maurine Levenson and ten other women, all most sympathetic, called to express their sincere regret over my broken engagement, before giving me the phone numbers of sisters, cousins, nieces and kind aunts. (Dating them, I suspected, would be akin to trying to make out in Macy's window.)

For the next few days, till the Sunday of my formal installation, I was kept busy answering the question "Why did you become a rabbi?"

I'm always asked that. (A thousand to one it's never asked of doctors, lawyers, accountants or millionaires—and only by Jews, come to think of it, never by nons-.) Clearly people worry about a rabbi: Does he believe in God *that* much? Didn't he know it takes longer to study for the rabbinate than for medicine or law? Couldn't he stand the sight of blood? Doesn't he want to make something of himself?

Each time automatically I thought of Zayda, Dad's Orthodox father and the saintliest man I've ever known; he knew every grandchild's teacher by name and his report card by heart, he treated his employees like family and paid them the highest wages in the industry, he could quote from the Bible and Midrash at the drop of a yarmulka. I was a child when he, a man in his seventies, left the United States to settle in Israel, and during his farewell party he came over to where I was sulking in a corner. "Please don't be mad at me for leaving," he said. "I have to go live in the Land; I'm a Jew. Soon they'll be declaring Israel the first independent Jewish State in two thousand years." I said everybody was a Jew, but they weren't going anywhere, and he told me, "In America? Who's a Jew here? Here Jews are inside-out Marranos." When I denied being a moron, Zayda explained: "Not morons, Marranos. They were Jews during the Spanish Inquisition who made believe on the outside they were Catholics; but all the time on the inside they remained Jews. In America now it's the exact opposite; on the outside Jews here are making believe they're Jews, but inside they're all of them Rotarians."

Yet I never mentioned Zayda, because even to me there seemed no direct connection between his leaving a million-dollar business to live in Israel and my becoming a rabbi. (Or was the rabbinate my way of memorializing Zayda's murder, while at prayer in a Jerusalem shul, by an Arab soldier at the outbreak of the Israeli War of Independence?) Instead I kept previewing my installation sermon, quoting from Abraham Heschel ("Where could one learn the eternal wisdom of compassion? The fear of being cruel? The danger of being callous? . . . We are in danger of sinking into the darkness of vanity; we are all involved in worshiping our own egos. . . . We are constantly in need of self-purification. . . . It is in the Synagogue where we must try to acquire such inwardness, such sensitivity") and Jacques Maritain ("Judaism gives the world no peace, it bars slumber, it teaches the world to be discontented and restless so long as the world has not God; it stimulates the movement of history").

Yes, you are absolutely right: I do lean on quotations. But they're my way of saying, "You wouldn't have the nerve, would you, to disagree with Moses! with Isaiah! with Maimonides! with Freud! For shame."

My parents drove out to Hillendale the morning of my installation. Undemonstrative family that we are, we didn't kiss or even raise eyebrows at each other; we never do. Nobody has ever so much as seen my parents shake hands or heard them go so far as to say they like each other—to this day I suspect I must have been voted into existence—except at their silver wedding anniversary party, when Dad toasted Mom with words so beautiful they sent a neighbor into the kitchen, bawling, "Why doesn't *my* husband say things like that about me, the sonofabitch!" and the next day another guest at the party brought divorce proceedings against his wife.) Mom, the only plump middle-aged woman in her circle who also doesn't sport premature blue hair, had come to kvell from her son the rabbi, while Dad, whom Belafonte resembles, was there to kvetch. "I promised your mother I wouldn't say a word," Dad said, "about what you're doing to yourself and to me."

Mom poked him in the tie pin. "Sol, you're starting?"

"Lena, all I said was—"

"Too much. You can nod every once in a while; that'll be plenty. Look, if *I'm* not saying anything—and I'm a *mother* yet—"

It was an old story, Dad's antipathy toward my vocation. He'd had other plans for me—namely, Treasure Chest, which Zayda had founded. Dad's also Jewish, you see, and it's an unnatural Jewish father who doesn't yearn to give his only son the business. In the beginning Dad created scenes that played like *The Jazz Singer* perverted. "A rabbi you want to be? What kind of *Jew* are you!" he exploded. "A Jew is somebody who's in business for himself. Which rabbi is? And why have I worked so hard all my life, building up Treasure Chest into the fourth largest independent business of its kind in the whole world? Why do you think? It was for you, Gideon, and all my grand-children you're going to give me." And more: "Did I ever say a word to you about your goings and doings? Did I? Did I ever try to stop you from majoring in English instead of business administration? Or from running around on freedom rides and sit-ins and God knows how many orgies at Fort Lauderdale in between? I did not. Because I had confidence your hormones would finally balance themselves out. But now—*now!* Throwing away the fourth largest independent business of its kind to work for five hundred bosses. With the richest ignoramus in the congregation the chief boss. The rabbinate! I can't think of an occupation better designed for making a man an anti-Semite."

I had quoted William James ("The great use of a life is to spend it for something that outlasts it"), Karl Jaspers ("What a man is, he becomes through the cause he has made his own") and Freud ("Only religion is able to answer the question of the purpose of life"), but Dad had rebutted them all with "Strangers you listen to instead of your own father? What kind of *son* are you! You know in 1942 the United States government no less gave Treasure Chest top priorities, they thought it that important to our country's defense? Top priorities, mind you, in the middle of the Second World War! It's so hard to take, Treasure Chest is? A useful business, a respected business, a growing business, a business a person can take *pride* in."

When I tried to explain that while I appreciated his generosity, what excited me were people and values, not brassieres (which is what Treasure Chest is, and not, as you might have jumped to conclude from Dad's description, the Holy Grail), he had snorted, "Appreciate? Is that a word to use to a father? Who wants appreciation? Who needs appre-

ciation? Just accept, take over the business, prosper.
Later, when you're older and smarter and a father
yourself, you'll understand things; *then* you can appreciate what I'm doing for an ingrate like you."

Where was my mother during my five-year argument with Dad (on the night before ordination, he
had taken me aside to ask, "Gideon, you're actually
going through with this?")? Also hoping for a change
of heart. Mom, you see, always wanted me to become
a doctor. When I announced my plans to enter the
rabbinate, she said nothing at first, and then, "If I
seem shocked, Gideon, it isn't because I'm not happy
with your choice; I am if you are. It's just that people
we know—well, they don't *do* that sort of thing."
Which, of course, is the curtain line in *Hedda Gabler*,
after the woman has committed suicide.

But don't get us wrong. The truth is, and I blush to
admit it because nowadays it's so way out, I love my
mother and father very much despite all my faults.
Oh, the bull sessions I've sat through where parents
were blamed for everything from halitosis to tight ids
to loose stools to orgasms of non-earthquaking pro-
portions. Me, I shep nachas from my parents (in
addition to everything else, Dad is not only his industry's biggest contributor to charity but also its only
anonymous one, and Mom does volunteer work twice
a week at the Chronic Diseases Hospital, a place I
can't visit without having nightmares), and if this be
treason against billions of motherfaulters and father-
damners, screw 'em.

Showing my parents around my apartment—that
was easy: they could see its two tiny rooms from the
front doorway—I related its history as servants' quarters, and Dad remarked, "Who was the butler, Tom
Thumb?"

"I like it," Mom said. "The grounds outside are lovely, the refrigerator looks roomy. Come, Gideon, help me unload."

Over my protestations—it was easier for me to eat out all the time; besides, there was no room in my apartment for food—Mom shlepped out five cartons from her car trunk; one packed in dry ice was marked Meat, and the others were full of enough S. S. Pierce canned goods to see me into the twenty-first century. I don't know why Jews have this hang-up about food, but we do; food is meat and drink to us, and sex too. Even in the Marines the Jewish personnel would sit around, munching salami and canned gefilte fish provided by the Jewish Welfare Board; then everyone would lick his lips, give such a sigh, sometimes moan, as if he were undergoing a religious experience. As for Jewish mothers, I don't have to tell you; they have this tremendous feeling of guilt because their breasts provide their babies with only milk and no variety.

(You want examples? I got examples. My first overnight hike in the cub scouts: we gather around the bonfire, and the thirteen gentile boys pull frankfurters out of their knapsacks. I, the only Jew in the group, open *my* pack, and right then there was nothing that would have given me greater pleasure than immolating myself, together with the marshmallows; Mom had packed two lamb chops and three chicken livers.)

My mother opened the refrigerator. "Books?"

There was no place else to keep them—the kitchen cabinets and stove were also filled with books, because my office had no room even for a window—but did that deter her from emptying the refrigerator, loading it with meat and shifting the books to my car trunk? Of course not. Then she served us a seven-course brunch, before asking to see the temple.

"Yes, we're dying to see it," Dad said, his face looking like a black armband.

On the way over, Mom gave me a run-down on who recently became engaged, who got married and who looked like she was late that month. Dad, a less oblique type, said only, "Even Frankenstein found a bride, Gideon. So what's with you?" (Parents, according to my own unpublished survey, are people who nag you to get married when you're single, when you get married they nag you to have a baby, when you have a baby they nag you to have a second, and when you have your second child they nag you to stop.)

Dad's expression gradually brightened as we toured the converted mansion. The seven upstairs bedrooms were classrooms and a storeroom, the linen closet was the library, and several walls of the first floor had been torn down to form a sanctuary that seated almost 193 people. "Nice!" he said. "Why didn't you tell us the place was so nice?"

"Who cares about a building? It's what goes on outside the temple on account of it that makes a temple a temple." (Now there was a homily worthy of Bing Crosby at his priestiest. If I wasn't careful I'd soon start calling congregants "My son" and begin Sabbath services with "Good Shabbas, dear friends, and welcome to another service of the Hillendale Temple," which Rick Adler wanted me to say in order to advertise that ours was the *friendlier* synagogue.)

"Gideon, Gideon!"

"Sol, you promised."

I took them through the kitchen and into my office, formerly the pantry. "The temple is overextended financially," I explained, "but they did assure me a window if the bazaar goes well."

"Not a word!" Dad swore.

It was time now for Mom to take my emotional temperature. "All I want to know, Gideon, is if you're happy." She's the kind who when anything happens to anyone, it happens to her too. When somebody marries, or gives birth, or makes Dean's List, or gains weight, my mother shares in the joy; and if misfortune strikes anyone, God forbid, she feels that also. Don't think it isn't wearing, growing up with a woman who's elated one day because Elliott Roosevelt just took his fifth wife and this time it looks like the real thing, thank God, and his mother is such a fine person she deserves some nachas already from her son; or who's depressed another day because Adlai Stevenson can't seem to find himself a mate, what a pity such a fine man should be lonely in addition to having been gypped out of the Presidency by some ten million votes. "*Are* you happy, Gideon?"

Dad beat me to an answer. "Why shouldn't he be happy? He has five hundred bosses to *make* him happy. That, and the knowledge that he'll always be in the wrong. It stands to reason: how can a rabbi ever be right when whatever he does, he can't avoid antagonizing somebody? Ask him enough questions during the year, let him take enough stands, and a rabbi's lucky if by June, seventy-five percent of the congregation don't vote to throw him a lynching party."

"Thanks a lot, Dad! Tonight's my installation, and already you're having me canned."

"Gideon, when you were a little boy, I was on the shul's board, and in all my life the one time I saw trustees happier than when they were interviewing and hiring rabbis was when they *fired* them. But I promised your mother not to say a word, and I intend to keep that promise." (Mom sighed.) "Gideon, you know what I wish you now, don't you? All the mazel in the world. The brassiere industry's loss is certainly Judaism's gain. I mean that sincerely. May God have mercy on you."

Mom intervened. "Suppose we change the subject now altogether. Gideon, there's an article in the Hadassah Magazine I want to show you—about Maimonides, the rabbi. Did you know that in addition Maimonides was a doctor?"

After having stayed up till four o'clock that morning, revising my installation sermon, I spent all afternoon revising my revisions, wishing all the while I could have tried my sermon out in New Haven to see whether the reviews warranted my bringing it into Hillendale or closing myself out of town.

(Do I sound overanxious? Well, I sure as hell am. It all goes back to my youth, Doctor, to the first time the seminary sent me out to preach—someplace in Long Island, where a group of Jewish families were meeting in a school auditorium until they had acquired enough members and their money to plunge into the great American religious sport of building. The service is about to start when I discover something missing. "Where," I ask, standing on the stage, clutching my twenty-one-page manuscript in two sweating palms, "where is the lectern?" Well, nobody knows. Nor could anyone find me a music stand or so much as a high chair, because the storeroom had been locked up for the weekend. But I *had* to have a stand; how could I preach, shuffling twenty-one pages of manuscript with the insertion on the back of page seven, and the asterisk at the bottom of page ten telling me to proceed to the first two paragraphs at the top of page thirteen, then return to page eleven?

"Service time!" somebody shouted, and there was only one thing to do: panic. Pulling out a grand piano from the wings, I set up shop on it, and that's how I conducted the service: snuggling into the curve of the piano with my prayerbook on top—I was lucky at that; the piano could have been an upright— feeling throughout like Helen Morgan reincarnated, so that when the time came to preach, it seemed inappropriate for me not to start with "He's just my God, an ordinary God . . .")

In the evening I drove my parents to the railroad station to pick up my installer, Dr. Isaac Tchernichovsky, dean of the Rabbinical Seminary. A broad-shouldered, erect seventy-six-year-old six-footer, with whirling white hair and brows that topped his olive skin and bright black eyes like whipped cream, his entrance into Hillendale was that of a Moses; indeed, he made all the passengers there look like a sea waiting to part before his mahogany walking stick.

"Installation," he snorted, when I thanked him for coming. "Wouldn't you think another term could have been found to distinguish between a rabbi and a washing machine?"

We all got into the car, I with a dozen prepared questions about Spinoza, Buber, Niebuhr and God. (Making small talk with the dean would be as sacrilegious as playing Ghost with Einstein; besides, I feared what Dad might say.) On the subject of God alone, there was much to ask. For the dean regarded man not only as the partner of God but His challenger, whose function was constantly to remind God of *His* function—to ensure the triumph of goodness in the world; and whenever He falters, man should take over for the Lord, who draws strength from the struggles of His champions. Perhaps—this was the dean's fascinating idea—the Lord was not perfect or omni-anything in the beginning, but is now *growing* toward perfection, which He cannot achieve without man's help; for his faith will compel the Lord's total emergence in the end. "'On that day,'" Dr. Tchernichovsky was fond of quoting from Zechariah, "'the Lord shall be One and His name one.'"

Alas, while I was starting the car, Dad jumped in with the first question. "Dean? You think my son has a future here?" he asked, as if the temple were a get-rich-quick scheme, in which case he'd no doubt offer to set me up with a chain of synagogues, and I felt like drowning myself in the gas tank.

"Mr. Abel, do you think Judaism has a future?"

"Here in Hillendale, you mean, or in general?"

Mom interceded to keep Dad from giving the dean the benefit of his doubts. "The reason my husband asks is, on the drive out I mentioned maybe we should move our cemetery plots nearer Hillendale so Gideon shouldn't have to travel so far to visit. But that's only if he'll be remaining here, you understand."

The Dean sighed. "There are storm clouds in the Jewish future, that's true. Judaism no longer dominates the life of our people, and there's no rabid anti-Semitism to force us to be Jews. Today a new threat looms: success, Jewry's mass entry into the middle class—"

Dad interrupted, aghast. "Success—that's a failing?"

"Mr. Abel, a story's told about Czar Nicholas the First reproaching the Emperor Franz Josef for emancipating Austria's Jews and granting them citizenship.

Do you know what Franz Josef replied? 'Nicholas, you destroy your Jews your way; let me destroy my Jews my way.' Moses warned that a fat and contented Israel would stop kicking, and it's true. Today we well-off American Jews are slowly assimilating—and not the best of America's cultural values, but its worst. You see what happens at funerals: if it's a plain one, as Jewish law requires, the departed will be eulogized for his spiritual qualities; if it's expensive, the deceased will invariably be eulogized for his material success. But I don't mean to prophesy gloom, Mr. Abel, not on a glorious occasion like tonight's installation. Splendid young rabbis like your son are to me what the rainbow was to Noah: a sign that we will persevere—and indeed be a blessing to many peoples."

When I parked in the driveway beside the lush Beardsley garden, the dean said, surprised, "Is this your temple? Oh, yes—there's the thermometer." He pointed to a nearby nine-foot cardboard thermometer, half inked in red, which bore the legend:

TEMPLE EXPANSION FUND
Have YOU contributed yet for GOD'S sake?

Rick Adler came running over in a tuxedo, his eyes shining more than when, as chairman of the installation committee, he had suggested staging this evening like the Second Coming, with publicity releases, engraved invitations, printed programs, newspaper articles and, possibly, the gunning down of an archduke. (His choice for guest speaker had been Robert Frost, whom he had given up on only after learning the poet had died since the Kennedy Inauguration.)

I introduced Rick Adler, who exclaimed, "Abentley!"

"Pardon?"

"Bentley." The trustee pointed behind me. "Bentley."

"Tchernichovsky," I whispered, "our guest speaker."

Rick Adler gave me a dirty look. "I meant the automobile." Before I could ask Dad what had happened to his Lincoln, the trustee asked, "Whose Bentley is this?"

"Mine," Dad said.

"It's a beauty. You have taste." Which would have been a nice compliment had Rick Adler emphasized "taste" instead of "you." To me he said, "You should feel honored. Dr. Lipton is here."

"Fine." I explained to my parents and the dean: "He's the rabbi of Hillendale's Orthodox synagogue."

Rick Adler corrected me. "No, no, that's Rabbi Jacobson—and he wouldn't be caught dead inside our temple. Dr. Lipton is a congregant, a psychiatrist, who usually comes to temple only to lecture."

Entering the temple, I was suddenly taken with nostalgia—no, not for Zayda's shul of my childhood, but for the old neighborhood appetizing store. For all kinds of mouth-watering odors washed over us from the lavish smorgasbord that was screened from sight in the lobby.

The dean could smell too. "My nose tells me," he remarked, "your sisterhood has prepared an orgy for the middle-aged."

We were approached by a portly gray-headed woman who stood out in the gathering crowd like an Arab; in this congregation, where life revolved sveltely around forty, she was some two stout decades older.

"Are you the rabbi's mother and father?" she asked my parents. "Oh, you must be *so* proud!" She introduced herself as Mrs. Greenwood, who was living in Hillendale with her son, Jerry, and daughter-in-law, Eve, the president of sisterhood, then took charge of my parents. "Now don't worry about your son one bit," she said. "If you'll tell me what his favorite foods are, I'll never let him go without."

"You say you have a married son?" Mom said, instantly alert. "How did you manage that?"

Before following the women into the sanctuary, Dad drew me aside. "He's such a fine man, the dean," he said. "Find out what size his wife is, and I'll send her a gross of bras."

Rick Adler guided the dean and me through the kitchen to my office, leaving us with the trustees who would be sitting on the pulpit. All eighteen had been assigned pulpit seats until it was pointed out that so many people couldn't fit on the small pulpit even lashed together on tiptoes, and it took only a few hours of discussion to narrow the group down to a seatable number. Dore Redmont, with the starlet's name and a punching bag's build, welcomed me warmly. "Good luck tonight, Rabbi. I'm sure you'll lay them in the aisles." (Well, he meant well.)

Pete Schuster handed me another of his lists. "Now these are the people I want you to thank from the pulpit for preparing the hors d'oeuvres, champagne punch, melon sloops . . ."

I donned my clerical robe, which always made me feel funny because the rabbi of Zayda's Orthodox shul had never worn one; the closest to it in my impressionable childhood had been Batman's cape. So you'll never see me raise my hands aloft in the pulpit: waving those black balloon-shaped sleeves, I'd be afraid of substituting "Jumping Jehoshaphat!" for the benediction.

"Eight-ten, twenty minutes to go, ninety-two people in the sanctuary," Rick Adler announced, popping into my office. "What happened to the carnations for the ushers?"

Nobody knew and he left.

Pete Schuster turned to the dean with a testimonial: "Religion means everything in the world to me. I put in more time running this temple than I do in my own belt business."

"Why?" the dean asked.

"Because I'm determined ours must become the most important temple in the county. So I knock myself out chairing four committees, serving on four more, going after delinquent members, negotiating loans for our expansion fund, reminding the rabbi of things to do ..."

Too true. My self-appointed adviser on how to succeed in the rabbinate, Pete Schuster is forever telling me how to galvanize the congregation spiritually, never to cross my legs while sitting on the pulpit nor to wear anything that isn't black or blue, and to raid Hillendale's other temple for members. Well, at least he balances a few congregants who, I suspect, regard me as their wicked step-rabbi; they seem unable to say a sentence without beginning "But *Dr. Terman* ..." Pete Schuster prefers me, praise be; didn't he tell me, "I also had great hopes when your predecessor came here, but he was such a disappointment. He was one of those know-it-alls; he hardly heeded me"?

Dore Redmont sighed. "My ambition is more grandiose. After having made it—which my settling in Hillendale proves—I want to find in temple an answer to: *Now,* what?"

"Huh?" Pete Schuster said.

Rick Adler returned. "Eight-twenty, a hundred forty-nine people here, and they're still coming. Where *are* those carnations?" Exit.

"Yes, we had great plans when Dr. Terman was here!" Curt Langer exclaimed. "If not for him, Dean, we'd still be meeting in the old firehouse. *Irv* was the one who went to the bank president and got us a second mortgage at a full half percent cheaper than any of us could swing it. Now there was a rabbi!"

Dore Redmont shook his head ruefully. "When we were meeting in the firehouse, we didn't need to raise twenty-three thousand every year above our income from dues. At the firehouse we never had to turn the temple into a piggy bank."

Everyone had a comment on that which he believed the others deserved to hear at once. The gist of the ensuing uproar, I gathered, was that some trustees claimed membership never would have doubled if the temple hadn't bought the Beardsley estate, while others maintained that without the Beardsley estate the budget never would have quintupled. Things quieted down, however, when several trustees ended up not speaking to each other. The last word heard was Barney Singer's "Some people just don't realize: the temple is a *business.*"

"There's only one difference," the dean commented wryly. "A business is organized for profits, and a temple for *the* prophets."

Rick Adler reappeared. "Too bad we can't install a rabbi every week. We had to move some sweet tables upstairs to make room for more seats." He checked his wristwatch. "Okay, line up now."

"Size places?" Dore Redmont asked, but I was too nervous to chuckle. My mouth was so dry I feared my tongue would break off like a piece of stale angel cake were I to move my face.

"Okay, let's go!" Rick Adler marched us out into the kitchen, where Maurine Levenson was asking, "You think the herring salad might turn bad with so many people warming up the sanctuary? Oh, I wish we were air-conditioned." A sisterhood member, busily stuffing something into pastry shells, prayed in response, "If only they don't drag out the service."

Pete Schuster held up a manicured hand. "Wait! People are still arriving."

"What difference does that make?" Rick Adler asked. "We don't want to get a reputation for starting our services late. Look, I'm not even waiting for the carnations."

Barney Singer called for a discussion.

During the debate I slipped back into my office to pray. Help is what I needed now, and plenty of it, for I am not what you would call preach-happy. To tell the truth, even before my experience in Long Island, I had been leery of sermonizing—no, not leery; overwhelmed is more like it. Overwhelmed by preaching, though—this is odd—not by public speaking. Addressing groups I enjoy, and the give-and-take of questions afterwards exhilarates me because sometimes I don't know my own thoughts till I hear them. Yet when I get up to preach in a synagogue—mama mía! The thought of acting as spokesman for God and four thousand years of Judaism and the prophets and ancient rabbis and martyrs, it makes me feel—well, presumptuous. Standing before the Holy Ark with the Torah scroll inside and the Eternal Light overhead symbolizing the Divine Presence, sometimes I can't help thinking that Big Deity is watching me and He's shaking His head, saying, "You have feelings of adequacy, do you, My son?" And all I can think of by way of reply is "Lord, Thou preferest *Billy Graham?*"

"Rabbi?" Pete Schuster was standing in the doorway. "What are you doing back here?"

"Looking for my prayerbook."

"With your eyes closed?" He handed me another list. "Look this over before tomorrow's meeting, will you? It's suggestions for enlivening our Sabbath services."

Enter Rick Adler. "We're five minutes late. Let's get this show on the road!"

Pulling us out of my office, he marched the group through the kitchen and into the crowded sanctuary. Comments trailed us down the center aisle, making me feel like a television set that had come to the temple on approval, which, come to think of it, I had; in June it would be up to the congregation to extend my option. So *that's* why they called this an installation.

As my companions took their assigned seats on the pulpit, I stepped up to the lectern. A hush damped down the congregation, but not my jitters. Sweat ran down my back, collecting in a pool at my waistband. It was a good thing I had prayed before in my office; with all those people watching, I certainly couldn't pray now, during the service. The weirdest thoughts kept surfacing in my brain while I led the congregation in prayer:

Where did I mislay my manuscript!

Who was banging that bracelet, which, from the sound of it, held enough charms to flail a yoke of oxen to death!

If only that man in the first row wouldn't always be three words ahead of me during congregational reading!

Why did that lady in the second row keep staring up at me like Dracula!

Did I accidentally skip a page!

Why was that woman wearing such a low neckline!

How could my mouth be so dry with my body floating in sweat!

If that kid drops those marbles one more time . . .!

She's *still* staring!

My sermon stinks.

Barney Singer succeeded me enthusiastically in the pulpit. With a reddish-brown suit encasing his massive frame, he looked like a spreading chestnut tree when he flung out his sturdy arms and cried, "Welcome, my friends!" He beamed down at his wife and children seated in his shade, then addressed the congregation. "As president of the Hillendale Temple, it is my distinct pleasure to welcome you all to tonight's installation. More about that in a moment; first these few announcements." Twenty-one minutes later he got around to Dr. Tchernichovsky, introducing him at flowery length.

The dean commented to me wryly, "After that build-up I can hardly wait to hear what I have to say." Then he stepped up to the lectern, a majestic figure, whipping his fingers through his creamy white hair. "Such a glorious introduction. I do hope the good Lord was listening. At my age one needs all the references he can get."

The congregation chuckled. I relaxed and stopped

trying to dry my palms on my robe, an impossible task, anyway.

Facing the people alone—without notes—the dean repeated some of his earlier remarks before exclaiming, "Today we have our greatest opportunity in history! For we Jews of America need no longer use up all our lives in making a living or defending ourselves against persecution. Now we can devote ourselves to our ancient covenant with the Lord, enjoining us to be a kingdom of priests, a holy people and a light to all nations . . .

"Our purpose on earth is never merely to anoint what is. As sparks fly upward, Jews are born to be gadflies of the soul; licensed skeptics and idol-smashers we have been ordained. Yes, American Jews *do* have a dual loyalty—let us never deny it. We are faithful citizens of the United States, this noble country, and we are at the same time *trans*-Americans, for we are also God's citizens. Indeed, reflecting society instead of ever-refining it would mean our spiritual death.

"This is why Rabbi Abel is joining you now: first, to *teach* you the mitzvos the living God requires of us, because 'the ignorant cannot be pious.' (Do you know, a school is considered holier even than a synagogue? The rabbis allowed a synagogue building to be transformed into a school, but forbade a school's conversion into a synagogue.) Second, Rabbi Abel is here to help you *perform* the commandments, because 'not learning but doing is the chief thing.' Or, as Martin Buber wrote, 'Judaism has no room for a truth remaining abstract, hovering self-sufficiently above reality. Judaism, instead, comprises the whole life: economy, society, state, the marketplace. And where Jews, especially the possessors of power and property, try to limit the service of God to the sacral sphere, or limit His authority to words and symbols —this is where the prophetic protest against social injustice for God's sake sets in.'

"What kind of rabbi Gideon Abel is, his actions will soon tell you, just as what you truly believe and whom you actually worship, your actions will tell him. Know one thing, however: though Rabbi Abel is a man of dedication and kindness, intelligence and good humor, he cannot serve you if you do not assist him. Your rabbi is not a soloist, and you are not his audience; he is not a professional Jew, and you are not amateurs. But together you are a holy congregation, born of Israel's yearning to sanctify this world for the sake of heaven . . ."

Finally it was my turn to preach in Hillendale for the first time. No match for the dean in eloquence, I concentrated on the nitty-gritty, announcing adult Jewish-education courses (Bible, history, philosophy, *Ethics of the Fathers*) and a social-action program to aid Jews abroad (support of Israel and combat of Russian anti-Semitism), Negroes at home (new housing, improved schools, guaranteed jobs) and other fellow Americans (a preschool kindergarten for disadvantaged children, a two-dollar minimum wage). Several noble causes may have gotten lost in my diction, for nervousness ejected my words with the slippery speed of spitballs; surely those who blew their noses during my sermon missed one project with every blow.

After the service dozens of people graciously came over to congratulate me; even more did so when the smorgasbord ran out of food. There were, however, a few comments like "Rabbi, I think you're *entitled* to your opinion" and "After completing all those projects of yours, Rabbi, what'll you do here *next* year?" and "Marvelous sermon, simply marvelous! Tonight you preached everything I've been telling people for years, and here they've been calling me a crank."

Yet it was now official: crank or no, I was the Hillendale Temple's rabbi, and these people were my congregation, even as it is written in the Song of Songs, "I am my beloved's and my beloved is mine." Hosanna.

ℵ

——*Rabbi Abel?*
——Speaking.
——*This is Rochelle Levenson.*
——Yes?
——*The niece of Maurine and Jim Levenson from Boston. We met at your wonderful installation.*
——I remember. How are you?
——*Fine, thanks. Rabbi, I haven't seen you since your installation, but I imagine you've been busy.*
——Well, yes. I'm still getting myself organized, and since the temple can't afford a secretary—
——*I wanted to tell you how much I enjoyed your sermon.*
——Well, thank you very much.
——*Dr. Tchernichovsky spoke nicely, but I thought you were far superior.*
——You're very kind, but my sermon was only a paraphrase of his.
——*My, but you're modest.*
——Nobody's ever accused me of *that* before!
——*You're remarkably straightforward, and I won't let you refuse that compliment. Rabbi?*
——Yes?

——*I'd like to see you.*

——Of course. Next Thursday all right? At two?

——*In the afternoon?*

——Well, yes.

——*But I work during the day; I'm not a rabbi. Let's make it eightish.*

——In the evening or the morning?

——*You do have a sense of humor. I prefer a late hour because when I was in Spain this past summer, I got into the habit of eating late. They eat dinner after nine in Spain, did you know that?*

——Really? Well, eight P.M. it is then. Care to tell me now what's on your mind?

——*Oh, I'll leave you to discover that for yourself, Rab. Tell me, how good an explorer are you?*

——Actually I haven't had much experience, so I'll need all the cooperation you can give me.

——*Boy, what a line.*

——What?

——*Gideon, you are one swinging rabbi!*

——Perhaps it would be better—for our relationship to be productive—if you would call me Rabbi.

——*You're very conscious of being a rabbi, aren't you?*

——Well, I am one.

——*Your aloofness now in contrast to your warmth in person and the pulpit. Do all rabbis take the rabbinage so seriously?*

——Rabbinage makes it sound like we live in a hutch. The word is rabbinate.

——*Holy hell, you even take the pronunciation seriously!*

——Well, we all sometimes make mountains out of molehills, don't we? And usually things aren't as bad as they seem, are they? And often asking for help is so embarrassing or painful that one turns on one's counselor—

——*What's with the maxims? You sound like a fortune cookie.*

——Rochelle, what seems to be the problem?

——*Problem? What problem?*

——The problem that seems to be causing the difficulty.

——*What difficulty?*

——Well, where do you think is the area of difficulty?

——*What area?*

——All right now, Rochelle, what's the trouble? Okay, *your* trouble.

——*My trouble?*

——The trouble you want to discuss with me.

——*You think I'm in trouble?*

——I didn't say that. I never said, in trouble. I'm just interested in hearing about the problem.

——*For God sake, what makes you so sure I have The Problem? Or do you mean The Curse?*

——You did call me, Rochelle.

——*Yes?*

——Yes?

——*Yes, what?*

——You did say you wanted to see me, Rochelle.

——*Of course.*

——Well?

——*Holy hell! Doesn't anyone want to see you when they don't have The Problem?*

——What?

——*Don't you ever see girls who aren't in trouble?*

——Of course. Not everyone I see is pregnant out of wedlock.

——*Oh, is that the kind of girl you like to date?*

——Date? Did you say date?

——*Yes, date. What do you think we're talking about here?*

——This—a *date?* You *don't* have a problem?

——*My only problem, Rab, is The Rabbi.*

ח

SEPTEMBER

You probably don't believe it, but that was the truth I told Rochelle Levenson when I humbly confessed modesty isn't my long suit; as a matter of fact, the one thing they were always hocking me about in Rabbinical Seminary was humility. Just because that's the only virtue the Torah ascribes to Moses—and you know what a big Jew he was—a couple of professors pushed modesty a lot, especially in my direction, so much so I feared flunking out of school for downcasting my eyes at an improper angle. (Not Dean Tchernichovsky, however; his classic remark to a classmate of mine who went around trying to outhumble Uriah Heep: "Bricker, don't make yourself so small. You're not that big.") Even the president of the seminary carped at me at ordination for not scrunching down far enough when he laid his hands on my head; we did not present a humble picture, he said, since he's nine inches shorter than I. "Well," I replied with all the good humor in the world, "you can't bless 'em tall"—which remark he accepted with growl instead of grace.

Happily, nobody at the temple seems to realize that humility is my one and only lack. Oh, occasionally Pete Schuster says, "Rabbi, you're not listening to me again," and Sam Warren tells me, "Not a hundred percent of the congregation approved of your Rosh Hashanah sermon, you know." But nobody's come right out and said, "Rabbi, where the hell is your humility?"

Then came that Erev Shabbas dinner at the Redmont's. Retribution is what they call it in Greek tragedy.

I was delighted to be asked; Rona Redmont, a very pretty blonde, is reputed to be the best cook in the congregation. The three children are bright and sweet and admire my ability to wiggle my ears and thumbs at the same time, a feat they swore Dr. Terman couldn't top. Their father, Dore, is the one who confided to me over matjes herring at my installation, "There must be something dreadfully wrong with a man whose public relations are better than his private ones! I hate my job; I hate working all day on nonsense; I hate peddling people, corporations, products—some of them noxious. Yet what can I do? I can't quit my P.R. firm, when I'm fit for nothing else, not at the age of forty-three with a wife and three children. And I'm making Rona as miserable as myself. She tells me, 'You think there'd ever have been a *Death of a Salesman* if Willy Loman had made sixty thousand dollars a year with stock options?' She's absolutely right too. I'm looking, Rabbi; can you tell me for what?"

Dore must have been good at his job because for someone in the image business, his looks didn't match the image of a public-relations man; he was as plain, dumpy and swarthy as his wife was pert, slender and blonding. Yet he had qualities which made for an attractive man: intelligence, intolerance of cant, and candor—about himself, which is a switch, instead of about others.

I was alone with Dore in the living room, swallowing my first gefilte-fish hors d'oeuvre, when he began anew: "Well, Rabbi? Have you thought of how to save me from my sixty-thou blues? I've been thinking since our little talk, maybe if I got religion, found God—"

Frankly, the man made me nervous. The religious equivalent of the mythical nymphomaniac of every man's dream, Dore, confronting me each time with ultimates alone, made me wonder whether I was rabbi enough for the job. "Why don't you do something like what my mother did," I said, "when her menopause began?"

Dore bridled. "Your mother? Menopause?" He looked mad enough to stone me with Rona's gefilte-fish balls.

Damn! I must learn to speak professionally. "What I mean is, give yourself to a noble cause. My mother, when she got depressed some years ago, she started doing hospital volunteer work. Not just anywhere, but in the Chronic Diseases Hospital; volunteers there are hard to get because the patients are in terrible condition. Since then she's been fine."

"Rabbi, I ask you about religion, God—and you tell me to become a Gray Lady?"

"That's what religion is mostly about—helping others, individually and collectively." Double damn! That was too simple; I must learn to speak more *profoundly*. "That's why I intend for our temple to go whole hog—I mean, with all our hearts—into social action in addition to adult education. If you'll help along—"

Rona and the children entered just then, and Dore said drily, "The rabbi is soliciting me for further temple duty, dear. Tell him what you're doing for our house of God."

"*My Fair Sadie*, the temple's biggest fund-raiser this year," Rona said, then reported on the show committee, which she was co-chairing with Pete Schuster, and summarized the plot. "You see, there's this Reform Jew, Hymie Higgins, who meets this Chasidic Jewess, Sadie Doolittle, selling knishes off a pushcart in Williamsburg, and he decides to teach her to speak like a Yankee so she can open a crêpes-suzette shoppe in Scarsdale. Isn't that clever? And wait till you hear our songs! 'Get Me to the Shul on Time,' 'At the Office Where You Give,' 'I've Grown Accustomed to Her Race,' 'I Could Have Hora'd All Night . . .'"

This put me in a bind. Could I say to Dore in Rona's proud presence, "I'm certainly not suggesting you do anything like *that*"? I was even afraid to point out—are rabbis supposed to recognize double-entendres?—that the cast would have to be awfully careful in pronouncing "Hora'd," lest ours be the first temple to be closed down by the police.

"Rabbi? Would you join us at the table?"

Gathering around the beautifully set dinner table, with its exquisite white linen cloth and centerpiece of sweetheart roses, we all watched Rona light the

Sabbath candles. She recited the ancient blessing over them, slowly circling the flames with her arms in the mixing motion of my mother, who always gave me the impression that on Sabbath Eve she was re-arranging the atoms of the world by hand, improving on their permutations and combinations, and by the time she'd be through praying in silence after cover-ing her face with those same hands, tranquil at last, life would emerge as it would have been had God only had the good sense to consult her in the be-ginning.

Uncovering her lovely face, lambent in the candle-light and serene, Rona said, "Good Shabbas," and all of us wished each other a Sabbath of peace.

Dore asked me to chant the *Kiddush*. I complied in exceptionally good voice, and we raised our glasses to our lips to drink, an occasion which always makes me feel grateful I'm not a Baptist, when what do I see floating atop my wine?

A big black fly.

First of all, I want you to know I didn't scream, the Marine Corps can take pride. Shaken I was, but out-wardly I remained cool as a corpse, watching the fly breast the waves made by my quivering hand. Yet after remaining calm, what was there to do for an encore? Everybody else was drinking up; soon they'd notice I wasn't and want to know why.

"Rabbi, why aren't you drinking your wine?"

See what I mean? That was Rona, a lovely woman whose personal hygiene was impeccable, dressed im-maculately herself and the children, kept a spotless home, cooked like an imported chef, and would drop dead with embarrassment in front of her credenza should I point out the fly in my glass—and that would be a great sin. No, I'm not exaggerating too much, for

Judaism teaches that one who shames another in
public, it's as if he had murdered him. Moreover, the
Talmud declares, "It is better to throw oneself into a
burning surface than to humiliate a human being
publicly."

What was a fellow to do in a situation like this,
where no burning surfaces were handy? That the
Talmud didn't say.

Well, I don't know about other rabbis, but I lie;
that's another lack of mine. "I don't drink," I gulped.
Actually, the truth was only one word away: I don't
drink *flies*.

"You don't drink?" The whole family was astonished
—even the six-year-old.

"I'm allergic to alcohol." Look, if I tell one lie, I
might as well buttress it with a few others to make it
look good and not feel lonely.

"Really?" They were aghast. For a rabbi to be allergic to wine is equivalent to a psychiatrist develop-
ing an allergy to sex.

"Makes me break out," I said, crossing my fingers.

"But I've seen you drink—every Shabbas in temple
after the *Kiddush*," said Dore, the observant Jew.

"I fake it."

"You *fake* it?"

"What I do is this—so as not to void the blessing."
I stuck my tongue into the wineglass, praying it
wouldn't hit the fly, then yanked my tongue out,
straining it through my lips just in case.

"Well!" everyone said, and, "What do you know
about that?"

After praising God for bringing forth bread from
the earth, we sat down to eat, I rather proud of
myself, if slightly nauseated. Sure, I had used up my
daily quota of lies, and the Bible forbade the inges-

tion of insects' bathwater, but I had saved the Red-mont honor. Now the family would still attend services, adult education and religious school without thinking every time they saw me: He found a fly in our wine, I could *kill* that rabbi.

The fruit cup was delicious—fresh too, none of that canned stuff for Rona, and no fly in it, praise be, though a watermelon seed gave me a nervous moment. The chopped liver was also superb, not too much schmaltz, and plenty of onions, one piece so brown it resembled a you-know-what; by then, however, I could relax. So working on the theory that people invariably end up believing what they practice, I started listing social-action projects for Dore to lead.

But he interrupted me to herald the next course. "Rabbi, if you don't agree this is the best chicken soup you've ever tasted, better even than you'll be getting tomorrow at the Evans bar mitzvah, I'll eat my yarmulka."

Rona said, "Oh, Dore." Yet anyone could see here was a woman tremendously ego-involved with her chicken soup.

"Great!" I exclaimed. "Chicken soup was my first love."

The ten-year-old, helping her mother, served me. Boy, did that soup smell *good*. Like a good steak, as my father would say of anything that smelled or tasted exceptional—whether it was fish, chicken or perfume. "Like a good steak," he would say, for he had cast his first vote before eating his first steak.

Swaying in the middle of the soup and setting off its rich golden color was a royal matzoh ball, as tantalizing as stretch pants, and fluffy too. Swiftly my spoon lunged into the broth. At the same moment

I saw something which made my stomach heave. Another fly floated in the matzoh ball's wake.

"Hope you like it," said Rona, the Jewish mother.

Now I couldn't even lie! Who in the world is allergic to chicken soup *also*, coming down with the allergy thirty seconds after his love object is offered him nakedly on a plate? And could I say, "Hey, look who drowned himself in *my* soup; what a wonderful way to go!" Of course not. One word about the fly— no, it wasn't my imagination; the fly was still there, and growing larger, it seemed, from absorbing all that nutritious broth—Rona would die of shame, and her with three young children and *My Fair Sadie* to manage. What about extracting the fly? Yes, I could do that, but where would I put it? The soup had been served in individual tureens, with no dishes under them, so if I parted my fly from its pool, all I could do was slap it down on the white tablecloth for all to see, or shove it in my ear.

There was no out. For Rona's sake, Judaism's too, I had to down the flyed soup. Yet why should that be traumatic when the fly was a good seventy-five inches shorter than I and 190 pounds lighter? Pushing my spoon at the fly, I tried to beach it on the side of the tureen. Alas, Rona used too much schmaltz in her chicken soup, as a good cook should, and the fly kept sliding back. Finally I broke off a piece of matzoh ball, lodged it against the side of the dish, forming a harbor of sorts, and wedged my fly in it.

Dore was watching me like another Jewish mother. "The soup's not too hot, Rabbi. You can eat it."

"Swell." Taking a deep breath, I exhumed a spoonful of fly soup and in one horrible gulp swallowed it.

Rona: "Well? Well? *Well?*"

Dore: "Isn't it *fantastic?*"

"Never tasted anything like it," I said. (Ordinarily I'd have asked for the recipe to give to my mother, but this one probably started out: Take one horse-fly . . .)

"You see?" he exulted. "I told you, Rabbi!"

Rona beamed. "I try my best."

"Next time," I felt like saying, "instead of Irish linen napkins for your guests, better give them fly-paper." It was natural, a snide thought like that. Look what I was doing for the woman, after all, and who would note or long remember?

"Don't let us interrupt with our chatting," Rona said. "Eat, eat."

I plugged away at the soup. Just a little more now, a little bit more; you don't have to finish the damn stuff, just about three quarters of it, then say you want to leave room for the main course and *its* inhabitants.

Six more spoonfuls now—who could bear to look? Five more . . .

Four . . .

Three . . .

Happy ending coming up . . .

One more only and—HORRORS!

Where the hell was the fly?

Not in my tureen, not any more. The matzoh-ball mooring had broken loose; it floated now immaculately in the middle of the bowl with no speck on, around or under it. And chances were, the fly hadn't flown the soup; the fat in it would have weighed down a B-52. Now *if* the fly wasn't in the soup, and *if* the fly wasn't on the matzoh ball, and *if* the fly was nowhere to be seen, *where* could the fly *be?*

I dropped my spoon and nearly coughed the middle ear out of my head.

Dore and Rona pushed glasses at me. "Drink," they urged.

Drink? In this house, whose liquids all the flies in the state used for lovers' leaps?

The eleven-year-old smacked me on the back too hard, and I sputtered to a halt. What alternative was there? Not all the coughs in the Western Hemisphere would resurrect my fly.

"Rabbi, you've eaten only five eighths of your soup," Rona pointed out. "Don't you really like it?"

"How can you ask?" I groaned. "Your soup, Rona, is an experience."

"My! Nobody's ever called my chicken soup an *experience*." Her eyes sparkled. "You're so appreciative, Rabbi—that's one reason everybody likes you."

Valiantly I finished off the entire watery graveyard. And that's the story: Thomas Becket went around washing the feet of the poor in order to teach himself true humility, I eat flies.

"You got to be *kidding!*" the photographer says to me the next morning, when I forbid his setting up floodlights in the sanctuary in order to take three-dimensional color slides of the Sabbath worship service during which the Evans boy will become bar mitzvah.

I tell him, in all humility, not on his life.

"That's why I'm here—to take pictures of the whole bar mitzvah from soup to nuts."

I explain that one reason for *my* being here is to stop him.

The photographer runs to tell Mrs. Evans on me, the same Mrs. Evans who had originally asked me to conduct the bar-mitzvah service in Mountain Tiptop, a catering hall whose furnishings she preferred to the temple's; besides, it would be more convenient for her guests not to have to traipse from the temple to the hall—what if it rained that day? the hair-dos would be ruined—and she comes to ask me, charmingly at first, to make believe we're all on *Candid Camera;* when I decline, she accuses me of being rigid, authoritarian, Pharisaic and, in addition, a bad sport.

Next, enter a guest to rage that an usher barred her husband from bringing her bar-mitzvah present, a saddle, inside the temple. This is a synagogue, I say, not Korvette's. The woman, insulted now, fishes a charge plate out of her bag to prove she buys at Saks.

Time comes to start the service, and where are the Evanses? Mother is in the ladies' room, fixing her strapless bra; Father is outside, greeting guests; the boy is at the front door, pocketing envelopes like a bookie. When the dramatis personae are finally assembled, we ascend the pulpit.

Stepping up to the lectern, I am momentarily stunned by all the women there whose décolletages suggest they came not to pray to God so much as to vamp Him. As the service gets under way, they start trooping in, all the latecomers, to catch the Evans boy's act. Clickety-clacking in spiked heels, they wave to friends and relations, pointedly avoid those they're not on speaking terms with, admire each other's attire, then sit down with folded arms, not picking up a prayerbook, and ask neighbors who had arrived five minutes before them, When does the bar mitzvah *start?*

Finally the Evans boy gets up to do his turn, chanting a prayer, the blessings, and Hebrew portions of the Bible. I follow with my sermon, to which everyone

listens intently so long as I'm speaking about the
bar-mitzvah boy and his parents. Through the rest
of my talk—about people the guests had never met
personally, like Moses and Isaiah—guests adjust their
plunging necklines, look at their watches, check the
time with a neighbor, inquire about directions to the
catering hall and how the food is there.

Later everyone recesses to Mountain Tiptop—decorated in the style of an interdenominational bordello
—where the first thing to transfix the eye is the
Evans boy immortalized in colored cardboard. That's
right, there in the lobby is a life-sized cutout of the
bar-mitzvah boy, resplendent in maroon trousers and
gold-lamé dinner jacket, and off to one side is the
photographer, snapping away at amazed guests being
greeted by *twin* Evans scions.

"Just look at those faces!" the father keeps exclaiming. "Just look at them when they see that picture!
Isn't that something?"

I ask how much the photograph cost.

"Rabbi, I'm surprised you're so materialistic," says
Evans, who can't wait for me to ask again. "One
hundred fifty dollars, and worth every penny. Just
look at their faces!"

I tell him to send me a check in the morning for
three hundred dollars made out to UNICEF.

"Why, of all the nerve!" swears Mrs. Evans, so
furious I hurry away before she can hit me in the
head with an item the *New York Times* had written
up on its fashion page that week, a four-hundred-
dollar black crocodile purse designed in imitation of
a Gideon Bible.

Entering the Mount Ararat Room, I see laid out
there a cornucopian smorgasbord of such vast propor-
tions it looks like the last supper for the whole world,

a sight as exciting as a naked girl weighing five hundred pounds. The affair is strictly kosher, so the pike is dyed pink and curled to look like shrimp, beef short ribs masquerade as spareribs, chicken pretends to be lobster, and the egg rolls are genuinely nontref. The centerpiece is a huge six-pointed mold of chopped liver, which, so help me, rings out with the theme song from *Exodus* whenever anybody takes a smear.

I repair quickly to the bar, where someone is saying, "You got any idea how much this affair costs? I inquired for my son, who'll be bar-mitzvahed twenty-two months from now. For two hundred guests—the meal itself is twenty dollars a head. Filet of prime beef costs two-fifty cheaper than filet mignon, but look, if you're going to make a bar mitzvah, you make a bar mitzvah, know what I mean? That four thousand is only the start of it." The man then goes through a list as long as Biblical begats—of gratuities, checkroom, rolling bars, bartenders, birthday cake, orchestra, flowers, valet parking, Viennese Table, personalized color-schemed napkins, candles, gift matches and escort cards, plus sales tax—before concluding: "Grand total—$6,845. And I can swing it too, provided my wife goes back to work for the next twenty-two months."

Arming myself with a triple Scotch on the rocks, I retire to a corner table, to eavesdrop on:

"One thing you got to say about that rabbi. He sure is no speaker."

"You're one hundred percent right. He phumphas."

"That sermon of his, I've heard better on TV from Dr. Gillespie. And did you hear how he mispronounced my father-in-law's name?"

"He never even mentioned how Jack got his company to donate twenty-four goose-down pillows to the temple bazaar. That's a lot of pillows, you know."

"And he certainly doesn't dress up a pulpit, that rabbi."

"He's not so hot at funerals either."

"I hear he's *death* at funerals."

"You think you're being funny? Well, it's not funny to invite all your friends and the boss to a funeral, and they all come away very unimpressed. Embarrassing is what it is. Especially when he calls the corpse by the wrong name."

"Boy, I'm certainly happy I'm a Jew."

"Why?"

"Catholics are stuck with the same priests forever."

I'm considering either slinking away in embarrassment or slugging a few guys with delight when one of them says, "Hell, we'd better not vote him down before *my* son's bar mitzvah, else Rabbi Brun will take it out on Sonny. He's just that kind, you know— a vindictive bastard." Only then do I realize I've mistakenly scaled the wrong peak, which isn't hard to do, since Mountain Tiptop's six caverns process a dozen thirteen-year-old men every weekend.

On my way to the Sinai Room, where the Evanses are making whoopee, I am stopped in the pass by somebody coming out of the men's room. "Steingut," he says, giving me a wet hand to shake, or maybe to dry. "Of Steingut and Romano. We're members of your temple also."

"You are? I mean, that's—"

"Yeah, we belong to loads. You know how it is when you're in catering: you want to give every shul a break."

"Oh, do—"

"But what I want to talk to you about, Rabbi: have

you been telling people to boycott our Mountain Tip-top?"

"Boycott? No. Why—?"

"What *did* you tell your people?"

"Only not to blow a fortune or go into debt for a four-hour—"

"Mama mía! Are there *more* important days in a family's life than a wedding, bar mitzvah, sweet sixteen? You tell people not to borrow money to buy a new car or vacation in Europe?"

"No. But bar mitzvahs and weddings are religious occa—"

"Look here, Rabbi, I want you to lay off us from now on."

"Lay—?"

"Or else."

"That's funny. You sound like one of those old gangster movies."

"Funny? Rabbi, don't you know who owns Mountain Tiptop?"

"You and your partner, Roma—"

"Nah, we're only window dressing. I thought everybody knew that."

"Oh! You mean you're fronting for the—"

"We never say that word. Just remember, there's more than one way to skin a rabbi," Steingut says. "*Arrivederci.*" And he vanishes into a crevice.

Looking over my shoulder to make sure nobody's fingering me, I enter the crowded Sinai Room in time to hear the band strike up our new national anthem, "Enjoy Yourself, It's Later Than You Think." We all sit down at our tables, to work our way through ten courses to the accompaniment of the snake, monkey, kangaroo, mule, bunny hop—everything except the golden calf.

For dessert the waiters, dressed in baseball uniforms (the reception's theme is a baseball game because the Evans scion is a Little League biggie), bring in platters of bird cages which hold red parakeets, representing Cardinals, perched beside baseball bats of pareve ice cream. When the cages are raised to a drum roll, the noise panics the birds, and some do on the ice cream what they usually do only on newspaper; the rest fly off, six ending up in screaming women's hair.

As soon as the mess has been cleared away, the master of ceremonies brings on the floor show, a couple of apache dancers who smack each other around in time to their shrieks, and twenty-one people who light twelve candles on a birthday cake larger than a pitcher's mound. The lights are turned off, everyone sings "Happy Birthday" by candle glow; then, carrying a prayer shawl on a red velvet pillow, the Evanses' five-year-old daughter enters the hall. But halfway to the dais she trips on the long fringes, falls on her head and bawls until the sexy band singer pulls her into the ladies' room. Now enter the bar-mitzvah boy himself, in a dugout lowered from the ceiling; scooping up the fallen tallis, he joins his parents at the dais. Together they all light the thirteenth candle as the band segues into a medley of "My Yiddishe Mama," "O My Papa," "Sonny Boy" and "Dayenu" (which means, appropriately, "It Would Have Been Enough for Us").

The woman next to me leans over, wiping tears from her eyes. "Oh, Rabbi! I just *love* ritual."

I cringe.

When the lights go up, the bar-mitzvah boy trots by my table with a bottle of champagne. I warn him, only half in jest, not to show up the next morning in Sunday School with a hangover.

"My father says I don't have to attend any more," he says, "so I'm not."

Feeling like Moses after his descent from the original Sinai, I look around for Tablets to smash. There's a pair, sure enough, atop the birthday cake, and I half rise from my seat when I realize that *these* Ten Commandments are pareve butter cream, alas—shatterproof.

Later, still resentful of having been used as a shill for an extravaganza, I hand the Evans scion an envelope before leaving.

"From you, Rabbi? You shouldn't've," he says, grabbing it.

Maybe the kid's right, for what the envelope contains is a note: "You're going to have to return all your gifts, man, if you don't return to religious school. Because I'll revoke your bar mitzvah and declare you a *boy* again."

My humility jag had lasted all of one day.

ℵ

MAN IN THE HILLENDALE *NEWS:*
RABBI GIDEON ABEL
Meet the New Spiritual Leader of the Hillendale Temple

Q. How do you like Hillendale, Rabbi Abel?
A. It's a lovely community.
Q. And the people—how do they strike you?
A. They're lovely too. So warm and hospitable.
Q. Is it a thrill to be undertaking this your first congregation?

A. Yes, it is. And an enormous responsibility.

Q. *How do you plan to discharge this responsibility?*

A. By demonstrating that Judaism is a study-and-do-it-yourself-and-right-now religion. I've begun our adult-education courses, and I'm planning a comprehensive social-action program. If I believed in slogans, I'd say ours at the temple should be: A Course and a Cause for Every Congregant.

Q. *You haven't mentioned the temple's new expansion program. How does that fit into your plans?*

A. Well, we need it, I guess. On Yom Kippur we didn't have enough room to seat all our congregants, and in two years we'll have to have more classrooms too.

Q. *But what about your temple kitchen?*

A. The kitchen? It's beautiful! Some houses of worship, you can't see the religion in them for all the chopped liver. My greatest ambition in life, you see, was to be the only clergyman in America with no kitchen in his house of God. So when I saw the Hillendale Temple's kitchen—it's just big enough to turn out coffee and cake and that's all—I was delighted.

Q. *You certainly speak your mind, Rabbi. Anything else delight you at your temple—aside from its kitchen?*

A. The children. I'm very fond of them. They're so fresh and responsive. Already they've started to collect clothing for the poor people of Appalachia and to tutor disadvantaged students. And sisterhood is sponsoring a prekindergarten class for needy kids . . . That's the greatest thing about being a rabbi: the world today is like some gargantuan civil service, but the synagogue is still an integral community, small enough to establish communion with and yet large enough to benefit society as a whole . . .

א

FALL

S OMETHING WAS WRONG.

I felt it as soon as I entered the temple for the first board meeting of its fiscal year. True, none of the trustees there belled me and shouted, "Unclean," but the message came through nonetheless when one woman approached, saying, "Well, you're young yet, Rabbi. *You'll* learn." Before I could ask, "Learn what?" she had made me a wager, "Oh, but I bet you don't remember my name."

"You win," I said graciously. The woman, one of my five-hundred-odd congregants, gave me such a dirty look and stalked away, heaven alone knows why; did she want to be a loser?

As we all took our seats, Eve Greenwood, the spirited sisterhood president, who is as quick-witted a' her mother-in-law is good-hearted, whispered, "I'm on your side, no matter what anyone else says."

"What did anyone else say?" I asked in surprise. She replied, "I mean, I'm with you in what *you've* said." That stopped me; how could I ask to be told what I'd said?

Barney Singer convened the meeting by slapping a J.K. Lasser tax book on the table, then motioned everyone to rise. The trustees did so in unison, for they are a homogeneous group; in addition to sharing similar incomes, homes, automobiles, politics and concern for help—to hear some of the women talk, it's a full-time job just to find a maid and keep her—they're all skirting forty, as if they had been promoted en masse into suburbia from the same grade. The president turned toward me. "Rabbi?" (I had asked not to be addressed by my first name, because does anyone want to be hatched, matched or dispatched by one of the boys? Whereupon Curt Langer had commented with his usual frown, "Dr. Terman insisted we call him Irv. Of course, he was an older man.") "The invocation, please."

Who listens to those spot loyalty oaths? If you were God, would you? All I can remember from auditing a million "O Lord" commercials with bowed head is trying to decide each time whether my shoes needed a shine. Yet I had no intention of tilting at invocations here; who yearns to play Cordelia in suburbia? Neither she nor Big Daddy Lear, I recall, had ended up on the sunny side of the street. So picking up the United Synagogue prayerbook, I read aloud from the ancient rabbis: "'Try to prevent poverty by teaching man a trade. Try all methods before you permit him to become an object of charity, which must degrade him, tender as your feelings with him may be.'"

The trustees remained standing when I sat down. Some kept their heads bowed while others looked up quizzically, as if waiting for me to say, "Hike."

"What about the invocation?" Pete Schuster demanded, in the manner of a district attorney out to maintain an unbroken record of convictions, which in his case I'd have bet were obtained by the third degree.

"That was it."

"That? But you neither invoked God nor prayed. Why, you never even said, 'Amen'!"

As the group resumed their seats, I explained, "Learning, according to Judaism, is a form of prayer. Therefore—"

Curt Langer, wearing the same nose as Judith Anderson who played Rebecca's maniacally faithful housekeeper in the movie, interrupted, "*Irv* never did anything like that."

Realizing that crying aloud, "Dr. Terman is dead; long live Rabbi Abell!" might be misinterpreted, I said instead, "Suppose we begin future meetings with such readings, then discuss them—"

"Christ!" exclaimed Rick Adler, who had asked after my installation why I had ever entered the rabbinate when my father owned a Bentley. "We'd never get out of temple then."

Barney Singer translated, "What Rick means is board meetings never finish before midnight. Tacking on irrelevancies might be all right for those who can sleep late in the morning"—one guess whom he meant—"but the rest of us can't do that."

"How about starting meetings twenty minutes earlier?" I asked.

A collective groan.

"That's a splendid suggestion, Rabbi," Barney Singer

said. "Only we don't have the time." (That made me feel right at home; Dad was always telling me my ideas were so terrific they would surely be executed just as soon as the Messiah arrived.) The president then cleared his throat and addressed the trustees for twenty-two minutes on our "quality product" (the temple), whose "splendid packaging" and "merchandising" should attract "customers" from the "untapped virgin market" so long as our "clientele" continued to generate "favorable word of mouth" about our wonderful "management." Concluding, he turned to a slightly built, rabbity-looking fellow who was gnawing his fingernails as if they were carrots. "All right now, Sam, the minutes."

"Right, Barney." Sam is Sam Warren, the worrier over the wrong petitions who always seems just about to be befallen by something. Earlier he had congratulated me that a "half-Jew" (as likely a state as half a pregnancy) had been nominated for the Presidency of the United States in 1964, because such things had to be done *gradually*, though Sam himself prayed that nobody with so much as a shot of "Jewish blood" in him ever be elected President, because once in office he might say or do something that not a hundred percent of the American electorate might like, and why antagonize Christians needlessly? Subsequently he had bravely asked why it was that every one of the Six Million hadn't at least died fighting. (Charlie Hecht, a lawyer whose diploma from Auschwitz is tattooed on his left forearm, had given the perfect answer: "They certainly would have, Sam, had they but known their fighting would have reconciled you to their slaughter.")

Dore Redmont passed me a note: "Nothing in the rules says we can't discuss over coffee *after* the meeting—you, me, Charlie Hecht, Eve Greenwood and whoever." A sweet note, but what did the postscript mean? "At the same time we can discuss your public utterances and maybe save you some aggravation."

Sam Warren's minutes reviewed the highlights of June's meeting, when the trustees had discussed, among other things: who would charge the least to fix the furnace, clues as to who was crayoning dirty words on the walls of the men's room, installing a soda machine in the temple and how much to charge per drink, what combo to hire for the President's Ball, whether it was necessary for guards checking admission tickets at the High Holiday services to wear guns, how to remove the cuckoo from the expensive antique clock a congregant had donated for the sanctuary, whether to dissuade the chief founder of the temple, Ed Geldzaler, from resigning from the synagogue after having been denied a fifth consecutive term as president, and, finally, what right the placement commission had to threaten the temple that they would send only one more rabbi, Gideon Abel, to be interviewed since the board had already rejected nine other candidates.

(So! There was a second reason for this shotgun marriage of ours. And it was worse than the first.)

Reports followed from the respective chairmen of nineteen different committees. I felt so *frustrated!* Here on my honeymoon with the temple, I'm eager to consummate our union via adult education and social action, yet how do we spend our evening together? On committee reports! Furnaces! Dirty words! It was as fulfilling as having your bride detail on your wedding night the intimate workings of her digestive tract.

The ways-and-means-committee chairman announced future fund-raising ventures: *My Fair Sadie,* the bazaar, football pool, Cadillac raffle, theater party, memorial plaques, rummage sale, duplicate bridge, carnival, white-elephant sale, cemetery plots, picnic, selling Christmas cards—

"You want to sell Christmas cards," I asked, "in the temple?"

Barney Singer said, "No comments now, please. According to *Robert's Rules of Order,* discussions come later—under New Business." He frowned. "At which time, Rabbi, we'll also discuss some of your other comments."

I almost shouted, "There's nothing to discuss! I plead guilty!" Yes, paranoia was revisiting me. What unspeakable things had I spoken? Why was I to be discussed here in public like cemetery plots and graffiti?

Eventually New Business was reached. The first topic was whether nonmembers of sisterhood should be allowed to join its weekly bowling league, a two-part question, since one woman who wanted to join was Catholic but a terrific bowler. When a vote was called for, somebody said, "Let's first find out what our rabbi advises."

Who knew from bowling leagues? Not I, who couldn't tell one pin from another. "I'm sorry, but I really can't say."

There was a silence which somebody's disappointed "Oh" did not fill; then the vote was taken. Results: Jewish nonmembers of sisterhood were barred from the bowling league, but the terrific Catholic high-scorer was accepted because she couldn't qualify for sisterhood anyway, not unless she converted, which

was unlikely since her five children attended parochial
school.

The next item was a coed junior-youth group that
Maurine Levenson proposed sisterhood form for children nine through eleven. The discussion:

——Maurine, what's the purpose of such a group?

——*It's important for children to make the right
contacts.*

——Isn't nine through eleven a little early for making contacts?

——*It's never too early to be making the right contacts.*

——Don't boys and girls that age have different
interests?

——*Nonsense. Boys and girls that age are both children together.*

——But preteeners want no part of the opposite
sex.

——*All the more reason for encouraging them to
mingle.*

——How are you going to get them to mingle?

——*Teach them social dancing together. They'll
have to mingle then.*

——And what if they don't want to dance?

——*What if they don't want to eat? You make
them.*

This time no questions were directed at me; apparently someone who didn't know about bowling
leagues couldn't know about children. "May I say
something?" I asked. (Perhaps if I began, as Pastoral
Psychiatry 1.1 had taught, with a word of praise
before criticizing.) "Certainly you should be com-
mended, Maurine, for your concern with our preteens.
But wouldn't it be wiser to limit coed groups to teen-
agers? Start them socializing at nine, they may very

well be going steady at thirteen and getting into trouble by—"

Maurine Levenson interrupted. "You never belonged to a coed junior-youth group, did you, Rabbi?"

"No—"

"Well, maybe if you had, your wife would be a member of our sisterhood," Rochelle's aunt said. "Understand now?"

That did it; a majority voted in the coed junior-youth group.

Not everyone was pleased, however. Nearby Eve Greenwood muttered, "Now my ten-year-old is going to make me buy her that twenty-eight-double-A training bra." Dore Redmont replied, "If your daughter fills the bra with Baby Ruths, maybe *then* my eleven-year-old Robbie will come near her."

Next item, the President's Ball, autumn's biggest fund-raiser. Sam Warren reported that half the tickets remained unsold and appealed for cooperation; otherwise the affair would end up in the red, like the Tumble-in-the-Hay Square Dance last June.

(Why the stress on fund-raising, when the temple could support itself through dues equal to the cost per member, then graduated upward or downward according to one's ability to pay, like income tax? But I said nothing; first I wanted to hear the list of particulars in my indictment.)

Up jumped Pete Schuster, breathing heavily. "All those members who never help out! You have to fight with them to take some lousy tickets to our affairs or to serve on committees—God knows we need people to buy and sell tickets, prepare the food and serve it, clean up afterwards, but they can't be bothered. Yet these are the same ones whose children attend our religious school and who frequent Sabbath services and adult education too—but they won't do a damn thing for the temple. These freeloaders, I'd like to toss them all out on their cans!" His face now the color of his tongue, he sat down and gritted his lips. "I had to get that off my chest. God knows the temple means *everything* to me." And he looked me straight in the eye.

Like a barroom tough who challenges every gun-fighter to a draw, Pete Schuster is plainly seeking to outrabbi me. The trustee has as many answers as Dore Redmont has questions, and it galls Goneril-Regan here that I've neglected to be taught of his ways, walk in his paths and install him as the power behind my pulpit. When I refused to devote my Yom Kippur sermon to a pitch for the temple's expansion fund, for example, he told me, "One thing about Dr. Ter-man: at least he knew his place." No smashing suc-cess in the belt business—beltless people don't heed him either, and it infuriates him no end that their pants stay up—Pete Schuster seems determined to make it big in the temple, and somehow he's got the feeling I stand in his way. Don't ask me why, ask Oedipus.

Sam Warren clapped his hands. "I only wish the temple had more fantastically dedicated workers like you, Pete, that's what I wish."

Pete Schuster bowed his red snaky-locked head. "Thanks, Sam. Thanks very much."

"I shouldn't be at all surprised, Pete," Curt Langer said, "if the board voted you Mr. Temple this year."

I saw Barney Singer flinch even before Maurine Levenson exclaimed, "But the Mr. Temple Award always goes to the president—unless, of course, he quits the temple, like Ed Geldzaler did."

Why should losing the Mr. Temple Award make a

wealthy, grown accountant wince? Don't misread me now; I think Barney Singer is a nice man—unfailingly cordial and conscientious. He attends as many meetings as I—remember too, this is after putting in a full day's work at his office—and no temple toilet overflows without his rushing right over to unstop it. Still, the president doesn't regard social action as the temple's concern, or adult education as his. In a way he reminds me of the chairman of my college hi-fi club, who knew everything there was to know about tweeters and woofers and stereophonics, but nothing about music. Turned out the fellow was tone-deaf.

Then came the menacing announcement: "Next on the agenda is Rabbi Abel."

Swiftly I girded my mental loins.

"I have here in my hand, Rabbi, a newspaper clipping and a letter." Unlike Senator McCarthy, Barney Singer showed me Exhibit A. "Did the Hillendale *News* misquote you perhaps?"

Was that all? Imagine! Worrying me about an interview in which I had hymned everything but motherhood. "You mean, when I confessed to being so fond of the children here?"

The president scowled. "I mean, when you proclaimed that your greatest ambition in life was to be the only rabbi in America without a kitchen."

"Well, I used a little hyperbole there—for effect —but I'm sure readers got the point, that I'm delighted to be leading a shul like this which places first things first." Could Dale Carnegie have been more winning?

So why all the grumblings? "The point is," Barney Singer said, "our expansion program. Don't you know that what we're expanding this year is not the sanctuary or classroom space, but our inadequate kitchen?"

I was astounded. "The kitchen?" But Pete Schuster's impassioned plea on Yom Kippur for the expansion fund had mentioned only "our temple," "Jewry," "faith" and "God."

"Certainly. The temple is crippled without a new kitchen. How long can I ask my girls to do our cooking at home and shlep it to temple for our affairs? Secondly, I want ours to be a total temple, so a person can live, give birth, bar-mitzvah, marry off his children and hold his golden wedding anniversary right inside these hallowed halls. Thirdly, just think of all the kickbacks from caterers that we're losing." The orator, unsurprisingly, was Maurine Levenson, organization man, whose husband had complained to me that the temple is ruining his sex life because when his wife isn't too tired she's too busy. The executive vice-president charged me now with her electric-blue eyes. "Rabbi, I think you owe it to our expansion-fund campaign to write the Hillendale *News* that you were libeled."

"But I wasn't."

"Then say you were misunderstood. A man with five degrees like you, Rabbi, I'm sure can juggle words around."

"I wasn't misunderstood either. Well, it isn't my greatest ambition to become the Carrie Nation of the kitchen. On the other hand, neither do I set kitchens above my chiefest joy." A reference there to Psalm 137, to link the board and myself with four thousand years of Jewish history, affording us all some perspective here, don't you see? The trustees didn't; their looks indicated they thought I was being snotty. So I hurried on: "If I'd known the expansion fund was for the kitchen—But I simply assumed, after Yom Kippur, when we couldn't fit everyone into the sanctuary,

and with the projected increase in schoolchildren—
I *am* sorry."

"Irv told us," said Curt Langer, who if he caught me
picking my nose would surely contend that Dr. Terman did it better, "the kitchen table is an altar to
God."

Anxious to get me out of the kitchen, because I
didn't care for any more heat, I asked, "You mentioned something about a letter, Barney?"

The president held up Exhibit B, a note. "Is this your
handwriting, Rabbi? Did you write Bill Evans' boy
at Mountain Tiptop that unless he returned to religious school, you'd revoke his bar mitzvah?"

Out of the kitchen and smack into the catering hall!
"Well, yes, but—"

"Do you know," Barney Singer continued, "how you
embarrassed the Evanses? Everybody saw you hand
this gift envelope to the bar-mitzvah boy, something
nobody had ever seen a rabbi do before. Naturally
they asked how much it was—I mean, what you had
written. So the boy opened the envelope and read
your note aloud before he knew what it said. Mrs.
Evans tells me she almost dropped dead on the spot
—this after spending eleven thousand dollars on her
affair."

"*Eleven thousand—*"

Pete Schuster exclaimed, "I never heard of such a
thing—a rabbi revoking a bar mitzvah! Why, it's like
uncircumcising somebody!"

"You all misunderstand." Surely a man with five degrees could explain things to everyone's satisfaction,
or failing that, juggle them around. "That note was
simply my protest—a trifle melodramatic, that I admit
—of the Evans boy's quitting his religious education
on the very day he assumed his responsibilities as a

Jewish adult. It makes as much sense as a bridegroom
going off on a separate honeymoon."

"*You* misunderstand, Rabbi." Barney Singer then revealed that the Evanses weren't quitting the *temple,*
having three younger children in religious school;
what's more, they paid their dues promptly and always contributed to the bazaar.

"That doesn't entitle anyone to empty a religious
rite of meaning." And I declared, "From now on,
I'll refuse to officiate at the bar mitzvah of any child
who won't continue his religious education till confirmation at sixteen."

Edythe Loring (the woman whose name I hadn't
remembered before) burst out, ashen-faced, "Rabbi,
how can you deny our children their God-given puberty rites!"

"Suppose," I replied, "we *raise* the age of Jewish
puberty."

Half of the trustees applauded. But the other half
shouted, until Barney Singer gaveled everyone into
silence. Then he made his own position plain. "We're
not in business here to drive families to join the other
temple. Nor to provoke Steingut into making effigies
of our rabbi in chopped liver, to be eaten at affairs,
as Mountain Tiptop did last week; notoriety like that
we don't need. Let's vote on this matter right now."

"Vote?" I was startled. "This is a religious matter,
and as your rabbi *I* decide what's kosher and what's
a farce."

"Hear, hear!" Dore Redmont cried, and I silently
blessed him.

But several trustees regarded me as if I were a
Christian martyr who had bitten into a lion, while one
mumbled something about June.

God, they were a solemn bunch—more a jury than

fellow Jews uniting with me to sanctify God. "Perhaps now would be a good time to discuss what the function of a rabbi is," I said. "What do you think?"

"It's late," Sam Warren replied, then announced the last item on the agenda, the ladies' room, which Edythe Loring proposed carpeting wall-to-wall, because so many other synagogues and churches did so, and she knew somebody who'd install it whosesale.

Eve Greenwood raised her hand. "I second the carpet motion," the sisterhood president said, and Edythe Loring beamed. "Anything that will make us better Jews."

The howl that went up would have killed NATO.

Barney Singer asked for a motion of adjournment, while Edythe Loring told a neighbor in a stage whisper, "See Eve Greenwood's nose? It isn't hers, you know."

Swiftly I intervened. "What happened to the social-action-committee report? I've drawn up a number of projects for consideration—"

"We don't have a social-action committee," Barney Singer said.

"You *don't?* Well, let's form one now."

"We can't."

I said, "All the other temples have a social-action committee."

"That comes under the heading of New Business," said the president, "and suggestions for New Business must be submitted in writing a week before our meeting. That's *Robert's Rules of Order.*"

Sam Warren wrinkled up his rabbity nose. "That agitator minister who got thrown out by his church started with social action."

Before I could say more, Rick Adler pointed out

that it was already 12:49 A.M., and could I save it
for next time? Well, at least the meeting ended on a
happy note: nobody asked for a benediction.

א

———Pete Schuster, please.

———*Speaking.*

———Oh, hello. How are you? This is—

———*Yes, I know. What's on your mind, Rabbi?*

———Well, I was wondering if the two of us could
get together for a talk—

———*About what?*

———Well, about us. We seem to be at odds, and for
the sake of peace—

———*You're blaming me?*

———No, no. It isn't a matter of assigning blame.

———*Isn't it? I blame you.*

———For what?

———*A whole list of things.*

———Another list, Pete?

———*Packing my four committees with friends of
yours who've been trying to outvote me, usurp my
powers—*

———You've got me wrong. Didn't you complain that
nobody was giving you any help?

———*And ignoring all my suggestions. I bet you never even read my last three notes, did you?*

———Of course I did, Pete. But starting every Sabbath service by blowing a ram's horn, or having
committee chairmen like you give reports in the
middle of the service, or dimming the lights and
ringing chimes while reading the names of the
dead before *Kaddish*—

———*It would put some life into a drab service.*

——Perhaps, but no other congregation in the world does such things.

——*Why can't we be original?*

——Well, I try for originality in my sermons.

——*Your sermons—they're too original. You can find more ways to apply three-thousand-year-old laws to current events—*

——Thank you.

——*That was no compliment . . . and when I ask you to recruit us some new members from among all those who dislike Rabbi Jacobson—*

——Barney Singer agrees with me that it's not quite kosher to rustle congregants away from other—

——*You're always so negative. Barney! All he cares about is balancing books; why, he runs a temple the same way he'd run the city dump. Now when I become president . . .*

א

OCTOBER

I LOVE the kids! Even before the coed junior-youth
group's first meeting ended with the boys' rubbing
cheese dip into the girls' hair and the girls' pouring
punch over the boys in retaliation, I loved them.

Funny, it had never occurred to me at the seminary
that of all my congregational duties (I wear so many
different hats it's difficult for me at times to find my
yarmulka underneath), working with children would
be perhaps the most satisfying. (Remember, I'm the
one who restrains a homicidal response whenever a
congregant says his only reason for joining the temple
is, of course, the sake of the children. What ex-Marine
wants to be turned into a hairy Mary Poppins!) Yet
it is, for with the kids, who resemble their parents

the way clay resembles concrete, I can see myself affecting them. Weeks following the monthly family service, for example, children are still quoting my sermons, and at the Oneg Shabbas afterwards *kids* never tell me:

"I don't recall the Bible making such a fuss about civil rights."

"Aren't those Jewish values of yours really rationalizations of defense mechanisms and reaction formations?"

"I should think anyone who acclaims Israel so eloquently would want to live there."

"Well, Rabbi, that's *your* opinion."

Kids are so open to new thoughts and experiences, so full of spontaneity and grace, so I-Thouish. (One embarrassed mother to her son: "You got to remember when you talk to the rabbi, he isn't nine years old like you.") It's wondrous to go from kindergarten through confirmation class and watch, in a few hours, children span the years from early childhood to adolescence, like a Walt Disney nature film with photography speeded up so that flowers blossom in sixty seconds. (On one Sunday morning I can be asked questions ranging from "Are *you* God?" to "The older you become, the more sins you get to do?" to "Was Goldfinger Jewish?" to "*Who* says there's a God?")

My affection for the kids may know a bound or two—the only person who loves everybody is a liar—and one is the confirmation class, which I teach myself. They fluctuate so, these turbulescents: one minute they're out to save the world, the next minute they're reciting in unison, "Hear, O Israel, the Lord our God, the Lord is Two." Or after lauding the prophets for promoting social justice, my teen-agers can suddenly start comparing clothes, bank accounts and bust measurements.

Such materialism distresses those parents who recall their own youth as a time devoted to ideals, causes and poverty. "What do you and your husband talk about at home?" I asked one disturbed mother, an alumna of the thirties' Young Communist League. "Well," she replied, "lately, Acapulco and Hawaii. We're trying to decide where to go for Christmas, and it's hard because we've been everywhere."

There are thirteen in my class, most of whom look forward every session to getting hysterical together. The hormones of adolescent girls must be at least fifty percent giggles, while the boys are always intent to prove anything girls can do, they can outdo three times as loud—how else to explain the hysterics when we study, in *Ethics of the Fathers,* teachings of ancient rabbis like Ben Bag Bag and Ben He He? With the troops so restless, what does one do? Desert them or deport them. So periodically, in conjunction with our study of comparative religion, I take the class to neighboring churches, where my students don't giggle at all—this annoys me; why do they bug only Jewish clergymen?—and the boys can't tip over pews without first unscrewing them.

After attending the local Methodist and Christian Science churches—what impressed the girls most was the red velvet gowns worn by two women Christian Science readers; the boys liked the fact that the services were shorter than Jewish ones—I phoned the Episcopal church for permission to visit.

Its assistant minister, Father Vernon Rutherford, was not nearly as cordial as his colleagues, however, "Suppose you make it some other week," he said, after a long pause which suggested he'd prefer my selecting another century.

I had five successive Sunday fund-raising brunches to attend, I replied.

A longer pause. Then the priest said, "Well, all right. Come ahead, Rabbi, if you really want to."

. . .

Hillendale's St. James Episcopal Church—so wealthy it has *two* nicknames, the Country Club at Prayer and the Cathedral of the Ninety Percent Bracketeers —looked exactly like a fish, even down to a forked tail and glazed blue brick that glistened scale-like in the autumn sunlight.

"Holy mackerel!" one of my kids exclaimed. "It's a fish."

The others giggled, and I scolded them all for their bad manners.

As soon as we entered the church, Rutherford approached, greeting me with the handshake of an overstocked used-car salesman. One teen-ager asked about the unusual shape of the building. The young curate reacted with surprise. "Can't you tell?" he said. "It's a fish, a secret symbol that early Christians used for identifying each other in lands where they were persecuted."

"Christians were *persecuted?*" several kids exclaimed.

Guiding us to seats in the second row—evidently the church too had trouble filling front pews (someday I intend to research why people who clamor for front seats at plays, ball games and prize fights always sit in the last rows of houses of worship; you think things would be different if we also charged admis-

sion?)—Rutherford left us, saying he would be happy
to answer questions afterwards, the liar.

"He's boss," said one girl. The boys agreed because
the priest had asked if they were on the Hillendale
High football team, which they weren't, for, as he
damn well knew, the school had no football team.

Soon the service began—with more people in attendance than at a bar-mitzvahless Sabbath service, I
noted not without envy, but Judaism's been on the
boards twice as long as Christianity, and everyone
knows that attendance invariably slackens during long
runs, which certainly isn't the fault of the show or its
performers. Still, I find a half-empty house of God
demoralizing; it sets me to thinking of Stonehenge,
and wondering can it happen here.

That morning the rector, Dr. Bidwell, was away,
and pinch-preaching for him was Dr. Larrabie, a
cherubic-looking man of about sixty with rosy cheeks,
clumps of white hair and, probably, a ho-ho-ho. I
wished him well when he was introduced, because
my heart goes out to all preachers; there for the grace
of God go I. Now if only the priest would speak on
neither positive thinking (let *God* put you in the
driver's seat) nor the Lord (the way some of these
Christians preach about God, you'd think *they* had
invented Him).

Dr. Larrabie began with a hoary anecdote about a
Protestant minister, a Roman Catholic priest and a
"Jewish rabbi," one I had used myself to a respectful
silence; only this time the minister had the punch line,
not the rabbi. Then—I'm not sure how he got there,
because he sneezed (which made a clever transi-
tion)—Dr. Larrabie began to sell "swelling Revelation," contrasting "the Old Testament God of Law"
(here he made such a face, as if referring to some-

thing not only old but also decomposing under his nose) and "the New Testament God of Love."

"Swelling Revelation shows how, beginning at low ebb with the Old Testament's fierce tribal deity of primitive justice, Jesus force-marches humankind via the New Testament to the heights of apprehending the God who is Love. For example, the Old Testament's legalistic Yahweh pronounces this anathema: 'Cursed be he that confirmeth not all the words of this law to do them.' But in the New Testament our loving Saviour bids, 'Love one another: for he that loveth another hath fulfilled the law.' What low tide! What high tide! What swelling Revelation!"

Yessirree, it was stereotype time in the old bullpit—if Lifebuoy can change from green to gold and Rinso periodically add something new or blue, why can't preachers occasionally switch clichés?—as Dr. Larrabie hippety-hopped from Sinai (*Valley* Sinai, to hear him tell it) a million light-miles up to Calvary, implying that the Lord had given the Ten Commandments to the Israelites by mistake, in the manner of a cosmic Pantspresser mixing up trousers, while the Israelites, for their part, had accepted the Tablets of the Law under the impression they were reservations for two weeks, all expenses paid, at Miami Beach.

Dr. Larrabie continued, "The Old Testament vows, 'The Lord will rejoice over you to destroy you, and to bring you to nought.' But the New Testament warms us with 'God is love: and he that dwelleth in love dwelleth in God, and God in him.'

"The Old Testament's chauvinistic Yahweh loves only Israel, as it is written: 'Ye shall be a peculiar treasure unto me above all people . . . a kingdom of priests.' But in the New Testament, 'There is neither Jew nor Greek, there is neither bond nor free, there is neither male nor female: for ye are all one in Christ Jesus.'

"The Old Testament never forgives, vengefully commanding: 'Remember what Amalek did unto thee when ye were come forth out of Egypt . . . Therefore thou shalt blot out the remembrance of Amalek from under heaven.' But in the New Testament, Paul lovingly implores, 'Therefore if thine enemy hunger, feed him; if he thirst, give him drink.' "

He ran on like that for quite a while, demonstrating the Biblical scholarship of General Motors though, alas, not its taste (Ever hear GM knocking Ford in order to make Chevrolet look good?). To Dr. Larrabie the Bible was a treasure trove of great quotations to plunder out of context.

One teen-ager passed me a note: "Rabbi, are we going to take this sitting down?"

What did the kid expect me to do? Boo? Stamp my feet? Walk out? Start singing "We Shall Overcome"?

Rutherford was now staring at me, and I matched him stony look for stony look. His lips were pressed tight, as if biting off the words "Serves you right, smart-ass, for being so pushy. Couldn't you tell I didn't want you in my church?"

To the bitter end Dr. Larrabie blasted the Old Testament's tribalism, provincialism, legalism, chauvinism, ritualism, primitivism (bad Old Testament, it contained every nasty -ism except communism, and everyone knows who fathered that) while extolling all of the New Testament's pretty -ities: universality, egality, probity, fraternity, spirituality, morality. Correction: Dr. Larrabie did not blast; a gentleman of the old school, he spoke throughout in the genial manner of Barry Goldwater proposing to lob a hydrogen bomb into the men's room at the Kremlin.

Succeeding Dr. Larrabie at the lectern, the curate made some announcements. I waited for the one welcoming my kids and me to the no-contest we had just lost. Sure enough, it came: "We are most happy to welcome to our fellowship this morning several visitors, Rabbi Abel and his confirmation class, who come to us from"—I expected to hear "From Brand X, or the Greasy People's Synagogue," but he played it straight—"from the Hillendale Temple." Incredibly, Rutherford added, "Perhaps Rabbi Abel would care to say a few words to us. Rabbi?" The curate motioned me to take his place at the lectern.

I did so. Was he in for a surprise! (I also, come to think of it, because what could I say?)

"I can't tell you how happy my class and I are to join you today." Now what? Sit down, of course. No! Why should I? They started it. And isn't it the New Testament that counsels turning the other cheek? "It was especially interesting to hear about the theory of swelling Revelation. Because different sets of quotes might suggest another swell theory. For example"—well, here goes brotherhood and the good will of those congregants of mine who are all for having *weekly* interfaith services; but I hadn't been feeling too ecumenical anyway since the first meeting of Hillendale's ministerial association, when I, the only rabbi there, was elected treasurer—"in the Old Testament: 'Thou art a God ready to pardon, gracious and full of compassion, slow to anger, and plenteous in mercy.' But in the New Testament: 'He that shall blaspheme against the Holy Ghost hath never forgiveness, but is in danger of eternal damnation.'

"In the Old Testament: 'The Lord of Hosts is exalted through justice . . . Do justice to the afflicted

and destitute, rescue the poor and needy.' But in the
New Testament: 'Believe on the Lord Jesus Christ,
and thou shalt be saved.'

"In the Old Testament: 'Let the oppressed go free
. . . break every yoke . . . deal thy bread to the
hungry . . . bring the poor that are cast out to thy
house . . . cover the naked . . . hide not thyself from
thine own flesh.' But in the New Testament: 'Depart
from me, ye cursed, into everlasting fire.'

"*Swelling Revelation?*"

I'll say this for those Episcopalians: they were a
damn polite bunch. Nobody in the congregation raised
his hand to cast the first stone, no usher came forward to give me the bum's rush, neither priest took
my children hostage; they all sat there quietly, perhaps more concerned with quotations from the *Wall
Street Journal* than both Testaments put together.
(You suppose, really, that's what brotherhood is nowadays—regardlessness of *all* religions?) Out front my
kids were squeezing each other's hands, even the
boys, while behind me somebody was huffing and
puffing as if trying to blow me down or, maybe, up.

Relenting, I made a stab at graciousness, listing
briefly some of the Testaments' similarities: Paul's en-
joinder to feed one's enemies was a quote from the
Old Testament, as was Jesus' bidding to love God
and one's neighbor, for Jesus repeated much of basic
Pharisaic doctrine. But the minister's stunt still
rankled me so much that what emerged, alas, was the
implication that Jesus and Paul were copycats who
should be sued for plagiarism, not to mention two
thousand years of back royalties. Trying to make
further amends, I pointed out that the Testaments'
similarities were due to the development of the
church, Jesus and most of his teachings out of Judaism.

Double alas! That made Christianity sound like a hand-me-down religion and Jesus merely a nice Jewish boy who had made God.

Red-faced, I resumed my seat. Rutherford continued the service, and soon he was delivering the parting benediction with a probable unvoiced postscript that the Lord need not feel obliged to bless, keep, be gracious and grant peace promiscuously to *everyone* in church that morning. My suspicion was confirmed as my class and I departed; when Dr. Larrabie, standing beside the curate at the front door and shaking hands with congregants who filed by, saw me coming, the last one on line, he changed color and stalked away, leaving Rutherford to lie in wait.

What could I say to the priest? You must come over to *my* place sometime and let me work *you* over?

Rutherford clenched his lips, as if afraid to let his tongue have its head. But he lost out and his mouth popped open, to emit—a snarl? imprecation? anathema? A bark! Which swiftly developed into a full-throated roar. "It was magnificent," the priest sputtered, losing control to a laugh, "the way you shot Larrabie out of the saddle! Are you and your wife free for lunch today?"

A woman's voice called out in response to my knock, "I'm on the phone. Door's open."

I entered the Rutherford home. There was a clatter of giant feet, and before I could so much as say, "Gevaltgeshrigginer!" a hairy heavy-breathing something jumped me and tried to bury my head between my shoulder blades, all the while howling such obscenities that one ex-Marine had difficulty controlling his sphincter as he relived the time Dad had insisted on his five-year-old son's making nice to a neighbor's dog, who promptly bit his hand. Damn that Rutherford! For revenge's sake he had lured me to the parsonage to be massacred by a wild beast.

"Beauty!" Enter the Lorelei of that ecclesiastical deathtrap, probably miffed that my disembowelment was taking so long. "Beauty!"

Two paws dropped reluctantly from my shoulders, and now the monster's head reached only to the wild thumping in my chest. I saw then a hound large enough to enable a two-hundred-pound desperado to escape a posse of thirty hard riders.

The midtwentyish woman—a billowy honey-blonde with a broom in her hand and red harlequin glasses on her long upswept nose, which gave her a cheerfully sinister look, like that of a witch who really enjoyed her work—grabbed hold of the dog's harness. "You're going to the basement," she said, and I didn't believe she meant the beast until it was dragged, still howling, out of the room.

After counting my ears with one hand and with the other wiping animal saliva out of my nostrils, I looked around the lair. Two living-room walls were lined with books, and three shelves were devoted to works of and about Reinhold Niebuhr. That was comforting because the great Protestant theologian had often acknowledged what he called his long love affair with the Jewish people.

Reappearing without her broom, the blonde said, "I *am* sorry, Rabbi. Beauty's so friendly. Did she scare you?"

"A dog? Scare me? Don't be silly."

She introduced herself as Rutherford's wife, Iris; me she knew from church that morning, she said without commenting on my performance, which meant she had not approved. "Vernon will be home soon," she continued. "He's dropping our twins off at a birthday party, and there was some shopping to do."

Like a scab that insisted on being picked, the question had to be asked. "You didn't like what I did before, did you?"

"Well, it *is* a trifle unusual to have a rebuttal to the sermon right in the middle of the service; it's like hearing the eulogy challenged during a funeral. But that doesn't mean I cared for what Dr. Larrabie did, Rabbi. Anti-'s bore me; all they know is what they dislike. Still—" She hesitated.

"Yes?"

"I guess I'm a creature of order, that's what it is. Like all women. It's men who are the bomb-throwers. You couldn't have done what you did without Vernon's help. I only hope the parish won't think the two of you plotted the ambush. Worse stories have been spread about Vernon, and me too, with less provocation. You know how they run: my clothes are too dowdy or Vernon's are too flashy, he's too radical or I'm a snob, I'm always telling him what to do or we're not speaking to each other at all. Heaven knows it isn't easy being the centerpiece of gossip. Your wife is a fortunate woman, Rabbi."

"I'm not married."

"Yes, I know. Vernon told me. That's why she's fortunate, your wife. Last month my husband didn't spend a single evening at home till I dropped him a note, saying Mrs. Rutherford and the twins would appreciate a visitation. Please don't misunderstand; we're a very happy family. Only, someone marrying a law student doesn't expect to end up a priest's wife. Will you have some sherry, Rabbi? You're too good a listener."

Presently Rutherford returned, amazingly transformed. Ninety minutes earlier he had been half a foot shorter than I, sullen, sallow, skinny, bushy-browed, beetle-eyed, hook-nosed; now anyone could see that the handsome priest was amiable, swarthy, wiry, with deep-set black eyes commanding an aristocratic nose, and he had grown a head taller. "Sorry to be so late, but the delicatessen was mobbed. Don't any Jewish housewives cook on Sunday?" He began unwrapping one long package. "Iris had already prepared a Virginia ham for dinner, *New* Testament style." Out came a salami. "See? Strictly *Old* Testament kosher. For Passover too, just in case." He grimaced. "Well, now you know why I didn't want you in church this morning. Larrabie's sermons invariably contain a higher crap content than fertilizer. This is one Sunday I was happy the church was half empty— that must have surprised you. Jews take their Sabbath attendance much more seriously than we do, don't you?"

Could I admit that temple attendance was half of his church's? "Well, when you've been in religion as long as us—" I said. "What's Dr. Bidwell like?"

"Nothing like Larrabie, of course, but he has his silly days too. Take last week—Bidwell attacked the Communists for being atheistic materialists. In a three-million-dollar church full of millionaire parishioners, whose vestry has just appropriated four hundred thousand dollars for a new entrance and a pipe organ, a thirty-thousand-dollar-a-year priest denounces Communists for worshiping Mammon! Other times Bidwell's preached that Negroes must never flout any law whatsoever and that America should send *spiritual* resources abroad instead of mere foreign aid."

Smiling, I quoted a Chasidic saying which I had used in a recent sermon that I mailed to the *Times:*

"Why do you worry so much about my soul and your own body? Take care instead of my body and your *own* soul."

Rutherford chuckled. "You're lucky, Gideon: Jews excel in social justice and civic virtue—Reinhold Niebuhr says so, which is why he's always tried to strengthen the Hebraic prophetic content of Christianity."

I thought of October's board meeting, when the trustees voted not to form a social-action committee but an investigating committee to see what other synagogues were doing. "True."

"What a disgrace. It took the Supreme Court and Congress to end segregation, while it was initiated by the churches, who also supported slavery. And it was not until 1964's General Convention that the Episcopal Church finally banned the exclusion of Negroes from worship. What's more—"

Iris broke in. "Shall we eat? I think the salami's getting cold."

We sat down at the dining-room table, where Rutherford said grace, then looked at me. "You want equal time now too?"

I laughed and dug into the salad. It was delicious. "Best tuna fish I've ever tasted!"

The Rutherfords looked puzzled. "It's crab meat," he said—I gagged; for observant Jews, crab is the pork of the sea—and she added, "I called our Jewish doctor for kosher do's and don't's and he said I couldn't go wrong with fish."

Happily the phone rang.

Iris nervously watched her husband pick up the receiver, while I shoveled the salad into a roll and stuffed it into my pocket. At first the priest responded with one-word replies; finally: "But it's written. ' 'Tis incumbent to pay heed to both sides at all times, verily, for what shall it profit a man to hear a partial truth and close his mind to the whole.' "

When Rutherford resumed his seat, Iris began, "Was that call also about—"

"How about that?" the priest exclaimed. "People were listening in church today."

Iris dropped her fork.

"That quotation of yours, it's good. Where's it from?" I asked. "It sounds familiar, and yet—"

"I made it up." He shrugged. "Amazing how many arguments one pertinent quote can save you. So when I can't think of one on the spot—"

"Vernon! By now Rabbi Abel has enough on you to get you defrocked."

Rutherford sighed. "My wife's afraid I have a priestly death wish, perhaps because she's already witnessed my lawyerly one." He frowned, and his heavy black eyebrows met on the bridge of his nose. "Gideon? Are you accomplishing a lot with your congregation?"

"It's hard to say. I've only been here six weeks."

"I'm here over a year—*that's* hard to say. I thought I had enlisted in Christianity; instead I find myself inside the belly of the American middle class. It's middle-class concerns, you know, not Christian ones, that rule today's church. That's why Protestants have only one low-income church for every two middle-class ones—don't ask about us Episcopalians—and that's why the churches are still not integrated."

"I see." Rutherford was paraphrasing part of Dean Tchernichovsky's sermon! (could it be that Judaism and Christianity shared failings?)

"Vernon," Iris said, as she served me a platter of cole slaw, potato salad, salami and corned beef, topped

with a baked pineapple ring, "must you talk shop on
Sunday?"

"I don't often get the chance, Iris. You know Bidwell's concern is the church, not religion." To me:
"He helped raise a million dollars for a Protestant
church at Kennedy Airport. Because the Catholics
built one there. Can you imagine a place less in need
of churches? Unless they're using them as giant Saint
Christopher medals for praying down planes."

"Really?" I didn't mention the synagogue that was
constructed at Kennedy Airport.

"*Aaaaaaoooooooooooooooooooooooooooooowwwwwww!*"

Howling *My Fair Lady's* opening line, the monster
lunged at me again. But happily this time there was
a door closed between us.

"That's only our dog," Rutherford said, perhaps noting me spill tea in my lap, as he started for the basement.

"Vernon! Maybe Rabbi Abel isn't as fond of dogs as
you," said Iris, while I dried my fly.

Rutherford paused, turned to me. "I usually romp
around with Beauty after Sunday dinner. You mind?"

"Well—" He was such a decent guy, this priest, so
straightforward. When would I stop pretending perfection that was the Lord's alone?

"Gideon? Do you mind my bringing Beauty upstairs?"

"No," I said finally, "not if you stuff him first. The
fact is, I don't particularly love dogs. You see, when I
was five years old—Vernon, Beauty scares the hell
out of me."

§

——Who's there?
——*Sam Warren, Rabbi.*

——Be right with you.

——*Can you hurry? It's started to drizzle.*

——Good morning, Sam. How are—

——*You still asleep?*

——Well, I got to bed after four—I did some reading after last night's meeting—and I must have slept through the alarm. What time is it?

——*Seven-thirty.*

——Is that all?

——*That's the time we start out to work.*

——Yes, well, I'm lucky the temple is only five minutes away, aren't I? What brings you here this morning, Sam?

——*Your letter to the* New York Times. *I saw it at the station while I was waiting for the train, Rabbi, and—*

——You mean they printed it? How about that! Sam, it's awfully nice of you to stop by to show it to me. Let's see—

——*Don't you remember what you wrote?*

——Well, sure. It was about Frobusher. And the *Times* printed it? Sam, that's—

——*Terrible, just terrible.*

——What?

——*The letter is signed "Gideon Abel, Rabbi of the Hillendale Temple."*

——What's the matter? They misspelled Hillendale?

——*Rabbi, you have any idea what this means? Frobusher is a congressman in the House of Representatives in Washington, D.C., and you called him "a moral moron and an ethical eunuch."*

——Certainly. Have you followed his votes on—

——*Didn't your experience with the Hillendale News teach you anything?*

——What?

——*Rabbi, who empowered you to write that letter?*

——Wait, let's get this straight. You didn't come over to congratulate me, did you?

——*Congratulate you? For issuing a controversial public pronouncement on a United States congressman? Rabbi, a minority group like us can't afford to do that, conspicuously denouncing congressmen. Furthermore—*

——Sam, suppose you let me get dressed before we discuss—

——*You have no idea how shocked we all were to see your letter. Everybody was talking about it at the station. Dr. Terman never did anything like this, and I don't think Rabbi Jacobson even reads the* Times.

——At least let's sit down, Sam. I seem to have lost the drawstring to my pajamas— All right now, Sam, why are you so upset? My letter was only an extract from last week's Shabbas sermon, and didn't you praise it afterwards?

——*I was praising what you said within the four walls of our temple, not something printed on the editorial page of the* New York Times. *God knows how many of its readers are goyim!*

——You think I needed permission to write it?

——*Not to write it; you can write whatever you want. But to mail it! On temple stationery!*

——I don't follow—

——*Rabbi, you are our representative.*

——What do you mean, representative?

——*A rabbi represents his congregation.*

——Oh?

——*We elect you just as we elect our congressmen.*

——You pay my salary, if that's what you mean.

——*Yes, we certainly do. Don't we?*

——Sam, the word "rabbi" means teacher. You suppose a math teacher, for example, "represents" his students? Should he reflect their ignorance of math?

——*Are you calling me ignorant?*

——I'm trying to make the point that—

——*That I'm ignorant.*

——Of course not. Look. A rabbi doesn't speak for Jews, but for Judaism, so our authority originates out of tradition, not from congregations. Rabbis are religious leaders, not cheerleaders.

——*Okay, teach and lead all you want, but in religion. You're meddling in politics here.*

——And morals, Sam? What about morals?

——*What's sex got to do with congressmen!*

——I'm referring to the Civil Rights Bill, the Nuclear Test Ban Treaty, social-welfare legislation, antipoverty laws, foreign-aid appropriations. You know how Frobusher voted on all these issues?

——*Now you're really messing in politics. Rabbi, you're going too far afield.*

——What do you think the prophets talked about most of the time—bar mitzvahs and bazaars? Besides, as you say, I was only talking. What'll be your reaction, Sam, when the board forms a social-action committee next month?

——*Over my— Who says we will?*

——I've got the votes, Sam, a clear majority. What'll be your reactions then, when the temple starts doing things?

——*Doing things? Haven't you done enough already? Families leaving the temple because you refuse to barmitzvah their sons . . . Those kitchen comments. And your speech in the Episcopal church must have set the ecumenical movement back a good two thousand years. Agitating now for open housing and improved public schools and— Rabbi, that wild-eyed Protestant minister never went* this *far!*

א

NOVEMBER

IT was at the end of the November 12 sisterhood meeting, immediately after Program Chairman Maurine Levenson announced the date of the December meeting, that her face turned white, which, believe me, was a refreshing change from what preceded it in the temple:

". . . And here comes Kay Evans, in a fragile full float of polka-dotted silk organza, dimpled darlingly with handsewn tiger-colored beads over a nude crepe slip . . . and Rona Redmont, gorgeous in a cloud of drifting pale chiffon with a hemline of matching feathers plucked from the tender underbellies of swans . . . Can this be our own Trudi Warren, delighting all eyes in a dangerously low scooped-out gay print blouse and a shimmering skin-tight pair

of hostess slacks made of black lace over scarlet satin
dotted with tiny pearl seedlings . . . ?"

A fashion show in beaded Technicolor! I had entered my protest as soon as the program was announced.

But Maurine Levenson had an answer ready. "Why
not a fashion show?"

"In a house of God?"

"It's a *Jewish* fashion show, Rabbi. Sisterhood's
modeling the clothes, and they'll be coming from
Jewish shops."

(All she had omitted saying was that the models
would strut down the runway rendering chicken fat.)
"Maurine, I'm not asking you to Buy Jewish or Model
Jewish. That's not the point—"

"You want us all the time to *Think* Jewish—that
point is better? Well, is there anything un-Jewish
about a little fun? You yourself preach how this-
worldly and life-affirming Judaism is. 'A person who
doesn't take advantage of the legitimate pleasures
afforded by this world will have to answer for his
neglect in the world to come,' the rabbis taught.
Remember?"

Quick study, wasn't she? I trembled to contem-
plate what would happen to her and my small Shabbas congregation when they learned that it was a
mitzvah for a couple to read Song of Songs together
Friday nights and help each other to sex. *Nobody*
would attend Sabbath services then; they'd all stay
home, claiming to be busy performing commandments.
Could I prove otherwise? Or deny what for some
would be the only mitzvah they were likely to be
observing all year? "Maurine, sisterhood has ten general meetings annually. Why spend ten percent of
them on what the women shop for all week anyway?"

(You'd have been proud of me: I spoke calmly and with utter dignity, when I yearned to grab her by the ears and shake her and jump up and down and scream, "But I became a rabbi to get *away* from my father's business!")

"Okay, Rabbi, you win. I'll let you choose our next program."

Who says chivalry is dead? "That's very sweet of you, Maurine. I appreciate it. Tell me, what were the girls' top requests?"

"Well, first was the fashion show, of course. Their second choice was a wig party."

Foiled! By a bossy Miss Clairol blonde, who if she wears Treasure Chests surely packs inside them pure muscle. But I'm being unfair to Maurine Levenson, for she chairs even more committees than Pete Schuster, and all the menial work that she hires a maid to do at home Maurine does tirelessly in the synagogue— you suppose this is today's secularized form of penance and atonement? There, unfair again! I resent the fact, you see, that Maurine and her clique play a far greater role in temple life than their men, thereby feminizing Judaism (which traditionally has been adult male-oriented).

And so the fashion show took place, with my warm body in attendance . . . I was the only man present —as in this periodic nightmare of mine where I find myself in a lifeboat filled with a hundred and forty women—except for the Coke man, who paused to refresh himself with the sight of models slinking across the auditorium to an instrumental recording of *Fiddler on the Roof* and Maurine Levenson's intermittently Jewish narration:

". . . And if you want to be a Judith and slay *your*

Holofernes with something subtler than an ax, here's Edythe Loring in a Chinese mandarin evening gown, beaded over a field of stylized flowers bright as a million suns and slit up those zoftig thighs . . . Shirl Rosenman, in plain black beaded hip pants from France—pagan in their sensual appeal, yet Biblical in simplicity . . . Even the Bible couldn't have a word for Gladys Schuster's teenie-weenie iridescent sequeenie bikini—"

Bang! went a dropped case of soda bottles out in the hall.

Gladys Schuster covered herself with hands bigger than her bikini. "*A peeping Tom!*"

(Pray tell, naked lady, what was I?) "Let me take care of it." I stepped out gratefully into the hall.

The soda man, picking up broken empties, leered at me. "*Va-va-va-voom!*"

I waited till beads stopped rattling inside (the dean or Dad should see me now, top spiritual banana at a burlesque show, and I'd plotz) before returning to the auditorium to ogle Shirl Rosenman's benediction— delivered out of plain black beaded hip pants from France, which were garnished by a bare bellybutton. Afterwards, Maurine Levenson announced that the next meeting, on December 16, would have a Hanukah motif—with candle-lighting, present-swapping and an original Hanukah playlet, then said, "How's that, Rabbi?"

Gently I broke the news. "December sixteenth is two weeks *after* Chanukah. This year the holiday begins on November twenty-ninth."

And that, as I was saying before, is when Maurine Levenson turned white. Others gasped.

"Rabbi, are you sure? The twenty-ninth of *November?*"

I nodded. "Don't worry. There are still a dozen more shopping days till Chanukah."

"Our children," Shirl Rosenman exclaimed, "what'll we tell our children?"

Yes, Virginia, there *is* a Chanukah that falls in November. "The children have learned about it in religious school—that the Hebrew calendar, which we use for observing Jewish holidays, is a lunar one, with months of twenty-eight and a half days. Of course, every three years or so we add one entire month in order to—"

"Shirl was referring to Christmas."

"Christmas?" I was surprised. "We're talking about Chanukah."

They all stared at me, surprised in turn.

"Aren't we?" I asked.

Twoscore women shook their heads in such unison that the Rockettes, seeing it, would have dropped dead from envy.

"We're discussing Christmas?"

Heads shook again, up and down this time.

"But what has Christmas to do with Chanukah?"

A collective snort. "What can you expect from a bachelor?"

Finally the explanation came; it must have been the official one, for three women said it in harmony and five others rattled their charm bracelets. "It's our children." Trudi Warren elaborated, "All these years Christmas and Hanukah have been falling at the same time, which means everyone can celebrate something together. But if Hanukah comes in November—"

"Are you telling me you celebrate Chanukah every year in observance of Christmas?" (Back came the rest of my recurrent nightmare: I'm marooned in this lifeboat, the only man amidst a hundred and forty women, all holding a couple of children by the hand, and now I see the name painted on the side of the boat, S. S. *Judaism.*)

"Rabbi, *you* know how hard it is to fight off Christmas," Shirl Rosenman exclaimed, "what with it flooding us over radio, television, school, department stores, starting with Columbus Day already. This year even giving our children a present each one of Hanukah's seven nights—that won't help us in *December.*"

"You mean," Eve Greenwood said, "eight nights."

Shirl Rosenman tossed her Sassoon cut. "I was brought up Reform, so we celebrate seven nights. Of course, for our children's sake we give eight presents."

Kay Evans stood up. "Some of you girls might be interested in the tradition my husband created for Hanukah. Bill dresses up like Father Mattathias, with a long beard and a blue suit with a white Star of Judah on the front, and he distributes presents to our children. They love it!"

Eve Greenwood giggled. "And does Bill color matzos for them during Passover?"

Kay Evans sat down.

"Rabbi?" Gladys Schuster said. "Tell us—if Hanukah comes on November twenty-ninth this year, what should we do December twenty-fifth?"

"The same thing you do when the Chinese New Year rolls around," I said, and perhaps that was a mistake; for all I knew, some sisterhood women set off firecrackers on February second and ran around the A & P dressed up like dragons.

Edythe Loring of the zoftig thighs burst out, "Rabbi, you don't understand. *We* are *mothers!*" She paused for me to salute, and when I refrained, she placed a hand over her even more zoftig heart and saluted herself. "Our children would never forgive us."

You see what Chanukah has become in our time: juvenile blackmail. For this the Maccabees started the first revolution in history for religious liberty? For this they fought and died? For this we eat potato pancakes every year? "Ladies," I said, "you're not obliged to keep up with the Joneses religiously. Do they try to keep up with you?"

"Well," somebody said, "they do read *Exodus* and *Herzog* and *How to Be a Jewish Mother*."

Gladys Schuster came back at me out of the depths of her sequined bikini. "Yours is an intellectual answer, but we parents must deal with our children on an emotional level. Don't you see?"

"How many Christian kids living in the State of Israel," I said, "do you think will be lighting Chanukah candles this November and receiving eight gifts?"

Sudden silence.

Broken by a whispered "That's a *terrible* analogy."

"Why," I asked, "is that a terrible analogy?"

A mutter: "Well, if he doesn't know, I'm certainly not going to tell him."

Shirl Rosenman jumped up, fingering her navel. "Maybe if instead of lighting Hanukah candles for only seven days, maybe if we kept on lighting additional candles every night from November twenty-ninth through January first—how does that strike you, Rabbi?"

"Like a fire hazard. I mean, it wouldn't be in keeping with the true spirit of Chanukah, Shirl."

"Mmmmmm," she said, resuming her seat.

Edythe Loring pointed an excited finger at me.

"Well, *I'm* getting my family a tree. It's an American tradition, uniting us with all other peoples; why make our children second-class citizens?"

"Ah, there's one immediate dividend of being a member of a minority group," I said. "You learn at the start that it's perfectly all right sometimes *not* to follow the majority."

Opening up a second front, Edythe Loring heaved both breasts at me. "Your rigidity is shocking! Rabbi, don't you believe in peace on earth? Don't you believe in good will toward men?" Would she consider her questions answered, I wondered, if I bit that waving finger of hers or into those— "Actually there's nothing Christian about Christmas; it's a pagan festival, marking the winter solstice—I read that in *Time*. So why deprive our children of beautiful evergreen symbols of nature's triumph over winter?"

Clearly these mothers would do anything for their offspring except practice birth control. "You're right, Edythe; Christmas trees are pretty," I conceded, "so pretty I approve of Jews' putting them up during January, February, March and April, when you can get really good buys."

Upshot of the meeting: some nine hundred dollars' worth of clothes were sold, sisterhood made ninety-two dollars in commissions, two dozen women came over to congratulate me, one resolved to postpone her observance of Chanukah till the winter solstice on December twenty-second, Shirl Rosenman bought six hundred Chanukah candles, and Edythe Loring defected from sisterhood, stating in a letter: "It took me four years of analysis to work through my conflicts with an authoritarian father—and now Rabbi Abel's dogmatism threatens to destroy everything. That man is too much of a Jew, and he runs too

tight a temple. Sisterhood simply isn't big enough for
the both of us . . ."

This brought Maurine Levenson on the run to ask
me to pacify her. "Rabbi, if you knew how hard sisterhood works to get members—"

The implication was plain: rabbis were far easier
to come by because they were open stock. "You want
me to tell Edythe I'm not *enough* of a Jew? That ours
is a *loose* temple?"

"Maybe if you convince her you're not *too* Jewish—"

"How do I do that? By blessing her damn Christmas
tree?"

We let it go at that, and Maurine still hasn't for-
given me; after all, you can't hire a new sisterhood
member. So it was that Christmas headed for the Hillendale Temple this year, bringing not peace, alas,
but a swearword.

א

Dear Rabbi Abel,

I happened to be at the temple last Sunday when
the children of the fourth grade were putting on
the assembly program, and I couldn't help but be
impressed by the Wohl child in particular, who
spoke so beautifully and with such impeccable manners. I went over to congratulate his mother afterwards, Cheryl Wohl, who struck me what a lovely
young woman she is, with immense charm, intelligence, personality, breeding and such a tremendous
devotion to Judaism.

Hence this letter. Cheryl Wohl is a divorcee, you
might not know. (The divorce was her husband's
fault, which you also might not know, but everyone

in Hillendale can tell you what a terrible man he was.) I am writing this letter therefore not only as your congregant but also as a friend to suggest in all good faith that the lovely Cheryl Wohl might very well make a very fine life's companion for a rabbi such as yourself.

With all good wishes for your happiness,
A Friend

Dear Rabbi Abel,

You *must* have received my last letter (I sent it registered), so I really can't understand why you haven't acted upon my suggestion to look up Cheryl Wohl. She really is enormously charming, personable, intelligent, highly attractive, talented too (she paints) and with a tremendous devotion to our common religion.

Really, what have you got to lose—except your loneliness and what must be an aching void in your life?

Trusting that what they say about a word to the wise being true—

With greatest sincerity,
A Friend

Rabbi Abel:

What's the matter? Don't you like girls? Is that

why you spend so much time with that goy Rutherford when you can be dating a nice Jewish girl?

                                        Suspicious

Gideon:

   Mrs. Cheryl Wohl called me last night to say she's
quitting the Temple and ask for her dues back.
From the way she talked, it sounded like a personal
matter to me, as if she'd had a fight with you.
What was it about?
   Please let me know at once because I'm sending
the Sunshine Committee over to see Mrs. Wohl on
Thursday night to try and straighten things out, and
it's important for them to know *your* side of the
story. I think maybe an apology from you would
help.

                                        Barney Singer

                            א

THANKSGIVING

FOR Thanksgiving, Hillendale's Episcopal Church joined my congregation in a service at the temple. (We invited several outlying Negro churches and the local Catholic church too, but they had already been booked by other houses of worship.) The turnout was excellent, thanks possibly to Vernon and me inciting our respective groups with "Wouldn't it look *awful* if more of *them* attended than *us?*"

Several new faces showed up, like the couple in front of me at the water fountain who, noting my robe, asked about the Christies in my church.

"Sorry, I don't know them." Hold on—Christie? At the temple? "What are your names, please?"

"Claire and Jack Bernstein," the woman said. "We belong here."

"Happy to meet you. I'm your rabbi."

Don't worry, I hadn't embarrassed the couple, though that was my sincere intention. "Happy to meet you," the man said, "Rabbi Jacobson."

Dr. Bidwell, an aristocratic gentleman with sculptured features and graying temples who looked as if he could model aplomb, opened the service with an invocation: ". . . Teach us now, we pray Thee, never to take our munificent blessings for granted, but to count them daily. Make us appreciate, moreover, that religion's sacred mission is to instill the spirit of God into people's hearts, thereby regenerating them with Thy love, for it is only that love that can transform lives. Indeed, the regeneration of society is God's work alone, while ours is to save souls . . ."

(No wonder Vernon had described his rector as the National Association of Manufacturers given extreme religious unction: "His kind preached about the souls of the poor while opposing poor relief, even as the vast majority of Germany's Christian clergy concentrated on 'spiritual' matters during the entire Nazi period. To listen to people like Bidwell, you'd think Jesus was only Adam Smith wrapped up in a bedsheet. So while the church is dying for want of servanthood and public responsibility, our lay leaders take their cue from the Bidwells and conduct church affairs as if Christ died for our first mortgage. The entire Episcopal church allots for social action the cost of one Coke per member!")

I conducted the prayer service, and Vernon preached, opening with "What on earth is there to be thankful for today?" He followed this with harsh statistics: Negroes, who make up ten percent of the labor force, account for twenty percent of the unemployed and thirty percent of long-term unemployment; the year before, only fifty percent of all Negro men had steady full-time jobs. Meanwhile, the gap between the rich and the poor—nations as well as individuals—continues to widen, and three million children die of starvation every year; by the 1970's a billion people will be starving. Yet the United States allocates four billion dollars to limit food production, thirty-five billion dollars more to explore the moon and only one half of one percent of its gross national product for foreign aid. Vernon then suggested that church laymen train adults and teen-agers for jobs, float low-interest loans for middle- and low-income integrated housing, pair rich suburban churches with poor city ones. Concluding, he appealed for our government to appropriate two hundred billion dollars over the next ten years for the war on poverty and, as it did under the Marshall Plan, allot two percent of the GNP for foreign aid.

My friend's sermon did not please everyone. "Does he think people come to services to get depressed?" Maurine Levenson asked me afterwards. And Pete Schuster remarked, "Rutherford was like a foreign movie without the sex."

Dr. Bidwell fared better. "I just love your diction!" Edythe Loring told him. "Are you from England?"

"Well, not quite," the rector said. "Staten Island, actually."

I was leaving the temple later for Thanksgiving dinner at the Redmonts' when somebody drove up, calling my name. At first the driver looked unfamiliar, but the two lovely girls with him, eleven-year-old Carla and her eight-year-old sister Joy (UNICEF's biggest collectors on Halloween), made me guess he was their father, Sid Frankel, a temple trustee I had

seen exactly three times during the past five months—
once at my interview, the second time on Yom Kippur,
and the third time at a neighboring urinal in the local
movie theater.

"We almost missed you," Frankel exclaimed, "we
were so busy preparing this." He pointed to a tray on
the girls' laps, piled high with a turkey, fresh fruit,
nuts and candy, all wrapped in cellophane and rib-
bon.

Before I could thank him, Carla said, "There's nine
more packages in the trunk."

"Ten altogether," Joy said.

Sid Frankel gave a proud-father smile. "It was their
idea, Carla's and Joy's. My wife and I just helped with
the shopping and cooking, Rabbi."

"I see," I said, but of course I didn't, not yet.

Carla said, "I told them what you said to our class
last week." (What had I said? Clergymen talk so
much that it's easier to keep track of our silences
than our statements.) "Remember how you read to
us from Isaiah and Michael Harrington?"

Joy pointed to the tray. "This is for all the *poor*
people."

Touched, I kissed both girls.

"Rabbi," Sid Frankel said, "would you help us dis-
tribute the packages?"

"Sure, of course. Who are you giving them to?"

"We don't know," Carla said. "We came to ask *you*
who, Rabbi."

"Who to give the packages? Why, to—to—" I
stopped short, stricken. I had no idea! I didn't know
any poor people in the North. The closest I had come
to poverty here was shaking hands once with Sargent
Shriver's millionaire brother-in-law.

"Rabbi?"

I was a perversion of Abraham; he couldn't name ten righteous people in Sodom and Gomorrah to save the cities, because there was only Lot—and here were forty million poor in the Other America, and I couldn't think of ten to save my soul. "Excuse me . . . something I forgot . . . be right back . . ." I mumbled, and dashed into the temple.

What now? Where to look? Whom to call? To ask, "Would you kindly give me the names and addresses of ten poor people? No, this is *not* a scavenger hunt." Eve Greenwood, who taught the disadvantaged pre-kindergarteners, had flown to Aruba for Thanksgiving —Barney Singer! An eight-year resident of Hillendale, *he* would know. I phoned; he sounded as testy as if I had interrupted both his dinner and his nap at the same time. "Frankel made up those packages, didn't he?" he said. "Let him find somebody to give them to."

I can't figure my president out. The temple's hardest worker, he is nevertheless religion-deaf, as attuned to the still, small voice as to dog whistles. The week before, he wanted me to fire our best Sunday School teacher because her students often left clay behind on their classroom floor. Like Curt Langer is devoted to Dr. Terman, Pete Schuster to his own ego, Rick Adler to appearances, Sam Warren to his fears and Maurine Levenson to reliving her sorority days, the president dedicates himself to the temple organization instead of to Judaism and God. *Who* says the Second Commandment is obsolete?

The police were no more helpful. The cop who answered my call had me spell my name and address first, before telling me, no, the police didn't make it a practice to donate food to Jews on Thanksgiving, and he hung up. I phoned back to explain I wished to *contribute* food, and the cop said he'd call me right back. He did, but with no information. "You're on the level," he said. "I figured you for some crank, meaning no anti-Semitism, of course; a friend of mine used to be a Jew, you know. What happened, Rabbi? Got stuck with leftovers from some bar mitzvah? . . . No, how should I know anybody who's poor?"

Then—how could I have so quickly forgotten his sermon?—I called Vernon.

There was a silence at the other end of the phone. "Well," he said, "those migrant farm workers in the next town—they're bad off; they get paid below the minimum-wage level, well below. But they're not there now, at this time of— Wait! This Negro church just over the county line, the one I invited to join our Thanksgiving service—I imagine its minister could help you." Vernon gave me the church's address, adding wryly, "Thank God for the Negroes. The people they don't make feel superior, they make feel good and charitable."

I returned to the Frankels a conquering hero—I had succeeded in uncovering a lead to one four-millionth of the nation's poor—and told them of the Negro church.

Carla exclaimed, "Oh, I can hardly wait to see the people's faces when we give them the packages!"

"You don't want to hand the packages over personally," I said.

She looked at me with surprise. "I don't?"

"Carla, it's wrong to make people feel ashamed of their poverty or indebted to you for performing your duty as a Jew. That's not true tzedakah, *true* righteousness." Sound selfless, don't I? A semitic Mary Worth. Well, there's appearances for you, because all this while I'm thinking of maybe inserting some halvah and stuffed derma into the packages to tip off the recipients that the donors were Jewish.

"Would it be right for us to go along while you delivered the packages?" Carla asked. "We could just stand outside and watch."

(Like Miriam watching from afar over her baby brother Moses!) "Sure," I said. "Know what else you can do? You can write notes saying 'Happy Thanksgiving.' That would add a warm personal touch." Back inside the shul with the children I made sure to hand them temple stationery to write on—well, I conceded sainthood wasn't my glass of tea—to combat Negro anti-Semitism, I told myself before calling myself a hypocrite. Then I phoned Dore Redmont to explain my delay.

"I'm jealous," he said. "I wish my kids had thought of that idea. Hell, I wish I'd thought of it myself."

Thirty-five minutes later Carla brought me the notes. "It took so long because we thought it'd be nicer if each letter was different," she said. I picked up one of the notes and read it:

Dear,

Happy Thanksgiving is what we wish you, a *very* Happy Thanksgiving Day to the whole family. It would be very nice if all your other days in the year were happy also. We sure hope so.

Love,
Yours truly

Lovely. But wait now—what happened to the letterhead? I pointed to the ragged edge at the top of the stationery, and Carla said, "Yes, we remembered to tear off the temple's name. Now they'll never be able to trace the packages."

(Do you sometimes suspect, as I do, that God has this secretary who goes around tidying up after Him?)

The children chattered all the way to the Negro quarter—about the packages, how they decided what to include in them, why they chose *gold* cellophane and *red* ribbons—but they fell silent when the Frankel car entered the black ghetto of bleak row upon bleak row of shabby clapboard houses.

"Do people live in those things?" Carla asked.

Joy burst out, "Ten packages won't be enough. We should have made more."

Sid Frankel parked in front of the Zion A.M.E. Church. We got out of the car and entered the building. Nobody was inside; that we could tell at a glance, for the entire church consisted of one room.

"Where do they hold Sunday School?" Carla asked. "There aren't any classrooms."

Joy said, "They don't even have a kitchen."

"Let's find the minister," I suggested. "He usually lives near the church." Luck was with us, for as we stepped outside, I spotted directly across the street a big wooden six-pointed star nailed to the front door of a house. "Look, there he is."

"What would a Christian minister be doing with a Jewish star?" Carla asked as we crossed the street.

I explained that the six-pointed star was called the Star of David, and the minister probably used it because his church bore the name of Zion, a nickname for Israel, over which David had been king and which was a land holy to Christians as well as Jews.

"It doesn't make sense," eight-year-old Joy said.

I knocked on the door—a card in the middle of the Mogen David read: YOUNGER—and it was opened by a heavy-set Negro woman dressed in her holiday best. Introducing the Frankels and myself, I asked if she was the minister's wife.

"Minister?"

"Of the church across the street."

The woman snorted. "You say you a rabbi?"

"That's right."

She pointed at her front door. "Don't you see that Star of David?"

"Yes—?"

"You think a Christian nails up a Star of David like that, for all the world to see?"

"That's what I asked, Rabbi," Carla said.

"*She's* smart."

"Well," I said, "the church *is* named *Zion*—"

The woman chortled. "You think Zion and the Star of David go together like ham and eggs? You a rabbi, and you don't know no better than that?"

Already I was beginning to regret having enlisted in the Frankels' war on poverty. "All right. Why did you put that Star of David on your front door?"

"Why do you think? I don't want nobody here taking us for one of them Christians. We're *Hebrews.* Matter of fact, me and my family are leaving for our temple in Manhattan right this minute."

"Really!" I stopped myself from telling her about the several fine Negro Jews I knew: it would sound too much like saying black was the color of some of my best friends. Instead, I explained my mission, asking if the woman knew people in need, perhaps at her temple.

"We don't take no charity," she said curtly, then directed us to the minister's house around the corner.

The parsonage, it turned out, had a big cross on the door, and something told me that in this instance the cross had spawned the star. Inside, Reverend Hobbes, an elderly man with a degree from Union Theological Seminary framed over his threadbare couch, said his parishioners could put the ten packages to good use, and accepted them, thank God; I was beginning to fear having to bear to my grave these contemporary marks of Cain.

As we headed back to the car, the Youncers drove up alongside. "Tell them," Mrs. Youncer said, pointing to her two daughters in the back seat, "don't Chanukah come early this year? Next Sunday night, matter of fact?"

Delighted with the gutturalness of the woman's *ch*, I said, "You're absolutely right, Mrs. Youncer. And a *ch*appy *ch*oliday to all of you."

Carla expressed my own thought as the black Jews drove off: "If they belonged to *our* temple, Rabbi, they wouldn't have to travel all that way to Manhattan."

That night at a board meeting I revealed our exciting opportunity to be the first integrated shul in the county—tokenly integrated, to be sure, for there were very few black Jews.

"Hey, that's great!" Dore Redmont exclaimed.

"A good thing," Charlie Hecht said.

"A fine thing," others echoed.

Maurine Levenson asked, "Do they have children?"

"Four," Sid Frankel said, "all boys."

Sam Warren called for a discussion.

"A discussion of what?" I wanted to know.

"Whether to admit those people into the temple," Sam Warren said, he the membership chairman, whose only question of prospective members, heretofore had been financial, and everyone started to talk at once.

My civil rights experiences down South should have taught me, I suppose, not to expect an immediate overwhelming welcome for the Youncers. Still, some of the comments I heard now shook me:

"But wouldn't they be happier among their own kind?"

"They're so pushy nowadays. Take my maid . . ."

So we had our dicussion, and like most of our discussions on most other topics, the same suggestions were advanced:

——consider the pros and cons (Barney Singer wanted to list on a blackboard the debits and credits of having a Negro family join our congregation).

——appoint a committee (Sam Warren suggested two: one to request a statement of policy from the United Synagogue of America, the Union of American Hebrew Congregations, the Union of Orthodox Congregations, and Hadassah; and the second committee to investigate the Youncers).

——beware of hasty action (Pete Schuster advised us to proceed slowly with all deliberate dilatoriness).

——*"Mah yomru ha-goyim?"* (Rick Adler wondered what people would say, those in the temple and outside, Jews and non-Jews, agnostics and atheists, men of good will and bad, everybody in the United States).

——define terms (Charlie Hecht asked me for an exact definition of a Jew).

——realize the complexity of the Negro problem (Maurine Levenson explained that no temple could be expected to solve a three-hundred-year-old dilemma overnight).

——acknowledge that we were all guilty (Dr. Lipton implicated all mankind in systems that produced the oppression of minorities).

——ascertain why it was that Dr. Terman had never discovered the Youncer family (Curt Langer).

Dore Redmont stood up. "I'd like to ask Rabbi Abel a few questions," he said, facing me. "Rabbi? Did you teach us in adult education that Jewish tradition entitles a person to close a synagogue for letting a wrong go unremedied? Like if children won't support their destitute father, can he state his case publicly in shul and bar all prayers inside until the entire congregation rights that wrong?"

"Entirely correct."

"Does Jewish law further teach that a man's color is one hundred percent irrelevant to anything at all?"

"Correct again."

Dore slammed his fist down on the table. *"Then what the hell are we discussing here!"*

(I could have cheered; that was my student who said all that.) *"So* correct is Dore," I announced, "that if this temple barred black Jews, I'd be forced to resign." Don't worry, I was running no risk. The majority of the congregation would surely support me; besides, at this time of year there was no rabbi available to replace me.

By a vote of thirteen (enough to take pride in) to four (enough to be shamed by), the board accepted the Youncers as members. I could not restrain myself from saying, "It appalls me there were as many as four un-Jews who would blackball Negroes."

"Rabbi," Pete Schuster said, "what makes you think all four voted against the *Youncers?*"

After a sleepless night—you'd think I had just felled George Wallace with a slingshot, I was so elated! Somewhat depressed too; would Pete Schuster never stop regarding me as an interloper on his turf?—I knocked on the Youncers' proud Star of David early the next morning.

Mrs. Youncer opened the door. "You still looking for that heathen?"

(Apparently the woman's interfaith needed work.) "I'm here for another reason," I said. "To invite your family to join our temple."

"Your temple?"

"It would save you that long trip into the city, and you could make friends with—"

"But you're a Jewish temple."

"Certainly. Rabbi Jacobson may not think so, but—"

"I couldn't do that—"

"Oh, don't worry about dues. Whatever you can afford is fine—"

"Impossible—"

"Mrs. Youncer, it's un-Jewish to discriminate against people because they're white."

"Who's Jewish?"

"You have a lovely sense of humor, Mrs. Youncer, so Jewish."

"I'm Hebrew."

"That's why we'd like you to join our—"

"But you're not Hebrews. You're all Goldbergs."

"Of course. You remember: I'm a rabbi, a Jewish rabbi—" Finally it hit me: I was talking "Jewish," and she kept repeating "Hebrew." "You *are* Jewish, *aren't* you?"

"Do I look Jewish?"

"Huh?"

"Rabbi, I been telling you: I'm not Jewish. I'm a Hebrew."

"What is a Hebrew?"

Mrs. Youncer told me: the Hebrews were a Negro sect, somewhat similar to the Seventh-Day Adventists in holding to a literal interpretation of the Old Testament (yet Chanukah, which they observed, and the Star of David were post-Biblical) while rejecting the New Testament and Christianity; according to the Hebrews, each of the six points of the star represented—

But inside of me all this time a voice was drowning out her words, repeating: Gideon Abel is an idiot, an idiot is Gideon Abel—and what will happen when the board hears about this?

As soon as I left Mrs. Youncer, I called Vernon and asked him to join me at the Posh Nosh. I needed a friend to bolster my spirits before that evening's Sabbath service, when I'd be confessing my folly to the entire congregation. Yet when I met Vernon it was difficult to speak. How did one begin? "Hey, guess what kind of jerk *I* am!" Coffee was served, and I was still searching for an opener when I realized that Vernon had hardly spoken either.

I looked up at him; at the same instant he looked up at me. We both said, "What's the matter?"

"You first, Vernon; you're three years older. What's bothering you?"

Scowling, he extinguished his fifth cigarette. "I'm a complete and total fraud."

"You—a fraud? Don't be silly."

"You heard my great sermon yesterday. All those statistics, carefully researched like a brief—to stress the urgency of aiding the poor, the unfortunate. Fifteen minutes later you call me for the names of ten, and I can't think of *one*."

"Well, neither did I."

"You've been in Hillendale twelve weeks, Gideon; I'm here over a year. 'The poor are always with us,' Jesus said, but since He neglected to give Vernon Rutherford a map— Well, now you know the truth about me. When it comes to religion I'm like everybody else: I talk a great game. That's why I'm always bitching how un-Christian Bidwell is, and that's why he disturbs me. Because, God help me, I *am* Bidwell."

"I'd rather be Bidwell than an ass," I said, then related my experience with the board and the Youncers, hoping for Vernon to deny my asshood as I had denied his fraud.

But my friend didn't follow the script. "Don't say the Youncers aren't Jewish," he advised.

"You're telling me to lie?"

"It isn't a lie to say Mrs. Youncer refused to join the temple, is it?"

"But, Vernon—"

"Gideon, it all depends which you prefer: absolution from the congregation for acting hastily, or the opportunity to lead them to other difficult choices."

"That's the easy way out, for me not to tell the truth."

"I don't think so. *You'll* never forgive yourself for jumping the gun; that's not easy. Gideon, why discredit your leadership when it's needed for the future?"

"You're mixing me up. I don't *want* to tell them, so it *must* be wrong—"

"Gideon, haven't you told me of Judaism's stress on community? And you agreed with my criticism of pietistic Christians who concentrate on their own individual salvational navels instead of the good of the group. Well . . .?" He paused to light his sixth cigarette. "Gideon, are you now going to choose a personal emotional release, as I did with all my pious talk? (Remember my describing Pope Pius' outrage if the Nazis had issued the Jews condoms instead of only butchering them?) Or will you save your temple's soul?"

Well, you can guess what I told the congregation. But I bet you can't figure my motive. How could you, though? I'm still not sure myself.

א

My Dear Friends and Fellow Congregants,

As you know, in June the congregation will be voting on extending Rabbi Abel's contract for another term. Now I'm sure that our Temple is as dear to your hearts as it is to mine and that you too want what is best for it. This means, of course, that our Spiritual Leader must be nothing less than the best also, outstanding as administrator, organizer and galvanizer of men. Representing us also as he does to the community at large, we need furthermore a Rabbi everyone respects, gentiles and Jews alike, and not one we have to make excuses for.

I would therefore be grateful to you for communicating to me your feelings as to how Rabbi Abel is meeting our standards, if indeed he is. Please feel free to speak your mind frankly, because your letters will be held in strictest confi-

dence. After all, we both want our Temple to be
an inspiring success, and not just another synagogue.

May the Lord bless you ever with His most benef-
icent blessings.

> With kindest personal regards,
> Pete Schuster
> Chairman, Temple Improvement Committee

Dear Rabbi Abel,

Enclosed please find a carbon copy of my reply
to an official Temple query, which asked us in the
congregation to estimate your performance thus far
as our rabbi. I sincerely hope that my comments
herein might prove helpful to you.

> With all good wishes,
> Curt Langer

To the Temple Improvement Committee:

Without comparing Rabbi Abel to Dr. Terman
(for it would be unjust to measure a beginning
rabbi against a seasoned one), it is my sincere belief that Rabbi Abel shows a good deal of promise.
Certainly he tries hard and has enormous enthusi-
asm (though it does often impel his youthful blood
never to stand still, but always boiling to do something). I'm sure, however, that time will settle him
down, while experience will teach him that nobody
has all the answers by himself alone.

In this connection I recall how often Irv would consult me on issues facing the congregation (which he did *before* taking public positions), so personally interested in each and every congregant was he. Whether remembering everybody's anniversary with handwritten notes of congratulation, or joining men's club for a shvitz at the Turkish bath, or sending Valentine cards to the girls in sisterhood, Irv was always more than merely our rabbi, but one of the Temple Family too, happy with us, like a proud father . . .

א

DECEMBER·

I FEEL *awful* about Pete Schuster's letter," Eve Greenwood began. "Imagine, soliciting dirt to bury a rabbi with!!"

"Forget it," I said, for I thought it improper to discuss one congregant with another, or to curse in public. "That isn't why you asked to see me, is it?"

She shook her head. "No." Running her fingers through her long red hair as if trying to estimate how long it would take to pull it out by the roots, she said, "Rabbi, I'm going out of my mind!"

I was surprised. Eve was a very bright thirtyish woman who seemed able to take care of everything except perhaps choosing the right husband. Jerry Greenwood, alas, was no match for his wife in intellect, wit or kindness. "Tell me about it."

"It's my mother-in-law," she said apologetically. "She's driving me crazy."

Mrs. Greenwood? Again I was surprised, for she resembled Eve more than her son. Mrs. Greenwood was the warm-hearted lady who had vowed at my installation not to let me starve in Hillendale, and never reneging, she had sent me a different delicacy every week.

"You see, we live in the same house, all of us— Jerry and I, the children and Mother Greenwood. And she's always baking something for Jerry and the girls, or telling *me* what to bake. Jerry's put on twenty-five pounds this past year alone. And when it rains, his mother's telling him to put on his rubbers; he's thirty-five years old and saying yes. She stuffs the girls with so much candy they'll be lucky to have a tooth left in their heads for their confirmations. Then she's always improving on my recipes or taking the wrong side in an argument— Rabbi, she makes me feel so guilty."

"Why?"

"Because I love her! I really do. No, I mean it. Jerry's mother is so unselfish and giving; she's goodness itself. I'm an ingrate to complain about her. And that's the worst of it: Mother Greenwood is driving me smack out of my mind, and I can't even hate her for it. Because she's a darling."

"How long has this been going on?"

"Twenty-three months now, such a *long* twenty-three months. Since Mother Greenwood lost her husband and Jerry worried about her living alone in a big house."

"Well, that makes things easier. Since it was Jerry's idea for all of you to live together, it wouldn't be rejecting if you found Mrs. Greenwood a place of her own."

"Oh, we couldn't do that."

"Why not?"

"It's Mother Greenwood's home we're all living in."

"Oh."

"You see, Jerry hasn't been doing so well the last few years. A partner of his turned out to be a crook, so he had to start a new business. And living at Mother Greenwood's—she wouldn't take any rent, she's like that—has helped a good deal."

"What about outside interests? Service to the community—"

"She does that. She's a Gray Lady at the hospital, reads to the blind, helps out at Neighborhood House, works for sisterhood, and she never misses a Sabbath service, as you know."

True. Mrs. Greenwood had a better attendance record than Barney Singer, and her comments on my sermons afterwards were certainly more discerning. (She always loved them.) A good-natured, plump, fiftyish woman with loving brown eyes and salt-and-pepper hair, she looked like grandmothers used to look before they discovered stretch pants. "What about friends?"

"In suburbia? Suburbia is a coupled affair—haven't you noticed, Rabbi? There aren't any single people around, and she's too young for the Golden Agers. Besides, I wouldn't want to match lovely Mother Greenwood up with just any man."

I pondered for a while, then concluded, "Well . . ."

"Yes, I've run out of ideas myself." Eve Greenwood stood up. "It's been good ventilating, Rabbi. I'll be going home now"—she grimaced—"where I'll find

Mother Greenwood has bought a dozen more outfits for the girls, who'll be eating sixteen Baby Ruths while she's whipping up more blintzes for Jerry, who's getting to look more like Kate Smith every day."

After Eve left I typed my sermon, swearing anew as my two fingers came up with weird words. And that's when a possible solution struck me. I phoned Mrs. Greenwood. "Can you type?" I asked her.

"I used to," she said. "When my husband opened his first law office I— Oh, excuse me, Rabbi, my cake's in the oven—" She put down the phone, but I could still hear her. "Girls, *girls!* You promised not to eat more than two Hershey bars apiece. Now hide these wrappers before Mommy comes home."

When Mrs. Greenwood returned to the phone, I asked if she'd like to be the temple's part-time underpaid secretary.

"Delighted! And forget about salary. It'll be my pleasure."

She started work the next morning, bringing me a pineapple cheese cake. "People don't have confidence in skinny rabbis," she explained.

A few days later the mailman delivered a parcel addressed to "The Greatest Rabbi in the World, c/o The Hillendale Temple." Accepting it at once, I opened the package to find inside five pounds of Barricini's chocolates, with a card that read: "From a wildly grateful congregant and daughter-in-law."

I called Eve to thank her, and she exclaimed in a rush of words, "You've saved my life! When that darling woman comes home now, she's too pooped to pop Hershey bars into the children or blintzes into Jerry or recipes into me. And yesterday morning, when Jerry and I were having a terrible argument, she was so anxious to get to temple on time she

didn't linger to announce which one of us was right.
How can I ever thank you, Rabbi?"

But I ended up owing Eve. For Mrs. Greenwood
turned out to be a superlative secretary, dedicated
(she often stayed overtime), conscientious (she took
courses to brush up her typing and to learn speed-
writing), immaculate (she removed all the cheese
cake spots from my jacket, and the only thing that
stopped her from doing the same for my trousers
was my refusal to take them off), thoughtful (she
brought me breakfast every day because, she said,
rabbis shouldn't have waists smaller than Scarlett
O'Hara's), efficient (she corrected the English in the
letters I dictated), kind (she was always inviting me
home for dinner), inspirational (she had better ser-
monic ideas than mine), considerate (she wrote my
parents every week that I was improving).

In short, inside of one month Mrs. Greenwood was
driving *me* crazy. Unwitting saint that I was, I had
not solved Eve's problem; I had confiscated it. For
now I had to spend more time at the temple than I
wished (it embarrassed me that Mrs. Greenwood
often came earlier than I and left later); I found
myself writing my sermons to please her (how would
you like to see someone typing a sermon of yours and
wrinkling up her nose?); I started writing out my
letters at home the night before, correcting the English and memorizing them (so she wouldn't find
errors when I gave her dictation the following morning); I was putting on weight (my waist now rivaled
Scarlett O'Hara's bust); and each morning I had to
explain why a nice Jewish boy like me wasn't married yet, especially since congregants, she kept saying,
don't have faith in bachelor rabbis, even fat ones.

One day in self-defense I asked Mrs. Greenwood,

"How come a nice Jewish girl like you isn't *re*married?"

"Oh, who would want to marry me?" she said, not coyly but matter-of-factly.

"Anyone who's mad about cheese cake, ruggelach, honey cake and a marvelously good heart."

She smiled. "The way men my generation figure: why settle for an old heart when for the same two dollars you can get yourself a fresh one? Their accessories are in such better shapes."

"Since when is fifty-four old?"

"You forget, Rabbi—a man is young as long as he can exercise his passions; a woman is young only so long as she can provoke them."

"You provoked Professor Evans." (A stab of mine at matchmaking. I had invited an old bachelor college prof to dinner, then asked Mrs. Greenwood to join us.) "He talked so much that evening, and he's usually quite reticent."

"He talked, all right. But who understood him? Existentialism, angst, theater of the absurd, hexachlorophene. All I understood was the professor's pauses, the one time he did. He must be a wonderful swimmer, that man; he doesn't breathe."

"What about Mr. Kimmel, the butcher?" (Eve's try.)

Mrs. Greenwood snorted. "I was never so embarrassed. I had changed butchers last month, and Eve brings him home for dinner! That Mr. Kimmel—he's always angling for invitations. That way he sells his meat and eats it too. But enough about me." She pulled out a box from her shopping bag. "Here, tell me how you like these ties for your new blue suit that you should buy."

A few days later, following the morning Mrs. Greenwood had waxed my office floor to surprise me and sewn up the rip in my jacket after I slipped and fell on the newly polished floor, I was tracking an article by Barbara Ward on the underdeveloped nations of the world through brassiere and girdle advertisements in the *New York Times Sunday Magazine* when suddenly the idea struck me: my father's bridge crony, Ben Palmer, the Corset King and, better yet, widower. Of course! I telephoned at once, asking him to join me for dinner the next evening at a congregant's home, and he accepted.

In the morning I said to Mrs. Greenwood, as she was unwrapping antimacassars she had made for the couch in my office, "You haven't invited me home for dinner in a long time."

She beamed. "How about tonight?"

"Fine. Okay if I bring along an old friend?"

In his expensive black silk suit, white-on-white shirt and silver lamé tie, Mr. Palmer, when he showed up thirty minutes late at my apartment, would have looked like a stocky Dun and Bradstreet sweetheart if he hadn't smelled like the Bowery. "I didn't have much else to do today," he explained. "They don't change the movies till Wednesday."

I made him take a package of chlorophyll Chiclets. Then I had to remind him to spit them out when we drove up to the Greenwood home.

"Those weren't mints?" he said.

Nobody ever died from swallowing a dozen Chiclets, I hoped. Still, how many drinks did the man *have* that day?

Inside we were welcomed with joy, warmth and childish resentment—depending on whether the speaker was Eve, Mrs. Greenwood or Jerry. No, I

wasn't mistaken about Jerry Greenwood's attitude; on
previous occasions he had made such remarks as:

"What's this magic power you have over women,
Rabbi? If my wife and daughters aren't telling me
how super you are, Mother is."

"I don't have to attend services any more. Mother's
always previewing your sermons all week long, and
afterwards Eve quotes them."

"Well, Rabbi, what do you hear from God lately?"

A college thrownout and something of a failure at
business, Jerry Greenwood was the insecure man's insecure man, never appreciating the fact that anyone
with a lovely family like his *is* a success. This I had
preached in one pointed Shabbas sermon, and afterwards Jerry told me, "That was a long one tonight,
wasn't it?" The kind of man who would envy anybody's having a bigger chip on his shoulder than his
own, Jerry resented his wife's ability instead of taking
pride in it. Eve, for her part, had refused to become
a trustee until the board first offered Jerry a committee chairmanship, whereupon even then he had
disparaged the temple for accepting women as trustees. That anyone as sweet and good as Mrs. Greenwood was Jerry's mother led me to believe that
gipsies went around switching infinitely more babies
in their cradles than people ever suspected.

After we had some delicious canapés, I made the
mistake of correcting a mistake of Mr. Palmer's because I wanted him to appear in the best possible
light. "You mean you're a widower, not a divorcé."

"Yes, Alice died," Mr. Palmer said sadly. "But Dolores didn't."

"Dolores?"

"My second wife. Your parents didn't tell you?"
He sighed. "Maybe because my second marriage

didn't last much longer than the Huntley-Brinkley Report. It was annulled right away." He felt called upon to explain, heaven alone knows why. "Dolores was underage."

It was hard to discern who among the Greenwoods gasped the loudest. Me, I merely dropped dead inside of me.

Mr. Palmer offered a footnote. "Every person over fifty tries to recapture his youth. I was only being more literal than most."

Mrs. Greenwood started away. "Excuse me. *Something* must be burning in the kitchen."

"Dolores told me she was twenty-five. How should I know she'd turned her speedometer ahead?"

Mrs. Greenwood paused. "Even twenty-five! You're at least—"

"Twenty-five is what she said. And I was only too anxious to believe her. You see, I was afraid the A-bomb was getting me. And I had to get in my last licks before it was too late."

"Too late for what?" Eve asked.

Mr. Palmer hesitated. "Yes, I *will* have a cigarette." He took one out of a gold case and lit up, while Eve and Jerry made unhappy faces at each other and I cursed Barbara Ward. "Age—that's my A-bomb. The way I feel, Red China may not get me, but cholesterol sure as hell will. Oh, I've been married before, like I said. For thirty-six years. To the same woman. And Alice and I were very happy too—ask the rabbi's parents. But we had married very young, and every once in a while, especially after my two boys married and then Alice died, every once in a while I'd get to wonder maybe I was missing out on something. You must feel it yourselves sometimes, don't you? There's got to be *more* to life than *this*. And

Dolores had everything. Anyone could see that. She used to model my girdles."

"Oh!" said Mrs. Greenwood.

"Mr. Palmer," I interjected, "the new styles in women's fashions—how do they affect your business?"

He never heard me. "Ai ai ai, Dolores! Robbers demand your money *or* your life. Dolores, however, wanted both." A sigh. "Still, those four months were marvelous while I lasted." A chuckle. "She almost killed me, that girl! Intentionally, I think. She acted like she'd read somewhere that if your husband dies on his honeymoon, the bride collects double indemnity."

Mrs. Greenwood, annoyed now, paraphrased, "But ah, my foes, and oh, my friends, she gave a lovely night."

That, thank heaven, stopped Mr. Palmer. "You read Edna St. Vincent Millay too?"

"*You* read Edna St. Vincent Millay?"

"Alice," he said, "used to read poetry to me sometimes. Alice, my first wife."

"That calls for a drink." Tactfully—it was obvious Mr. Palmer was a bit high—Mrs. Greenwood asked, "What would you like, grape juice or vegetable juice?"

Mr. Palmer appeared stricken. "Grape juice or vegetable juice?"

"They're frozen."

"I don't doubt it for an instant."

"We also have a bottle of something I take a sip of when I can't fall asleep. Would you prefer that, Mr. Palmer?"

"What is it?"

"Oh, it's alcoholic. I just don't know what kind; we're not drinkers in this family, and the label fell off last June. But I'm sure it's good stuff; it tastes horrible."

"I'll take it. I'm not particular, I drink anything." Mr. Palmer shuddered. "Anything but frozen vegetable juice."

"I'll help," Eve said. Catching up to her mother-in-law, she whispered, "Isn't he dreadful?"

Mrs. Greenwood looked glum. She said, as the two of them exited into the kitchen. "This is the first night I've ever held my husband's death against him."

Jerry beamed. I had never seen him happier, not even the Shabbas when he told me what was wrong with my last three sermons. Evidently one man's turning out to be poison to his mother was his meat.

"You know," Mr. Palmer said, "your mother is very nice, for a person who doesn't drink." A shrug. "Alice never used to drink either before she married me."

"She became an alcoholic?"

Mr. Palmer laughed. "Only a bartender. At our parties. That's the only time I used to drink myself, when we had people over. We liked to entertain a lot. We used to—" Suddenly he turned serious. "I miss Alice, miss her very much. That's why I couldn't resist the offer of a homecooked meal tonight. Not that I'm crazy about food. I do love homes though. Mine is only a house now, as huge and empty as—as me, I guess."

The phone rang. It was the temple's answering service, asking me to call Dore Redmont. I tried, but his number was busy. When I returned to the living room, the women had returned too, everyone was sipping something, and Mr. Palmer was still going strong.

". . . and then she started calling me a *sexagenarian*.

Who knows where she had picked up such a word? It made me feel like some degenerate. As if Fredric March wasn't lots older than me when Kim Novak married him!"

Eve was surprised. "Kim Novak married Fredric March?"

"Of course," Mr. Palmer said. "Didn't you see *Middle of the Night* on The Late Show? Funny thing—I didn't mind when I found out Dolores was selling everything I gave her. But when I found out she was also selling what *she* gave *me*— She was only my wife, a private detective told me later with pictures, as a sideline."

Mrs. Greenwood, her patience wearing thin, said, "Oh, are we talking about Dolores for a change?"

Mr. Palmer refused the hint. "You know, to me Dolores was like—"

"Like a daughter."

"Oh, no. She wasn't old enough to be my daughter. Dolores was like—well, she was like the sun in the wintertime: she dazzled more than she warmed. Sex is a wonderful thing, Mrs. Greenwood, but sex—"

Mrs. Greenwood's patience ran out. "Mr. Palmer, I'm the kind of woman, when somebody starts talking about sex, all I can think of is Gimbels."

Mr. Palmer slapped his thigh and hooted. "That's funny! Like something Alice would have said. She'd say things that sounded funny on the surface, but underneath, bloody murder. I don't suppose you could fix me a Bloody Mary—this drink tastes bloody awful —no, I guess not. Know something? Alice and you— you're a lot alike. Maybe that's why I've been running on about Dolores. Maybe I wanted to see how Alice would have reacted if she'd known, whether she'd have been ashamed of me." He made a face. "Mrs. Greenwood, it's a terrible thing, growing old ... terrible."

(The outburst embarrassed Eve, Jerry looked disdainful, and I found myself thinking of the poignant verse "O Lord, do not discard us when we are grown old.")

Mrs. Greenwood regarded the man with compassion. "Mr. Palmer," she said softly, "you know an alternative?"

He shook his head. "Would you believe it? I still don't know why I married Dolores! Oh, she was pretty, and she was fun, and she certainly knew how to— But still. There's more to life than that . . . That's what everyone tells me."

Happily the phone rang again. This time it was Dore Redmont, who informed me that the deposit for the new kitchen construction was being handed over that evening; since we both insisted on writing an antidiscrimination clause into the trade-union building contracts, I had to be there to make sure it was done. Lovely! A mitzvah would enable me to escape the house now. It wasn't until after excusing myself that I realized the Greenwoods would still be stuck with Mr. Palmer; I couldn't very well ask for him to be excused also.

Eve and Jerry saw me to the door. "It was very sweet of you to try," she said. *He* said, "Nobody's asking you to try, try again."

Mrs. Greenwood came running out of the kitchen. "Don't worry about your old friend," she said. "What he's drinking now is a mixture of black coffee, tomato juice, vanilla extract and Maalox. He'll be all right." And then she pressed a whole roasted chicken on me. "Just in case you wake up hungry in the middle of the night, you should have something to nibble."

The next morning I beat Mrs. Greenwood to the temple. "I'm sorry to be so late," she said when she finally arrived with my breakfast, "but your Mr. Palmer kept me up till the end of The Late Show."

"I'm sorry too, about Mr. Palmer and his behavior."

"What are you apologizing for? It was thoughtful of you to bring me a dinner date. Made me feel like I was still in the race."

"But the way he spoke and all—"

"Well, he was feeling guilty. And guilt is soluble in alcohol, I've noticed."

"He *should* feel guilty. Imagine—a man his age marrying a twenty-year-old. Or was she seventeen?"

Mrs. Greenwood looked at me as if I were no older than Dolores. "Rabbi, lonely people sometimes do foolish things. Some marry teeny-boppers, others bake cheese cakes."

"You're defending him?"

"Well, I've played his games myself."

"What games?"

"Getting through the day and living through the night—I don't know which is worse. When you have nothing to do with yourself and nobody really your own to do it for—"

I felt sad. "Has it been so lonely for you, Mrs. Greenwood?"

She shrugged. "Two by two they went into Noah's ark, Rabbi, and things haven't changed much since. That's why I let the children move in with me— against my better judgment. Because I was lonely. Jerry told me he wanted to save rent money, and Eve he told he was worried about my living alone. Actually, Jerry moved in because he's always been too close to me. Too close for Eve's comfort, or his own good. It's impossible for two women to share the same kitchen, so how can they share the same man?'"

This was getting to be more like a murder mystery every minute. It began as an ordinary conflict between daughter-in-law and mother-in-law, and now it turned out neither of them was the heavy; it was Jerry.

"I'd better get to work now." From her shopping bag Mrs. Greenwood produced a yellow pad full of notes, which she handed me. "Maybe you can use this. It's some research I did for that Israel sermon you're planning." The woman was incredible: maybe I would solve her problem, Eve's, Jerry's and my own bachelor one by marrying her myself. "Oh, yes— mind if I leave on time today? Somebody's taking me to *Hello, Dolly!* tonight."

Several weeks passed, and either Mrs. Greenwood began mothering me less or I had begun enjoying her ministrations more. It did seem, however, she was spending less time in my office, more time in the beauty parlor, no time baking my favorite goodies, some time on a diet, and she even missed one Sabbath service and a day of work. Had she found an outside interest, perhaps male? I hoped so.

Occasionally Mrs. Greenwood mentioned Mr. Palmer, and once she commented, "People think they know everything about themselves by the time they reach middle age. But the trouble is, every new stage of life is another adolescence." And the following week: "Who's ever prepared for widowhood? Finding yourself technologically unemployed. Looking forward to the milkman and the mailman every morning, *anyone* to talk to. I'm sure Mr. Palmer never intended to marry that Dolores. But what with being so alone, his sons having their own families, also running the business now, watching *Middle of the Night* five times on television and—know something? I think that movie must have ruined more middle-aged men than all the prostate glands in New Jersey. Mr. Palmer only proposed to that girl to see if she'd accept. How could he know she'd take advantage of him and say yes?"

I assumed then they were seeing each other. It wasn't likely after all this time she'd be able to quote him verbatim, not without periodic refreshers. And it was so. Once Mrs. Greenwood was late for a date, and Mr. Palmer called me, worried. He phoned back ten minutes later to say she had finally arrived, explaining apologetically, "We didn't want people to know we've been going together. My sons would think I was being debauched again. They don't trust me since I brought them a stepmother younger than the Beatles and, worse than that, had to give her a settlement out of their inheritance. And that Jerry Greenwood thinks I'm a real bum. He acts like I'm bent on deflowering the woman."

The next morning Mrs. Greenwood apologized for not having made me a hot lunch all week, then said, "Well? Aren't you going to say anything about me and Mr. Palmer? He said he spoke to you last night."

"Praying is a rabbi's business," I said piously, "not prying."

"What if I want you to pry? Half the fun of going out is talking about it afterwards, and I can't talk about Mr. Palmer at home. Jerry doesn't approve of him. But then, just between us, I don't think Jerry approved of his father either."

"You like Mr. Palmer?"

"A lot more than cheese cake, certainly. Lately I've been getting awfully sick of baking."

"Should I start looking around for a new secretary?"

"Oh, don't be silly. Mr. Palmer would never marry me."

I bristled at the slur. "Why not?"

"Because Dolores was twenty years old, and I'm *size* twenty."

"What if he *would* propose? What would you say if he did?"

"If! If my grandmother had had heavy water, she'd have been a bomb."

"Mrs. Greenwood, if you don't answer my questions, I'm going to stop prying."

"Well, I know Eve would live happily ever after if I got married, but the question is, Would *I?*" She picked up her shopping bag and pulled out my clerical robe, which she had taken home to lengthen without my knowledge. "But it's an academic question, really. I'm working on something now that should settle things for good." And that's all she would tell me.

Three weeks later Mrs. Greenwood invited me to dinner, not at her home but at the Posh Nosh, where Mr. Palmer joined us as her second guest. Neither of us knew the reason for the occasion, and she waited till cocktails were served before enlightening us.

"I want you two to be the first to know—Jerry will probably have a tantrum, so like a coward I'm postponing telling him. I want your reactions first. You see, this is like a rehearsal of sorts and—"

"For God's sake," Mr. Palmer exclaimed, "tell us already!"

Mrs. Greenwood took a deep breath. "I'm moving to Israel. My papers came this morning."

Mr. Palmer gaped.

"You're moving to—?"

"The Holy Land, yes. Why so startled, Rabbi? It was that marvelous sermon of yours that gave me the idea."

"But it was directed at our teen-agers," I said, "to enlist a year of their lives for Israel—"

"Well, even the Peace Corps accepts fifty-year-olds," she said. "And the Jewish Agency assured me that people my age also can contribute—"

"But why?" Mr. Palmer burst out.

"You'll have to read Rabbi Abel's sermon. I'll send you a copy."

"Mrs. Greenwood," I said, "what's the other reason?"

"Other reason?"

"Tell us, Mrs. Greenwood."

She sighed. "Well, I think it healthier all around if I don't live with the children. Eve's a dear, but I'm getting on her nerves. And I'm spoiling my grandchildren; I can't help myself. It isn't good for Jerry either. How can you be a man when your mother's always around to remind you that you're a child? And since they can't afford to move out—"

Mr. Palmer cleared his throat, then spoke hesitantly. "May I suggest an alternative? May I? I have this huge house, Mrs. Greenwood. Move in with me."

She smiled. "I'm afraid the rabbi wouldn't approve of that."

He took her hand in his. "Mrs. Greenwood, I just asked you to marry me."

"*Mr. Palmer!*"

I kvelled with nachas! What, after all, was the very first thing the Lord had done after creating Adam?

He made Eve, of course. And if matchmaking was good enough for God—

"You have to call me Ben now—Ruth." He leaned over and kissed her on the mouth. "Come, let's call the children and tell them—"

"Tell them what?"

"Why, that we're getting married."

She shook her head. "But we're not."

I don't know who was more astonished, Mr. Palmer, or I.

"We're *not* getting married? But a second ago—"

"I was carried away," she said apologetically. "It's been thirty-eight years since anyone's proposed to me, and I was just carried away. Even a woman my age can get carried away—almost. Oh, it isn't that I don't like you, Mr. Palmer, because I do, I do."

"Then why—"

"I am fifty-four years old. No, that's not true; I'm fifty-seven. Mr. Palmer, I am too old for you."

"Too old for me? Hell, I'm sixty-three."

"Dolores was twenty. And she was pretty, and she was fun, and she certainly knew . . . things . . . things I've probably . . . forgotten by now. Mr. Palmer, I just would not stack up."

"Ruth, I don't have such a good memory myself, believe me."

"Marrying me after being married to Dolores—no, Mr. Palmer, I have no desire to be an anticlimax. Besides, I don't love you."

"You don't love me?"

Mrs. Greenwood shook her head ruefully.

"That's wonderful! Marvelous! Beautiful! I don't love you either, Ruth. Now you *must* marry me."

"What?"

"Listen, Ruth, when I asked Dolores to marry me,

I said I loved her—and when she accepted, she swore she loved me too. And we both knew we were lying in our teeth."

"But—but—but—"

"It's different with us. I like you, and you like me— you just said so, didn't you? I have the greatest respect for you, you know that, and I'd be so grateful to you for keeping me company during the long days and lonely nights. Ruth, Ruth, Ruth, *save* me from The Late Show!"

She clasped and unclasped her hands. "I don't know, I just don't know."

"What don't you know?"

"I don't know how we'd get along, and who wants to be bothered now? I mean, starting all over again at my age . . . wedding, honeymoon, new husband, new home, honeymoon . . . Now I prefer talking to— It's too unnerving. I may not be ecstatically happy now, but at least I have my peace of mind."

"Peace of mind? Peace of mind can drive you right *out* of your mind! That's what's wrong with the two of us now. Neither of us have any problems to solve, decisions to make, troubles to worry over. So I marry Dolores, and you run away to Israel."

"That's not so—entirely."

"You know who has peace of mind? A vegetable has peace of mind. Ruth, do you want to marry me and have problems and troubles? Or do you want to be an eggplant the rest of your life?"

"Oh, Mr. Palmer, I don't know . . . I just know I'm afraid . . ."

Mr. Palmer grabbed both her hands. "Ruth, you're fifty-seven, and I'm sixty-three. What in hell do we have to *lose!*"

I tried to slip away in the silence that followed.

But Mrs. Greenwood gripped my arm. "Don't go, Rabbi!" she implored. "Tell me, what should I do?"

"Well, if you ask me—" I checked my counsel though rooting for their marrying. "Mrs. Greenwood, what do *you* think you should do?"

She wailed, "Why does a Jew always answer a question with another question!"

It was the first marriage I'd ever officiated at, and I was so nervous that the florist took me for the groom. To pass the time till the ceremony, I helped set up the wedding canopy and decorate it.

The first guest to arrive at the temple was a lovely olive-skinned Latin type, whose long, wavy black hair made me appreciate that woman's curves could begin from the crown of her head. No relative of either bride or groom, Gina—that was the name on her gold necklace—had been befriended by Mrs. Greenwood at the hospital, she said, where she had recently begun working as a therapist and the bride did volunteer work. She also mentioned giving Mrs. Greenwood the address of an aunt in Rome to visit on her around-the-world honeymoon; no, she was not another blind date for me, alas, because she was Catholic. Such a pity! For Gina was a beauty, with huge eyes that were exquisite mosaics of greens and blues, and not caged in her high-cheekboned face by mascara.

"You have eyes like stained-glass windows," I told her, and isn't it lucky I'm an eye man? How would it be for a rabbi to be a breast or behind man? This way, while girls think I'm looking them so steadily in the eye out of sheer attentiveness, secretly I'm being demoralized.

The girl smiled. "Even your words are flowery." She

touched one corner of the wedding canopy. "It's a beautiful chupah."

The way she pronounced the *ch!* "Are you Jewish?" I asked eagerly.

Remember that poignant scene in *Marty* when the butcher asks the old maid if she's Catholic, because *he's* Catholic and his intentions are entirely above bed? Well, that's not the way it played here, not by a moon shot; making an ugly face at me, Gina snapped, "Are you bigoted?" And she started to lecture me on anti-Semitism.

I burst out laughing. "Hey, I'm a rabbi."

"A rabbi?" The girl was astonished. "But you don't look— I mean, the florist truck outside says, 'Lars Jensen,' and with your hair and then that question—"

"Why does it upset you to be asked your religion?"

"Well, I thought—"

"Would you get so insulted if I asked if you were an American?"

"I'm *proud* to be a Jew, I'll have you know. Where's the ladies' room?"

Presently the wedding party arrived. Lest I conclude that Gina was Mrs. Greenwood's matchmaking tit for my tat, she said to us at once, "The two of you shouldn't get the wrong idea. I think you're both *much* too good for each other."

The ceremony began. My voice kept cracking with emotion as I prayed aloud . . .

Mr. Palmer was also nervous; I imagine that's why he stamped on my foot instead of the wineglass at the end of the ceremony. Then, furtively looking around at his children and grandchildren and his new wife's family, he kissed the bride on the ear, as if to demonstrate he was on his best behavior.

"Mazel tovl" everyone cried.

Afterwards dinner was served, and each of Mr. Palmer's sons took turns toasting the bridal couple. Jerry made a toast too, but not for them. "Here's to Super-Jew, Rabbi Gideon Abel, who steals women's hearts and gives them away with equal ease."

All the Palmers laughed at the jest.

But the bride started toward her son with arms outstretched for hugging. (I knew that's what she intended; how else does one comfort a sulking child?) At the last moment, however, she clenched her hands into fists and pulled them down to her sides. "Dear, you must learn," she said quietly. "Mothers also have to leave home one day."

Jerry forced a smile. "Sure, Mom." He embraced her. "You know what I wish you."

And me? What did Jerry Greenwood wish me? I wondered.

א

——*It's awfully nice of you to come visit, Rabbi.*
——My pleasure, Mrs. Levine. What a great week. Yesterday I officiated at my first wedding, and now you've given birth to my first congregational baby.
——*LeVine.*
——Pardon?
——*Our name is pronounced LeVine. Didn't you know? Rhymes with shine, not sheen.*
——Oh. But don't you spell it—
——*The same way—yes. But our V is capitalized.*
——I see. The baby—how's he doing?
——*Eleven pounds, nine ounces; he's so big the doctor says he could have been twins.*
——That's wonderful. What have you named him?

——*Well, Ralph wanted the baby named after his father, Samuel.*

——*Samuel LeVine—sounds feen. I mean, fine.*

——*Oh, we're not naming the baby Samuel. We're naming him after Samuel. With an S, you know. We picked Sean.*

——*Sean?*

——*You don't suppose people will think we named him after those James Bond movies, do you? But we did want a name that wasn't run of the mill. You understand.*

——Of course. Let me see now—Sean's bris will be next Friday. What time—?

——*Bris?*

——The circumcision.

——*Oh, that.*

——It's done on the eighth day, and since the baby was born Friday—

——*Well, to tell you the truth, Rabbi, we've told the doctor to go ahead and circumcise Sean whenever he feels like it.*

——What?

——*It's hygienic, we know. But to make a whole religious thing out of it with a ceremony and special Jewish doctor, well—I'd never say this to Rabbi Jacobson of the other temple, because he's so old-fashioned Orthodox—it just strikes me as barbaric. You understand, don't you, being a modern rabbi?*

——Barbaric?

——*Besides, when we attended Ralph's brother's son's bris last year, as soon as the mohel started cutting away at the baby—I'll never forget it as long as I live—Ralph grabbed hold of his—you know—and keeled over in a dead faint. It was awful! He almost skewered himself on the doctor's knife.*

——I can get your husband a chair to sit on this time.

——*No, thanks, Rabbi. A bris still seems too voodooish for anyone living in split-level times.*

——Mrs. Levine——

——*LeVine. You're not going to give me a Jewish pep talk now, are you?*

——No, no. I'd merely like to ask a favor.

——*Favor? What is it?*

——Please don't repeat what you just said to Queen Elizabeth.

——*Who?*

——Queen Elizabeth, you know, had all her sons circumcised by the official mohel of the London Jewish community. Now I don't know about Prince Philip——

——*Queen Elizabeth of England?*

——That's the one. Here, you can read about it in this news clipping I happen to carry in my wallet.

——*Imagine that! Queen Elizabeth!*

——Yes, Mrs. LeVine.

——*Well, we want our son to have every advantage; we're very Jewish that way, Rabbi. Suppose I speak to Ralph about a bris, and meanwhile would you keep Friday open for us? We certainly want to start Sean off on the right foot. Oh, I just remembered, Rabbi—next Friday is Christmas Day. Would that make a difference?*

א

W I N T E R

S O L S T I C E

I was in the shower that evening when the phone
rang, and the only thing that made me answer it,
dripping wet, was my hope that the board meeting
had been canceled. Who yearned to discuss whether
General Electric or Hotpoint would give a house of
God's kitchen more for its money? Besides, I needed
to husband my resources for the following night, when
the stockbroker who had spoken to the Episcopal
church brotherhood the week before would offer tips
to men's club on blue chips.

"*Gideon! Oh, Gideon—*"

"Iris? What's the matter? The way you sound—"

"Can you come right over? I'm at Hillendale Hospital."

Hospital? I threw on some clothes and raced to the

hospital, scared. Iris wasn't one to get upset easily. Vernon or the twins—had one of them been in an accident? God, no!

She was sitting in a corner of the lobby, staring at the clock over the information desk. Her face looked so drawn and chalky that I hesitated to approach; I wasn't sure I wanted to hear her news. She saw me, however, and ran over; clutching my hand, she told me it was Vernon. No, there had been no accident, thank God; my friend had undergone a series of tests that day—lately he had not been feeling well, I knew that—and the doctor was operating in the morning to remove part of his stomach.

My voice cracked as I said, "Stomach—?"

"Ulcers, the doctor says. But sometimes ulcers turn— Oh, it's all my fault!"

"What are you talking about?"

"You know how unhappy Vernon's been in Hillendale. He never wanted this kind of church, he wanted to minister to the inner city. Only, I wouldn't let him. *He* heard a call, I *never* did. A future lawyer is the man I married, so I wouldn't let him take a slum parish; why subject our children to slums? He's been eating his heart out ever since. That's what's given him ulcers or—"

"Iris, Vernon never told me he was miserable here, least of all that he stayed on because of you."

"He didn't? Too bad. Maybe if he had told you . . . maybe he wouldn't be lying upstairs now. But he probably didn't want to sound disloyal to me. Gideon, the operation's tomorrow; they'll find out then what it is . . . Oh, how am I going to get through tonight . . .?"

She took me to see my friend. I didn't know what to say—against the white linens, his swarthy complexion

looked green—and Iris forced cheery remarks, so
Vernon led the conversation. He joked about all the
church meetings he could miss now, regretted not
having bought a Christmas tree for the twins, told
Iris not to tell his parents about the operation, and
asked her to bring his Bible, adding for my benefit,
"*Both* Testaments." A deep sigh. "Everything I've
urged on hospitalized people, about God and faith
and prayer—now I get to find out if I really meant
it, don't I?"

The nurse came in to say visiting hours were over.

Vernon kissed his wife and shook my hand, a
formality we hadn't observed since the Sunday we
met. "Gideon?" he said. "Pray for me."

Intellectually I'm offended by the notion that God
must be bribed with prayers before deigning to heal
the sick and relieve the oppressed. *The Song of
Bernadette* always infuriated me with its implication
that the Lord couldn't care less for those who didn't
acknowledge Him king of the hill. Yet I replied in-
stinctively, "Sure, Vernon. Of course." No, God doesn't
need our prayers; we do.

A Gray Lady approached Iris and me in the hall.
"Oh, my dear, is it true? I just heard they're operating
on Vernon tomorrow. But it isn't *cancer*, is it?"

Iris gulped. "Of—course—not."

"Oh, that's a relief," the woman exclaimed. "Cancer,
when you're opened up, it spreads something awful—
the air hitting the cells, you know. Oh, my dear, I'm
so glad it isn't cancer!"

Iris burst into tears.

Without pausing to step on the Gray Lady's tongue,
I hurried Iris to her car. "It isn't what that woman
said," I kept repeating all the way home; she would
say, "Of course not," and then we'd switch lines.

She started to prepare dinner for her seven-year-old twins, while one asked if Vernon was at another meeting and the other wanted to know why all the kids on the block had their Christmas trees up and decorated for two weeks now, when *their* fathers weren't priests or even Episcopalians. But she dropped the first plate she handled. It broke, and she cut her hand picking up the pieces.

"We're all eating out," I announced.

Mark and Luke whooped. I asked where they wanted to eat, and the boys cried together, "Chinese!"

We drove to Kublai Khan's Nationalist. While the family was being seated, I phoned Barney Singer to say I'd have to skip the board meeting that night.

"But we're discussing the new kitchen," he said.

I'd explain at the men's-club meeting, I told him, then joined the Rutherfords without removing my overcoat; in my rush to the hospital I had left my apartment without a jacket, tie or belt. I ordered for the four of us: dinners for the boys, Jell-O for Iris, tea for me. It was good that the children were with us: she wouldn't let herself break down in front of them, and their fight over who had more noodles distracted her; it was bad too, for the boys resembled their father so much one couldn't look at them without thinking of Vernon in the hospital.

"I remember once telling you," Iris said, playing with her dessert, "how shocked some ministers' wives are to discover their husbands have weaknesses, like ordinary men. But not me. I was different—because I had married a law student. Yet when the doctor told me Vernon might have—" She checked herself. "Character weaknesses I was prepared for, but not this. My first thought was: It can't happen, not to a clergyman. God wouldn't *allow* it."

Poor God, He gets it in the neck every time. If only He didn't let Himself be publicized as all-powerful. But he probably had His pride, like everybody else. The Lord guides us in living a good and creative life—only an ingrate would demand He do anything. I couldn't say this to Iris, of course, not now. Besides, at this moment I myself didn't accept it.

"*Do* it, Rabbi."

"Do what, Mark?"

"Wiggle your ears."

"And your thumbs, Rabbi."

"Okay." Would you believe it? Nothing I had learned in divinity school had stood me in such great stead in the rabbinate as having been born double-jointed and loose-scalped.

"Having a good time, Rabbi?"

Sam Warren was standing beside me. I stopped in the middle of an intricate double-wiggle to introduce Iris and the twins.

"Say, who you voting for, Rabbi? Hotpoint or General Electric?"

"What? Oh, the meeting. Well, neither. I'm not going tonight."

"You're not? But it's such an important meeting."

Iris intervened. "Don't miss your meeting on my account, Gideon. You don't have to stay with me." Which was a mistake.

Sam Warren's eyes opened wider than Little Orphan Annie's, as his eyebrows raced for his hairline.

I couldn't very well explain, not with the children there. Besides, it would seem I was granting Iris some kind of favor. "I can't go tonight. But I'll see you in temple on Shabbas."

Sam Warren threw me a look which clearly stated, You don't come to my meetings, why the hell should

I come to yours? (I know that's what he was thinking, because a few weeks earlier his wife had told
me, "Roberta never invited us to any of her parties;
why should we attend her funeral?")

After Sam Warren left, Iris said, "I can manage
now. You really should go to that meeting."

"Oh, my congregants can get along without me."
Not to give the game away, I added, "For one night."

The Rosenmans descended upon us. "I thought
that was you, Rabbi," Shirl said. "I told Max here,
but he said, 'It couldn't be the rabbi, not without
socks,' and I explained that that was the height of
fashion now, no socks, among college boys."

So I was also sockless. What would Shirl Rosenman
think when she found out I wasn't wearing underwear
either? "I was in such a rush—"

Iris tried to help again, alas. "It's my fault. I called
Rabbi Abel before and he's so obliging—"

"Isn't he though?" Shirl said, and Max commented,
"I see you go in for Chinese food, Rabbi, spareribs
and all."

"Only Chinese tea. They make swell tea, the Chinese. I believe Rabbi Jacobson *also* drinks Chinese
tea." I stood up. "Would you excuse us? We were
just leaving."

On our way to the cashier Rick Adler hailed me,
and I only had myself to curse for not having remembered that Chinese restaurants outdraw synagogues every day of the year except Yom Kippur.
"Mind if I ride to the meeting in your old green
thing, Rabbi? It would save me a trip. I could give
my wife the car now."

I flinched. "Sorry, I'm not attending the meeting.
Something important came up. I mean, something
more important. I mean, something *even* more im-

portant." I couldn't change my mind now if I wanted to, which I didn't. What, trustees would want to know, had been pressing enough to keep me from the meeting that became *un*-pressing as soon as everyone saw me dining out on spareribs in public alone with a married woman and wiggling myself? Now if only Iris would *not* say—

"Go, Gideon. You don't have to keep me company any more."

For centuries mathematicians have been talking about the perfect circle; Rick Adler's mouth now formed it.

"Maybe I'll stop by later," I said. "The meeting will probably be going hot and heavy till after midnight, like always."

Rick Adler regarded me coolly. "Sorry you think we blabber too much, Rabbi."

We left.

"Gideon, want to know the truth?" Iris said. "I'm glad you're staying with us tonight. It helps." That made all the gossip that was sure to follow worthwhile. It also eased my embarrassment to discover in front of the cashier that I was not only without a jacket, tie, belt, socks and underwear, but also with no wallet. So when I asked Iris for money, I pretended nonchalantly not to see the Rosenmans, Adlers and Warrens pretending not to see her hand me ten dollars to pay the bill.

I drove the Rutherfords home—all the way the twins nagged about a Christmas tree, worse than Edythe Loring—and dropped them off there, saying I had to pick up the rest of my clothing. Returning to my apartment, I finished dressing and got my billfold, then went out looking for a tree; it would cheer the kids, and decorating it would help Iris pass this long night. I found a mart in a lot off Main Street—its enormous size implied there were more Christians in the world than I had ever realized—and asked the proprietor for a nice tree.

"Nice trees is all I got, mister," he said. "What color?"

"What do you mean, what color?"

He pointed to an assortment of pink, white, red, blue and green evergreens. "Where you been living, mister—in a monastery?"

"Well, I'm a rabbi, you see—"

"A rabbi? No sh—" He checked himself. "Really?" He shook his head. "Boy, this ecumenical thing is really something, isn't it? I can't go to church any more without tripping over a bunch of Protestants or Jews there. You have no idea how hard it is on my priest; he can't use his old sermons any more."

"The tree is for a sick friend—"

The man smiled. "That's what all my Jewish customers say." He held up one finger. "Hey. You being a rabbi, you should know. How come Jews have holidays thirty and forty days long?"

"No Jewish holiday lasts that long."

"Are you sure? Every night for a month now this Jewish neighbor of mine is lighting candles in her window; tonight there were twenty-five candles there. Which doesn't bother me, except this Rosenman woman gave her son his twenty-fourth present in a row last night, and my kids are calling me a Catholic cheapskate."

A traditionalist in religious rites, I decided on a green fir tree instead of a dyed synthetic, and the proprietor helped me tie it—the biggest tree there—to the roof of my car. "When you rabbis go in for something," he remarked, "you really go all out."

"Why, you look *exactly* like Rabbi Abel! Anyone ever tell you that?"

It was Kay Evans, of course, Christmas shopping. God, I hate small towns. You can't blow your nose without people noticing, debating its necessity and commenting on your style. They always knew whose relative I blind-dated, with how much success, and they were still asking me about Rochelle Levenson. I said, "The tree is for a friend—"

"A *sick* friend?" Kay Evans asked.

The children hugged me when they saw the tree—what a sad holiday for them without their father at home—and tears filled Iris's eyes. But putting it up would present a problem, since the tree was taller than the house. I hacked off a few firry feet (learning in the process that there are such things as pine-needle splinters), and the four of us stood the tree up in the living room, then decorated it with tinsel and foot-high figurines of angels. Around the base Iris arranged the nativity scene, with the Magi, animals and onlookers. "Vernon buys me a few of these every year. Aren't they lovely? This year he—" She stopped.

I asked for the star to put atop the tree.

"I'll hang it up," Iris said.

"Sure. I understand. You should put up the Star of Bethlehem yourself."

"You think I don't want an unbeliever tainting our star?" She almost smiled. "I just don't like chancing your falling off the ladder. What would your congregation think of a rabbi who broke his neck while trimming a Christmas tree?"

"If that's your only reason," I said, ascending the ladder with the star in my hand. "It's less risky for a man to hang than a mere woman."

"Please be careful, Gideon," she said.

Reaching out from the top of the ladder—my hand was two feet from the treetop—only then did I realize that Christmas trees are shaped like triangles, not rectangles, but after all, this was my first Christmas tree. Down I climbed from the ladder, pushed it closer to the tree, though not two feet closer because the thick branches blocked me; then back up I went. Now only nine inches or so wide of my mark, I leaned over nearer, with the twins cheering me on and Iris again cautioning.

Seven inches to go . . . three . . . I stretched myself just a little bit farther.

"Let's help Rabbi," Mark said.

I smiled—they were such adorable kids—then gasped as the ladder began to wobble.

Iris clapped her hands. "All right, into bed now. We can't have you knocking down the rabbi."

The boys resisted, Iris insisted, with me silently rooting for her, and they left the room after bidding us good night, they were such well-mannered children —so well mannered they even stopped to say good night to their dog, which since my first visit was always locked away in the basement when I came over; they were a most considerate family.

"Sweet dreams, Beauty," the twins said.

It replied with a howl that was much too clear and far too close; evidently good manners dictated that one must never say good night through a closed door, and when the boys had opened the basement door Beauty bounded past them into the living room. Spying me, the beast howled the equivalent of "Long time no see!" and lunged to complete what he set out to do at our first dialogue, knocking the ladder out from under me.

"*Beauty!*"—that was the last thing I heard Iris cry

as, below, a wide-open drooling mouth rose to meet
me—"Be *careful* . . ."

א

——*How's your head, Gideon?*

——Fine, thanks, Barney. It wasn't a concussion,
after all.

——*That was a nasty spill you had. Lucky the dog
broke it.*

——Good old Beauty.

——*I'm surprised he didn't bite you, your landing
on him like that.*

——Well, it seems *I* scared *him.*

——*And Reverend Rutherford—how's he doing?*

——Thank God it wasn't— I mean, the doctor said
the operation was a complete success. Vernon
will be home in two weeks.

——*Good. I explained to Doug Bettleheim that
that was the reason you didn't visit him in the
hospital—you were all banged up yourself.*

——Doug Bettleheim? In the hospital? What's the
matter with him?

——*A stone in his bladder. And he was put out you
didn't visit him, especially when he heard you
were on the same floor that day, seeing Reverend
Rutherford.*

——Why didn't the Bettleheims call me, like Iris
Rutherford did?

——*Doug was sure somebody would tell you. You
didn't know, Gideon, did you? I mean, just between us.*

——No, Barney, I didn't. I'll visit Bettleheim tomorrow.

——*Well, he's home now.*

——*Oh?*

——*He was just there overnight. He passed the stone right away.*

——Then I hope to soon have another chance to visit Bettleheim in the hospital.

——*There are a few other things, Gideon, I want to discuss.*

——Yes, Barney?

——*The new temple kitchen, for one. The contractor is ready to start building—only we don't have enough money to finish. And some people say the reason we don't is because of you, because you never supported it in any sermon or temple bulletin column. Why, you never so much as mentioned the kitchen. People find that odd, you being our spiritual leader.*

——What could I say about a kitchen?

——*When we were considering this old Beardsley estate, Dr. Terman compared our buying it to the Maccabean recapture of the Second Temple.*

——I'm sorry, Barney. I honestly can't think of anything appropriate.

——*Well, doesn't the Torah recount at length the building of the Tabernacle?*

——Yes, but the Tabernacle housed the Tablets of the Law, Barney, not a walk-in freezer.

——*All right, if that's the way you feel about it. Gideon, there's another thing that needs discussing—our Sabbath services.*

——Yes?

——*Only seventy-four people attended last week.*

——There were eighty. Well, I also counted.

——*You probably included the Shapiros and the*

*Goldins, didn't you? But they're way behind in
their dues. And those two strangers aren't members, they just came in off the street.*

——Oh.

——*What's worse, attendance has been decreasing.
Take the last four services: eighty-nine, eighty-
seven, seventy-nine and now seventy-four. I'm
not counting the family service—that always
draws over two hundred, since the children like
you—or last Sabbath, when a hundred and
eighty-six people came because they heard you
almost killed yourself trimming a Christmas tree.*

——You think I ought to fall off ladders more often?

——*I'm serious now. Gideon, you're just not drawing at Sabbath services. Yet business is booming
at all our other affairs. The Sisterhood Gourmet
Supper was a sellout, so was the Father-and-Son
Dinner, the Valentine's Day Darlings' Dance is
half sold out already, and when that stockbroker
spoke to the men's club, even the women came,
and I don't know how many Christians. So evidently people are dissatisfied with Sabbath services; it stands to reason. If more people were
satisfied, we'd be drawing more people.*

——I guess so. It works that way with *Bonanza.*

——*There! That's another thing I want to talk to
you about.*

——What?

——*Your sense of humor. It rubs people the wrong
way sometimes. Not me, understand, because I
always enjoy a little humor; it's important, I
think, whatever your religion. But at the last
board meeting, after Curt Langer got through
telling you exactly the way Dr. Terman ran
things around here, you said, "Thank you very*

much"—which was fine, very polite. But why did you add, "Mrs. Danvers"? You have no idea how insulted Curt got, hearing his masculinity impugned. He's a married man, you know, with four children and a pregnant wife.

——That wasn't my intention. Mrs. Danvers was Rebecca's devoted housekeeper in—

——*Well, that's very nice, but not everyone understands your Biblical references. And at that same board meeting, when after the success of our special services—the birthday service, anniversary service, Sisterhood Sabbath, Men's Club Sabbath, Young People's Sabbath—when Maurine asked you to come up with ideas for more special Sabbaths like that, you suggested a Witches' Sabbath. Really, Rabbi.*

——I was only trying to point out that the Sabbath itself is reason enough to attend services.

——*Well, evidently the message hasn't been getting across. Here we're talking of enlarging the sanctuary because it's too small to hold the entire congregation on the High Holidays; yet it's never more than thirty percent full on ordinary Sabbaths. Why is that, do you suppose?*

——Good question. After all, the congregation *invited* me to preach to them; how would they like it if *I* didn't show up?

——*Well, you're paid to be there. Which reminds me—there's something I want to ask you, Gideon. It isn't public knowledge yet, but that director we hired for My Fair Sadie—he's quit to do an off-Broadway show. Worse, he won't give us back our fifteen hundred dollars—*

——You were paying him fifteen hundred dollars?

——*The temple show is always our major fund-*

raiser, so it has to be professional, to keep people coming back every year. Well, we remembered your degree in the drama and— Gideon, would you take over the direction for us?

——Me? Direct *My Fair Sadie?*

——*We don't have the money to hire another professional. And there's this to consider: if the show doesn't open, we'll have lost so much money I don't know how we'll be able to keep paying your salary.*

——Barney, you know what you're asking? You want me to go over to the *enemy.*

——*What enemy?*

——*My Fair Sadie!* Thirty-five people are involved in that damn show, and they rehearse so often they can never attend services or adult education. You want me to aid and direct my biggest competitor?

——*But, Gideon, you know our financial troubles; we rely on the proceeds from the Coke machine to pay our phone bill. Don't forget that the temple is, after all, a—*

——Yes, I know, a business. But people work so hard at keeping it solvent they never have time to use it for religious purposes. Sometimes I wonder why they joined in the first place! Why did you join, Barney?

——*That's a very personal question.*

——Sorry.

——*Not that I mind telling you, Gideon. It's an obligation, I feel, to contribute to the community. For years I devoted myself to general charities like the Community Chest. Until I realized that not once had any of the non-Jews in those organizations ever invited my wife and me to their homes for social reasons. I was good enough for heading drives because of my contacts with Jews, who are far more charitable than other groups—that's statistics—but otherwise they wanted no part of me. So I turned to the temple, hoping to be of service to people here. That's the real reason, Rabbi. I'm sure you don't believe any of Pete Schuster's stories. He's been slandering me because he wants to be president himself next year, that egomaniac. Because he can never join anybody, he's always trying to beat them. But what's all this got to do with your attracting more people to services?*

——Well, maybe if I understood the congregants' motivations——

——*That's what we're trying to do, Gideon—motivate members. The telephone squad is reminding them to attend services, I'm appealing to their loyalty to the temple, the ritual committee is involving more people and cutting down on the Hebrew, we're expanding the refreshments served at the Oneg Shabbas. So you see, Gideon, we're doing our part.*

——I appreciate it, Barney. Though after checking around, I find that we draw better at services, percentage-wise, than most synagogues. Seems that we Jews, who gave prayer to the world, may have given it away; we who led peoples into religion may be now leading them out.

——*Well, you could help by doing something about your sermons.*

——What about my sermons?

——*For a change, can't you preach on things that people don't feel quite so strongly about? Or*

*maybe if we lined up some guest speakers, like
David Susskind—*

——Barney, there's something else we can do. Instead of sermons, what if we had lectures, followed by discussions after services?

——*Lectures?*

——Yes, I could lecture on Friday nights, and later we could sit around and discuss. It would be a real learning experience.

——*Look, I'm trying to boost your popularity, Gideon, and you won't let me. Springing lectures on the congregation! And when I give you the chance to take over something as important as* My Fair Sadie—

——Barney, I have no choice. The rehearsals conflict with adult education. I'd have to drop my whole program to direct the show.

——*Still and all, twice as many members are involved in* My Fair Sadie *as in adult education. And you know our annual meeting is only a few months away, when people will be voting on Dore Redmont's proposal to give you a four-year contract.*

——Oh, I don't care about any four-year contract, Barney.

——*You don't? Why not? The other rabbis do.*

——Because they're family men. To me a yearly contract is just as good. I only want to do a good job each year.

——*Gideon?*

——Yes?

——*I hope you won't take this as an insult, but—*

——What is it?

——*You're no businessman. Oh yes, Gideon, before*

I forget—Curt Langer is going into the hospital next week for a tonsillectomy. Now be sure to visit him.

——Yes, Barney. I'll accompany you.

——*Oh, I'm not visiting Langer. We aren't that friendly.*

§

JANUARY

NOBODY can accuse my congregation of not being as modern as tomorrow's war. Jesus, according to the New Testament, drove moneychangers out of the Second Temple, and what drove us out of the Hillendale Temple was George Bernard Shaw bastardized. When *My Fair Sadie's* cast began meeting nightly—throwing themselves into rehearsals with the feverishness of performers intent on crashing the big time, Temple Emanu-El on Fifth Avenue—all nonthespians were forced to congregate in private homes for the duration, except on the Sabbath.

My sole contact with the show came when Dore Redmont insisted that Rona, the co-chairman, have me judge the suitability of one of the songs:

All I want is a colored maid
Who doesn't vanish when she's paid;
I'll not find her, I'm afraid,
Though wouldn't it be mazeldik!

A maid who doesn't chase the men,
Who takes her day off and not ten—
Let her even be Zen!
Oh, wouldn't it be mazeldik!

Oh, so mazeldik relaxing without travail,
I would never budge till Saks
Ran its first summertime sale.

Someone to care for the family
Who will not run off on a spree
And doesn't envy me—
Mazeldik! Mazeldik!

I ruled the song out, then offered a substitute of
my own. (The way sales were going, this was my
chance, as a lyricist, to reach ten times my audience
as a preacher.)

All I want is a home somewhere,
Far away from the Negro lair—
No integration scare . . .
Oh, wouldn't it be suburban!

Lots of problems I could escape,
No more Negroes trying rapes
And getting into scrapes—
Oh, wouldn't it be suburban!

Oh, so suburban sitting absopositively quiet—
I would never budge till summer
Brought its annual race riots.

There we could live so happily
With not a trace of bigotry,
Because it's Negro-free—
Suburbia! Suburbia!

Pete Schuster, Rona's co-chairman, called for the
inevitable discussion, which resulted in my song being
replaced by a new one, "Mrs. Fish's Knishes Taste So
Delicious." Why? Because several people charged my
song with being anti-Negro, anti-Semitic, lewd, all
three, or none of the above but so preachy it would
damage ticket sales.

Alas, Dad was right: you can't wise up all of the
people all of the time. Now in the middle of my
freshman year here, I'm realizing that there's nothing
I can do or say—or *not* do or *not* say—without one
of my hundreds of bosses taking exception or umbrage
or muttering darkly about June, not because it rhymes
with moon but, rather, with screw'im. I'm beginning
to feel like the man in the Talmudic tale with two
wives—one old, and the other young; the old one
kept pulling out the husband's black hairs while the
young one pulled out all his gray hairs, until the poor
guy ended up bald.

Not that all is bleak; far from it: there are many
lovely Jews in the congregation. It's just that Gresh-
am's law infects me too; at times the few bad Jews
here drive all the good ones out of my mind. Still,
though the *My Fair Sadie*-niks outnumber those congregants involved in adult education and social action, there are enough to make me feel like a rabbi.

Take Dore Redmont, for example. At the temple's New Year's Eve Frolic, he told me soberly, "I never felt happier than when pushing through that vote for the Negro Jewish family, because I never stand up that way for principle in my P.R. firm. How could I? I'd be out on the street in no time. All this while, you know what's been making me so miserable? The feeling I was constantly missing out on opportunities without even knowing what they were. That made me feel guilty. For wasting myself. I wouldn't have turned alcoholic, but I'd have found *something;* when a man's looking, he's bound to find. But now I feel some small sense of purpose, having discovered there's a people I belong to and mitzvos to accomplish. So I put in my forty stupid hours a week at myth-making, then take the money and run to try to accomplish things with the rest of my life. Because one thing's suddenly become clear to me: people become what they do."

Only a few weeks old, Dore's social-action committee was meeting for the fifth time—in Charlie Hecht's home that night—to map out campaigns for open occupancy, the improvement of public schools, a survey of job opportunities, job training, a negative income tax, the Israel bond drive, the combat of Russian anti-Semitism, safe cars, restrictions on gun sales and more. "Aren't you proud of us, Rabbi?" Dore exclaimed. "We're coming up with as many causes as the new temple kitchen will have appointments!"

During the meeting, Vernon phoned to ask me to stop by his house afterwards and look over his Sunday sermon. "Iris agrees with the gist of it," he said, "but she thinks maybe it's a little too rough and should be toned down."

"Sure thing. And I'll bring you *my* sermons. Maybe

you can give me endings. I'm still having trouble with my third acts."

"Gideon, use this last sermon of mine, and you won't worry about endings ever again—only a new beginning."

Vernon was kidding, of course—wasn't he?—but I was serious: it isn't easy, you know, to knock off two good sermons a week. Edward Albee established a world-wide reputation on the basis of two one-acters even before *Who's Afraid of Virginia Woolf?* and here we poor clergymen must compose their equivalent every week of the year, then preach to the same audience each time—and look what overexposure did to Milton Berle and Lassie. Worse yet, we usually preach to sanctuaries that are two-thirds empty. You have any idea what that feels like? As if you've stumbled into the fabled lost graveyard of the pews, the place where sermons go to die.

I left Charlie Hecht's around midnight, while the others lingered over coffee and cake, and drove to the temple to pick up my unfinished sermons. As on every Thursday night, I mused about their efficacy. Most clergymen consider preaching their main duty, maybe because it takes some eight hours to come up with a good sermon, and anyone who's expended that much time doesn't like to think the hours could have been better spent paring toenails. Let Billy Graham boast that his preaching has changed men's lives—after all, that's his racket. Me, I rather suspect preaching resembles dropping aspirin tablets from the top of the Empire State Building in the hope they'll fall into the open mouths of people on the street below on their way to Ohrbach's with headaches. Ever know a clergyman to walk a block to *hear* a sermon?

The temple was dark, the *My Fair Sadie*-niks having departed, and I made my way by the red light of exit bulbs through the hall and kitchen to my office. Opening the door, I flicked on the light switch and—

"*Oh . . .!*"

The couple on the couch reacted to the light as to a movie director's "Cut!" In the middle of making nice, the woman threw her hands over her face, the man disentangled himself, she screamed out like one dispossessed, he whirled around—and it turned out to be not a foreign movie after all. I beheld Pete Schuster with friend.

"*Sonofabitch!*" he cried, jumping to his feet.

Though I appreciated that fate was being addressed, not I, nevertheless the Marine in me automatically lashed out at the chairman of four different committees. Lashing was easier, more satisfying too, than explaining at length that a married trustee does not behave like this at the scene of his noblest temple-waving speeches. Almost as quickly I realized that my blow, a karate chop aimed at his windpipe, could very well kill the man—hardly sporting and rather awkward; what could I do with a dead Pete Schuster? —so I pulled my hand up short in mid-swing, changing its angle to a slap, which maintained enough momentum to spin him around like a corkscrew and send him sliding across my desk.

Something of Pete Schuster hit an open drawer, and he disappeared with a clunk over the far corner.

The woman was still screaming, so loudly now you'd have thought her virtue was being wrested from her petal by petal. Who was she? It was impossible to tell, for she kept her face covered, her hair was standard Miss Clairol blonde, and she was wearing basic black.

Scarier though than her screams was the silence emanating from Pete Schuster, parts of whom were dangling in the wastepaper basket. Had I executed him by mistake? I rushed around the desk and bent over him. He was stunned but breathing, thank God, through a bleeding nose, and his left cheek was bruised. Suddenly something blushed by; looking up, I saw the woman hightailing it out of the room.

Now what?

I could tattoo a scarlet letter on Pete Schuster's nose, then drop him on his front doorstep. Yet what good would that do? After all, there were his wife and children to consider.

Stepping into the adjoining kitchen, I soaked my handkerchief in tap water, then returned to wipe the blood off the man's face. He groaned, picked a paper clip out of his ear, opened his eyes, saw me, passed out again, or probably only pretended to while he tried to think up a better line than "You realize, of course, you just lost my vote for the four-year contract."

"Hello. Anybody home?"

I jumped and Pete Schuster quivered as the temple door slammed shut.

"Rabbi?" Now steps were heading through the hall toward my office, which was the only room lighted. "Is that you?"

Fly! Away! I couldn't let anyone walk in on this: Pete Schuster on the floor, and his tie and a brassiere entwined on the couch like a family crest. No, it wouldn't do for word to get around Hillendale that as a special fund-raising feature, the temple ran midnight orgies. Besides, there was always the possibility that I had jumped to the wrong conclusion; maybe the blonde on my couch had been Pete Schuster's wife, and the two of them were merely trying to invigorate their marriage by romancing in new surroundings, as prescribed by the *Ladies' Home Journal*.

I darted to the threshold, turning around to close the door behind me.

"No, don't do that!"

"Oh!"

"I didn't mean to scare you, Rabbi, but it's dark as hell out here." It was Dore Redmont. "What are you doing in temple now?"

"Picking up—sermons—on my way—Vernon—"

"Everybody else gone?"

"What?"

"From rehearsal. I thought I'd get Rona and go out for a bite— Say, I never realized you were that much taller than me, Rabbi." He pointed to my stained handkerchief. "Bloody nose?"

"Uh-huh. Dore, how about us going for a cup of—"

A sudden noise behind me startled the two of us.

"Didn't you say everybody had left?" Before I could stop him, he stepped into my office.

I didn't follow him inside. What good was it? I had tried to shield Pete Schuster, why I'm not sure, but it was no use now.

A gasp. Moments later Dore stumbled out, looking shorter than when he had entered, now that I was no longer standing on my toes to block his view. "You hypocritical bastard!" he cried, and ran off.

Not until Dore's car roared away did I collect my wits; even then all I could manage was "Who? Me?"

I stepped back into my office, ready to clobber Pete Schuster again and repent afterwards. But one look around and my arm wilted. For all I saw was:

the couch, the brassiere and tie, a dress and jacket, the new window the board had finally installed, now wide open, and no Pete Schuster.

Gevalt! Dore thought he had caught me in flagrante delicto. Now I had to clear myself, and before morning, before Dore talked to Rona and she shared the gossip delicto with all of Hillendale.

Dashing outside to my car, I sped to the Redmont house so fast I beat Dore there. His Thunderbird was not in the driveway, where he usually left it; only Rona's station wagon was in sight. To make sure he hadn't been driving her car that night, I checked the motor to see if it was warm, and to my astonishment nobody popped up to inquire why the rabbi of the Hillendale Temple was going around at one o'clock in the morning feeling radiators.

I returned to my green thing to wait and aggravate. Of all the people to have stumbled into the temple before, it had to be the writer of this song for my fair Sadie's father, Rabbi Doolittle:

> So you founded
> Ev'ry shul in Passaic;
> If you're Judaic,
> Show me.
>
> Don't say you're religious
> All through and through;
> If you're a Jew,
> Show me.
>
> "A Jew at heart"—
> That's so bromidic;
> If you're Semitic,
> Show me.

Of social action
Don't be skittish;
If you're Yiddish,
Show me.

Pious don't speak,
Just do, do, do;
If you're He-brew,
Show me.

Don't wait till the Messiah or de Gaulle comes
To show you exactly how;
Show me now!

It was after four, closer to five, when Dore finally drove up. His Thunderbird came roaring down the street, bobbing and weaving as if through heavy traffic, only his was the only moving object in any direction. I ran over as the car stopped on his front lawn.

Dore swore at me with a hundred-proof breath. "Adulterer!"

"Let me explain—"

"From my rabbi I don't want explanations. Explanations is what I hear every day of my life from people doing rotten things. From my rabbi I want inspirations. Now will you get the hell out of here before—" He burst into tears.

There seemed nothing wrong with Dore's crying: it was that kind of night. I felt like crying myself. Only when he stopped crying as suddenly as he had started did I begin to wonder: Why was *he* crying if *I* had committed adultery? And how did he know it was adultery? I'm single, and the woman was gone.

"Dore, listen for two minutes." He said nothing.

That encouraged me to jump into the car beside him. I started talking even before closing the door and didn't stop till I had recounted every detail, omitting only Pete Schuster's name.

Dore said, "You expect me to swallow that?"

I threw up my hands—figuratively. Actually, my heart sank down into my small bowel, where it sat in mourning for me.

"You forget I'm in the business of creating lies, believable lies, and never have I heard a more incredible story. I expected better from a man with six degrees."

"Five, just five," I said, wearily opening the car door.

"Wait." Dore reached over and grabbed my throat. "Your tie!"

He was good and drunk. Here I'm aggravated to death, and he's concerned with my haberdashery! Or was it my garroting he had in mind? I pulled away. It was Friday morning, almost dawn now, and I still had my Shabbas sermons to complete and lady's wear to bury.

Dore jumped out of his car and ran around it to head me off, babbling all the while. Suddenly his words came through: "You're wearing a tie now, just like before, but before there was also a tie on the couch. Nobody wears two ties! Maybe you're telling the truth!"

Saved. By a tie. I should have felt elated, I suppose, thanked Dore for his faith in me, maybe even sat down on the grass right then to write an article for the *Daily News:* "Justice *Does* Triumph!" But I resented having been placed on trial; that made me a loser from the start.

"Swell," I said. "Good night." Yet several loose

threads remained untied. "Dore, what makes you think the woman was married?"

"The dress. It's a chorus costume from *My Fair Sadie*. And since all the women in the chorus are sisterhood members—"

"And why did you go out on a drunk?"

"I didn't go on a drunk. I went to a bar, but the bartender kept asking me with every drink, 'What's the matter, pal? What did your wife do to you?' What could I say? 'It isn't my wife; it's my rabbi. I caught him with another woman.' I mean, it was ridiculous. So I left and drove out to Westport, just me and Jack Daniel's."

"And the tears just now? Why tears?"

Dore's answer didn't come readily. He turned away before speaking. "In my business, Rabbi, there's nobody to trust or respect, not even yourself, *especially* not yourself. And outside of Rona, there's only one other person I've trusted and respected. You, Rabbi."

I felt—I'm not sure what. At five o'clock in the morning it's hard to feel anything.

"Look, I'd better get inside. I called Rona from Westport; she was hysterical. The maid told her I'd gone to pick her up at the temple a few minutes before she'd returned, and the poor thing thought I'd had an accident. I guess I did at that. What a night . . . Well, see you in temple, Rabbi. Rabbi—that's a lovely word, you know that?"

It was five-thirty by the time I got back to my office to tidy up. I put the dress in the storeroom with the other show costumes, hung up the jacket and tie, and went looking for a manila envelope to stuff the brassiere in before taking it away to burn. Then I saw it: on the other side of the couch, an alligator handbag.

It was easy now to identify Pete Schuster's partner,

who had cost me a night's sleep and two sermons. All
I had to do was open the bag and look inside.

But was it right? I wasn't sure. For what purpose?
I wouldn't drum her out of sisterhood. To preach at
her? It was more important for her to condemn herself. To scare her into behaving in the future? Anyway, she'd think I knew her identity; surely it would
never occur to her that I *hadn't* looked inside the bag.

So I didn't. Retrieving the bag, I stuffed the bra
inside—Dad would have been pleased; it was a Treasure Chest—hoping the woman had reached home
safely. The way my luck was running that night, she
might have been killed on the way by a pygmy's
poisoned dart, and the police could start an investi-
gation which would turn up charred belongings of
hers bearing my fingerprints. Automatically I wiped
my prints off the bag, wondering whether to rinse out
the bra too before I burned it. And then I saw them
on the clasp; so big, so golden, they were impossible
to miss—initials: RR.

No wonder she had been hysterical when Dore
phoned.

RR: Rona Redmont.

                                 8

"Next Saturday Mrs. Rutherford and I leave this
church for Chicago's Urban Training Center for
Christian Mission, and so I take for my text this
morning First Corinthians twelve: four through six:
'Now there are varieties of gifts, but the same Spirit;
and there are varieties of service, but the same Lord;
and there are varieties of working, but it is the same
God who inspires them all in every one.'

"Why am I leaving Hillendale for a different means
of service? In brief—because it's impossible to tell

St. James Episcopal Church

The County's Most Spectacular Church
Famous for Its Great Architecture

Rev. ALISTAIR F. BIDWELL, D.D., Rector

Sunday: 11 a.m., Holy Communion and Sermon

Preacher: REV. VERNON RUTHERFORD

"Religion in America"

The Friendly Church of Hillendale

---

from people's actions who are the churched and who the *un*churched; because churches with a hundred twenty million members exercise so little influence on domestic affairs, international relations and social change; because the church becomes something other than a church when it ceases generating values and merely sanctifies those of society.

"The tragic fact is that today's typical church, as segregated by class as it is by race, has restricted itself to the sidelines of life—to the suburbs, the familial, the domestic, the private, the sentimental, the leisured. Ministers, who have trained to offer witness in the world, spend their days supervising social activities and catering to egos. For parishioners want their minister to do everything except change them, regarding him as the plastic statuette on their Protestant dashboard, whose purpose is to give people some sort of identity, soothe their anxiety and never shake them up.

"Indeed, this is the function of religion in America

today: *to don't.* That accounts for its overwhelming material success: the institutional church is supported precisely because it *is,* for the most part, irrelevant, inoffensive and purposeless.

"Is it any wonder that today more than a third of newly ordained ministers don't enter the parish ministry—they choose instead the public sphere of causes over the private sphere of symptoms—while half of the young people leave our church never to return?

"What is needed today are new ministerial modes for all the structures of society that shape most lives. We need ministers trained in housing, automation, economics, race relations, drug addiction, alcoholism; we need ministers to work out of storefronts and apartments, in industry, business, penal reform; we need ministers to influence banks to grant mortgages and home-improvement loans to slum residents; we want ministers to speak out on the Cold War, Red China, Vietnam, the Middle East.

"God, remember, created the world, not religion.

"What is a church but a way station in time, where people come to be charged with their mission to live for each other and reconcile themselves in God? The church is not the billion dollars spent every year on building new houses of worship to serve as comfort stations for the bored housewife and the tired businessman. Rather, to quote Henrik Kraemer, the church is 'the interfering community'—a launching pad for, in the words of our Rabbi, 'the setting at liberty of those who are oppressed.'

"One thing I know as surely as I know that God lives: a church that lives to itself, preoccupied with survival and self-service, will die by itself—as it so deserves ..."

N

FEBRUARY

R EMEMBER that god-awful Evans bar mitzvah?
Well, the Margolin one, which was celebrated
the Shabbas after Vernon's departure, nearly wrecked
me altogether.

Sandy is the name of the boy, very withdrawn and
scrawny, with the look of an island castaway. In
class and at services he strands himself in the farthest
seat of the last row, his tentativeness suggesting he
might decide any moment to disembody himself entirely—portrait of the loser as a child. It's impossible
to engage him in conversation, for his favorite re-
sponses are "Uh-uh," "Uh-huh" and "Mmm." Three
words are the most I've ever coaxed out of him at
one clip, and they were "I don't know," preceded and
followed by a shrug, like body-English parentheses.

Several months before his thirteenth birthday, I called Sandy to my office to ask him to check with his parents on a bar-mitzvah date. This time the boy responded: with tears. Yet even they looked unsalted and dehydrated.

"Sandy, what's the matter?"

The boy wiped at his eyes.

"What's bothering you?"

"Nothing."

"Why did you get so upset?"

"I don't know."

"Something to do with your bar mitzvah?"

He shrugged.

"You do want to become bar mitzvah, don't you?"

The boy's eyes opened wide. "All my life," he said.

My lessons with Sandy soon revealed the trouble: he couldn't read the required Hebrew Biblical texts, not a word. Well, maybe a word, but that word he never read the same way twice in succession; the vowels (dots and dashes in Hebrew) were always mispronounced, and any two consonants that resembled a third were mistaken for a fourth. After a month, I told the boy the obvious: "Sandy, you're not trying."

"I am."

"Do you ever study your haftorah and maftir?"

"Every night."

"That's hard to believe."

"But I do."

"I'll have to speak to your parents about—"

The boy started to cry; that he did well.

"Okay, I'll give you another week. But only one."

I asked Sandy's religious-school teacher about him —there was something not quite right—and she said, "But didn't you know? Sandy's blind."

"Blind?"

"Oh, I don't mean totally blind. Legally blind. That's probably the reason he never says a word in class, though he does write nicely. In public school they give him books with extra-large print. Didn't you see those thick glasses he wears?"

Who notices glasses and braces on children any more than minks and wall-to-wall carpeting on their parents? The next day I asked Sandy why he hadn't mentioned his poor eyesight.

"I don't know."

"Here I've been bawling you out for something that isn't your fault. I'm sorry, Sandy. How bad are your eyes?"

He shrugged.

"What exactly do you see—rather, what part of the Hebrew don't you see?"

"The vowels. The *a* looks like the *ah,* and the *ah* looks like the *aw,* and the *aw* looks like the *eh,* and the *ee* and the *o* I can't see at all."

Who would have guessed the boy had so many words in him? Hurray for the Hebrew vowels. Helping him now was easy: I had a photographer blow up the texts to three times their regular size. In one week Sandy was reading his first three haftorah verses correctly.

"Why didn't you tell me about your eyes to begin with?" I asked again, after congratulating him.

"I was afraid."

"Afraid? Of what?"

"My bar mitzvah."

"What about your bar mitzvah?"

"You'd stop it."

"Why would I do that?"

Shrug. "I don't know." Shrug.

Within a month Sandy could read all his Hebrew

selections and chant them nicely. His next assignment was to compose an original speech. (I am a great believer in original talks, ever since my own bar mitzvah, when the rabbi gave me a canned speech to memorize, and bright sonofagun that I was, I memorized it so well that when I recited a phrase in the concluding paragraph: ". . . on this great day of my becoming a man of responsibilities and duties in the eyes of Jewish law . . ."—which phrase appeared in the first sentence of the talk, automatically I started the whole speech all over, while the people out front began whispering—they had never heard a broken bar mitzvah before—and I can still remember my growing terror as that same phrase loomed once more, and unable to recall what came after it, I feared never being able to end the speech, but repeating it again and forever, like the mills at the bottom of Davy Jones's locker that forgot how to stop grinding out salt.)

I was expecting some difficulty, a speech of twenty-five words or shrugs. But Sandy brought in a fine talk based on the rabbinic dictum: "If one destroys a single person, it's as if he had destroyed the entire world; if one saves a single life, it's as if he had saved the entire world." The boy wrote of his desire to become a doctor, which is what his mother wanted him to be (where had I heard that before?) because, he said, a person who is good only to himself is a good-for-nothing. In his conclusion he promised to continue attending religious school after bar mitzvah (alas, ninety percent of Jewish boys don't, while many families quit their synagogues upon returning from the reception) and expressed his filial appreciation in a way that made me wonder whether to revise it:

At this time I'd like to thank my parents for all they've done to me. My father and my mother have been very good and patient, which I appreciate very much. I know I have disappointed them sometimes, but I will attempt with all my might in the future to disappoint them not as much. I want them to be proud of me as a son, person, Jew and American, and I promise to try. When you're number two hundred, you try harder.

The last sentence was an excessive tribute to me, which, unhappily, revealed that Sandy's self-esteem had risen because he felt liked by me, a thought that in the long run would prove harmful. He had exchanged one wrong notion, his being a disappointment because he felt unliked, for another wrong one, his being worthy only because *I* liked him. So I suggested he add to the speech a few paragraphs about the Biblical verse that tells us all men are created in the image of God, and the next session we'd discuss them. "Sandy," I concluded, "I'm proud of you. Your speech is exceptionally good."

"You like it? *Really?*"

"Very much. Some of the English needs to be corrected, but that's usual. Here where you say, 'The temple is a special place, a holy place, a quiet place. Other places are quiet, like the beach in winter with only the sea gulls skipping waves, but temple quiet is *quieter*, quiet enough to hear yourself think and make plans as well as pray'—that's fine. But we'll have to substitute a word in this sentence, 'The words I hear in temple are *wordier*.' Sandy, you have such fine thoughts, how about speaking up more and sharing them with us?"

Shrug.

For his first scheduled rehearsal on the pulpit Sandy called in sick. He missed the second one too; when he didn't show up for the third, I phoned his house. He answered on the first ring, as if he's been sitting beside the phone.

"Oh, is it today?" he said.

When Sandy arrived I took him into the sanctuary and reviewed his cues for reciting a prayer, the blessings over Scriptures, the textual readings and, finally, his speech. I asked the boy to begin. Very pale and thin and clammy-looking, he approached the lectern as if it were a bull, he the bullfighter and the empty seats out front a crowd cheering—but for the animal.

From my pulpit seat behind him I said, "All right, go ahead."

The boy said nothing.

"You can start now."

Not a syllable.

"Sandy?"

Silence.

Annoyed, I stepped up to the lectern, where I glimpsed the boy's now beet-red countenance. Eyes popping, nostrils dilating, cheeks bursting, it looked as if all his features had panicked and were trying to flee.

"*Sandy!*"

His face caving in before a sudden downpour of tears, the boy darted out of the sanctuary.

I raced after him and grabbed him at the front door. "What is it? Tell me."

But he broke away and ran out of the temple.

I dashed to my office and dialed Sandy's home with a shaking finger. That horribly contorted face! Had he suffered a seizure? What was with this boy anyhow?

Mrs. Margolin, answering the call, made me fear that what was wrong was Sandy's genes, for she said, "What are you talking about, Rabbi?"

"The bar mitzvah—"

"Whose bar mitzvah?"

"Sandy's bar mitzvah—"

"Bar mitzvah?"

"That's right, your son's bar mitzvah, twenty-seven days from now."

"There must be some mistake. We're not having any bar mitzvah."

"You do have a son, Sandy? Small, thin, glasses, brown hair, mole on left cheek—"

"Yes, that's my Sandy," Mrs. Margolin said. "But I don't understand. We decided long ago Sandy would not be bar-mitzvahed."

I lectured the mother on the value of bar mitzvah, while every couple of minutes she responded, "I *agree*, Rabbi, I *do*." (She was such an irritating woman.) Finally, when I let her, she elaborated, "Rabbi, we would love Sandy to be bar-mitzvahed; you don't have to convince me. But how can he? Sandy's a terrible stutterer."

"Stutterer? Impossible! He's never stuttered— Oh." That's what had happened. "Well, just once—today."

"He doesn't always stutter, only in front of groups or when he's tired or nervous or ill at ease, which I'm afraid is most of the time. He'd been seeing a psychologist in Chicago before we moved here last June, and—"

"Why did you have him prepared for bar mitzvah if he can't go through with it?"

"*I* never asked you to prepare him. Why, we never even consulted a caterer."

"You gave me the date. No, Sandy did." And I had

automatically started his lessons, as I did with all the other boys entering their teens. "But why is it I never heard him stutter till today?" Then I realized: until now the boy had hardly spoken to me.

Mrs. Margolin replied: "You make him feel comfortable, Rabbi. Sandy's always talking about the long discussions the two of you have together."

The bar mitzvah was out of the question—on the pulpit Sandy didn't stutter; he simply couldn't open his mouth—unless I taped his recitation and played it back at the Sabbath service while he lip-synched it. To make sure—the bar mitzvah clearly was important to him—I called his former psychologist in Chicago, and he said, "I wouldn't want to rule out the bar mitzvah, no. Sandy's never felt himself the equal of other boys. His vision is poor, though that's not the cause of his stuttering. He can't play ball with other boys as a result, he's smaller than the others, he doesn't speak well. Now if a bar mitzvah is *also* denied him, that would be still another blow for a boy who thinks himself without a single accomplishment."

"But if he stutters—"

"Rabbi, doesn't the boy's part in the proceedings consist of singing?"

"To a great degree, yes—chanting."

"Well, then, maybe things can be worked out. Sandy doesn't stutter when he's singing. Many stutterers can sing without difficulty—don't ask me why, there's so little we know about either the cause or cure of stuttering—and Sandy is one of those."

"But, Doctor, boys *without* problems get nervous at their bar mitzvahs. Hell, *I* still get nervous during services. Even if Sandy can sing okay, won't he freeze up when he has to sing in public for the first time?"

"There is a risk of that, yes. Yet either way there's a risk. If the bar mitzvah is canceled, Sandy will be crushed; if it proceeds and he freezes in front of everybody, he'll be humiliated. On the other hand, if he is bar-mitzvahed successfully it will be an enormous boost, money in his emotional bank, so to speak, to draw on when he feels frightened or inadequate."

"What do you advise, Doctor? Should we chance it?"

"It's hard to say. What do *you* think, Rabbi?"

There's nothing like a counselor counseling a counselor: What do you think I should *do?* I don't know; what do *you* think you should do? *I* don't know; what do *you* think?

I called the Margolin family to my office to tell the parents in front of Sandy that he knew his Biblical portions as well as any other bar-mitzvah boy in history, and to tell Sandy in front of them that there was no religious necessity for him to go through with the ceremony.

"I want to be bar-mitzvahed," the boy said.

I related the history of the bar mitzvah—how it began among the Jews of Germany in the fourteenth century to celebrate a boy's assumption of religious responsibility, which he could do then because an intensive study of Bible and Mishnah had familiarized him with the mitzvos, or commandments, that were his obligations to perform—and confessed that since few thirteen-year-olds today underwent a comparably thorough Jewish education and since Jewish life in America was being devastated by today's bar mitzvah, which has become the literal as well as figurative end of most of Jewish education (with the result that most Jews are frozen with a child's-eye view of Juda-

ism, which evaporates as soon as the eighty-two percent of Jewish youngsters enter college), I favored
postponing all bar mitzvahs till eighteen—when adolescent turbulence subsides, his status crystallizes, and
emotionally and intellectually he is ready to study
and appreciate religion on a mature level—or even
twenty; in any event what was important in Sandy's
case, far more meaningful than a ceremony anybody
could undergo with a few months' training, was his
mature decision to continue his religious training.

When I concluded my speech, Sandy said, "I *have*
to be bar-mitzvahed."

Neither Abraham, Isaac nor Jacob had undergone
a bar-mitzvah ceremony, I pointed out, nor Moses,
Isaiah, nor Judah Maccabee.

But Sandy's standards were higher. "Please, Rabbi.
I *got* to."

Mrs. Margolin voted against it, admitting that she
had been told there was some connection between
her pressuring the boy and his stutter, while Mr.
Margolin voted for it because for generations all the
boys in his family had been bar-mitzvahed. Both decided to leave the resolution to me, and all I could
come up with was "I just don't know."

Sandy burst out, "Where's your f-f-f-faith?"

That line was the clincher, for each of us inter-
preted it in his own way: Don't you have faith in
God? (Mr. Margolin.) Don't you have faith in *faith?*
(Mrs. Margolin.) Don't you have faith in *me?* (Me.)

So back into the sanctuary to practice Sandy went,
relinquishing his speech and prayer. Happily, after
many stumbling starts and snags, he sang his portions well enough to get by. If only the boy could do
as nicely at his bar mitzvah, standing defenseless in
front of hundreds of people . . .

Nineteen days before BM-Day, Sandy called me excitedly into the sanctuary. "I've been practicing. Listen." He recited his speech and prayer—haltingly and stammering syllables beginning with *b* and *p*, but he made it to the Amens. Then: "I want to speak too."

"Sandy, let's not press our luck."

"*Please*, Rabbi—"

"It's not a good idea. No."

"I *got* to."

"We'll see."

To help Sandy with the prayer and speech I opposed his delivering, I substituted different words for all those with syllables beginning with a *b* or *p*— "mother and father" for "parents," "synagogue" for "temple," "this day" for "bar mitzvah," "Aunt Jane" for "Uncle Paul"—and eliminated all references to me, since the only substitute for "Rabbi Abel" was "Spiritual Leader Gideon." Moreover, acting on a tip from my cram course on stuttering at the library, I read the speech and prayer in unison with Sandy endlessly.

The rehearsals continued, longer than *My Fair Lady's* or even *My Fair Sadie's*. By now I was spending twenty hours a week with Sandy—from six o'clock, when religious school let out, till the start of meetings or adult education, and most of Sunday. (Devoting a proportionate amount of time to the rest of my congregants would mean a total of eight thousand working hours a week, which wouldn't be at all bad if I were paid by the hour.) Yet that was one reason for my becoming a rabbi: to enter into meaningful I-Thou relationships, and twenty hours a week was as person-to-person as you could get; did Romeo see that much of Juliet before killing himself for her? Still, I was

getting awfully tired of sending out every night for
hot corned beef sandwiches that were delivered always cold and never lean.

Fifteen days to go now, and all was going almost
like the preparations for a normal bar mitzvah, when
one evening Sandy, rehearsing for the thousandth
time, easy, sputtered to a halt. What now? Another
surprise? The boy came up with a new one every
month; I expected him any day to surprise me again,
maybe change into a bat and fly away.

"I didn't mean to interrupt, Rabbi. I was looking
for my hammer." It was the caretaker. Sandy had
seen him enter the sanctuary, and that was enough to
silence him. What would he do with hundreds of
people watching?

We had to start all over—now *I* refused to forgo the
prayer and the speech, for his obsession had become
mine; if Moses could make a go of it with *his* stutter,
why not Sandy?—this time dragooning as a representative audience the caretaker, stray sisterhood
members, the soda-machine man, the delivery boy
from the delicatessen. After a few days Sandy could
speak before all kinds of uninterested strangers, who
couldn't wait to escape. But ten days to go till BM-
Day, I sneezed—and Sandy froze again.

I conceded for the both of us. "Look, Sandy, we're
dropping the prayer and the speech. That's final."

"I want to speak."

"Sandy, it's not worth the risk."

"I *got* to."

"You don't want to be worrying throughout the
ceremony about sneezes. Then there are always people coming in late, making noise, talking—"

"All the boys speak."

"Not all. Most bar-mitzvah boys don't speak; they just chant their portions."

"Why do they speak here?"

"Only because I make them."

"Why do you make them?"

"Just chanting is kind of mechanical; the speech is creative, makes them think—I mean—"

So back into rehearsal it was, while I rambled around the sanctuary, sneezing, coughing, hiccuping, rattling candy wrappers, stamping my feet as Sandy spoke. The boy got used to all this—with eight days till BM-Day, but then a fire engine came screaming down the street, and that was the end of the speech.

Two days later I brought in a transistor radio, switching from one rock-'n'-roll station to another with the volume turned way up high. I also broke paper bags, sneaked up on the boy and yelled in his ear, and stepped on his feet. Sandy himself got into the spirit of things by stuffing jelly beans into his mouth as he talked, a candied Demosthenes.

And it was working. Four days till BM-Day, Sandy delivered his speech and prayer perfectly, though it embarrassed me to be caught by Barney Singer throwing Silly Putty at a bar-mitzvah boy while he spoke earnestly about God. The next day, on his own, Sandy restored his deleted references to me, but he never made it to "Abel"; between "Rab" and "bi," sure enough, he got stuck.

I thanked Sandy for his sweet thanks and excised them again. Peace of mind is what I needed, not appreciation.

"I want to say it," he insisted. "You've spent more time with me than anybody else besides my mother, and she spends too much time with me."

But I forbade it absolutely—even when the boy showed me he could say "Rabb-i Abe-el"—out of fear that by now every bone in the camel's back had been splintered by the last thousand last straws.

Two days before BM-Day, Mrs. Margolin called to ask if we were really going ahead with the bar-mitzvah. I said yes, and she said she'd now get busy on the phone, inviting people to the service, which she hadn't yet done in order to make it easier on Sandy if he had to back out. "Sandy will do all right, won't he?" she wanted to know.

"From your mouth," I prayed, "into God's ear."

Came the Shabbas of the bar mitzvah—surely the most unusual in the annals of contemporary Jewish history in the United States, for it was being held without the blessing of either printed invitations or caterer ("Don't you know affairs have to be arranged at least ten months in advance?" Mountain Tiptop had told Mrs. Margolin, when she called them the day before. "You some kind of greenhorn, lady?")— and Sandy came to temple an hour earlier for his last rehearsal. Not that he needed it; *I* did. The night before, it had come to me in a nightmare that Aaron had been delegated by Moses to do his speaking for him precisely because of his stutter.

As I watched from the last row of the sanctuary, Sandy stepped up to the lectern—angled, like my pulpit chair, to enable me to see his face during the service. Suddenly there was no more reason for apprehension, only panic. The boy had opened his mouth, nothing had come out, and he had vanished behind the lectern. I blinked twice—what had happened *now?* we had rehearsed everything that could possibly occur, omitting only the outbreak of World War Three—then dashed up to the pulpit.

Sandy was lying on the floor unconscious, like a sacrifice.

The first thing that sprang to mind, to be perfectly honest, was not to revive him. Instead, I gave serious consideration to fainting myself. After all these months, after all the effort and hopes and coming so close, the bar mitzvah would have to be canceled. Maybe the show must go on—because producers hate like hell to give refunds—but not a bar mitzvah, not with an unconscious boy.

When Sandy came to, I led him into my office, where I gently told him of the cancellation. There were better things in life to drop dead for than a bar mitzvah.

"I'm all right," the boy said.

"You looked all right—stretched out on the pulpit."

"You *can't* stop my bar mitzvah *now*."

"Sorry, Sandy. My mind is made up."

"I didn't eat any breakfast this morning or supper last night, I was too nervous. That's why I fainted, not because of the bar mitzvah. I didn't stutter up there; you saw: I didn't stutter once. I just fainted, that's all. Because I'm starved."

It sounded logical. I myself felt light-headed from not having slept or eaten since my dream about Aaron.

"Rabbi, have just one hour's more faith," Sandy said.

I gave in for the last time (who would ever be able to unearth that poor camel now from beneath all those straws?), when my inclination was to do what they did to the theater during the Restoration:

hang up a sign outside the temple saying: CLOSED ON
ACCOUNT OF THE PLAGUE. Well, at least the kitchen was
on our side; its refrigerator yielded us leftover sponge
cake, pickled herring, egg salad, tuna-fish croquettes,
gherkins and pastry shells. Then all we had to do was
sit around and tell each other how all right everything was going to be, just like in *The Song of Bernadette* . . .

Finally the service began, and an odd one it was.
Nobody came late, everyone took a seat without
greeting anybody, opened his prayerbook and followed the service intently; there was not a single
whisper. The unusual deportment unnerved me; it
was like leading services in a wax temple. And was it
safe? Silence was one thing Sandy and I had never
rehearsed; could the boy function without noise,
sneezes, exploding paper bags, tossed putty?

Finally it came, time for Sandy to stand up, step
to the lectern, and debut with his prayer, from which
I had also eliminated every syllable beginning with a
b or *p*. I broke into a cold sweat, to which the
gherkins and greasy tuna-fish croquettes contributed
nauseousness, as the boy rose from his seat and
walked up front. God help him . . .

Sandy opened his mouth. I heard nothing. Yet his
lips were moving. Then, like the time lag between
hitting yourself on the thumb with a hammer and
the coming of the pain, I heard the boy *speaking*. I
had been so fearful of silence that silence is what I
heard. Beautiful syllables were falling from his lips,
joining into beautiful words; the words formed
phrases; the phrases became sentences, then paragraphs; the paragraphs added up to a prayer, and
Sandy was finished.

The congregation heaved one great sigh along with

me. Relaxing, I wiped my forehead—there was time to tense up again before Sandy's speech—because now he would be singing. The Torah scroll was taken out of the Ark, uncovered, unrolled, blessed, read, and then someone with my voice called out, "*Ya-amod ha-bochur ha-bar mitzvah, Shlomo ben Binya-min;* let the bar-mitzvah young man arise, Sanford the son of Benjamin."

Sandy grabbed the little silver hand from me; clutching it like a dagger, he pointed to his place in the Torah scroll and sang out the blessings. Good! Now for the chanting of the Biblical verses. Again he sang out—*very* good!—and I felt so happy that— What was this?

The silver pointer was no longer moving from right to left over the Hebrew scroll, but up and down as if Sandy were reading a Chinese laundry ticket. He had lost the place—I knew another surprise was due —and between my despair (the boy would freeze-freezefreeze*freeze*) and his frenetic waving (upand-downupanddownandnowcrissandcross) I couldn't find the place for him.

Yet Sandy was still chanting his portion, correctly too. No, he wasn't looking at the scroll at all; he was singing it from memory. Hadn't he rehearsed it more times than his own name?

Crisis 139 over, next came the chanting of the chapter from the Prophets. That too was accomplished well, until something—a dozen of them— went rattattatting on the floor out front. "My pearls!" a woman exclaimed.

The entire congregation turned around and said in unison, "SSHHH!"

Without missing a beat—what were pearl drop-pings, compared to my boxing both his ears during

rehearsals?—Sandy continued till the end of the haftorah. Then he sang the final blessings.

All that remained now was the speech. Sandy stood
up straight in the pulpit, spread his legs apart for
better balance, licked his lips and swallowed a few
times to relax his throat muscles, fixed his gaze on a
spot I had marked on the back wall to keep him from
being distracted by eyes, then began talking, slowly
and loudly. We had rehearsed so much that his speech
came out mechanical, as if it were being delivered by
Ken doll to Barbie, but every word was distinct.

In the congregation, people were clutching their
hands or a neighbor's, nodding with nachas whenever he finished another sentence. Mr. Margolin had
tears in his eyes, and Mrs. Margolin silently mouthed
every word along with her son, and when he got to
the part about his parents she pressed a handkerchief
to her lips.

Finally, after a journey of only five months, came
the last sentence in the talk. Sandy had completed
everything—splendidly.

So why wasn't the boy returning to his seat? Why
did he remain standing in front of the lectern? Was
he *now* going to change into a bat and fly away?
Sandy opened his mouth, and out came additional
words, familiar ones but unrehearsed: "At this time
I want to thank also my very good friend who worked
so hard all this time with me so I can speak just like
everyone else on this great day—"

For a moment, just for a moment, I was touched.
How sweet. What's lovelier than doing a kindness
anonymously and then being found out? Then it
struck me: how terrible! The one time Sandy had
spoken that line—

"I mean, of course, Rab—" Sandy froze, his jaws

locked together as if in a battle to the death, and most likely it was my fault for terrorizing him about the *b*'s and *p*'s. *No no no no no no no!*

I jumped to my feet, and just as quickly—at such a moment who could remember that when turning my chair to face Sandy at the lectern, I had placed it catty-corner to Barney Singer, who always sat on the pulpit with his legs spread out as if he were watching the Army-Navy game on television?—I fell forward on my face.

Not a sound from the congregation at first; everybody was probably busy poking a neighbor, asking, "Am I seeing things, Gertrude, or did the rabbi just topple off his chair dead drunk?" All answers must have been affirmative, for six seconds later—it was really too much to expect people *not* to—they burst out laughing.

Poor Sandy! Unaware of what had happened—of what I, his very good friend, had done to him on this great day in his life—he was sure to think the congregation was laughing at him. Could all those months of practice end like this?

Reaching up from the floor, I grabbed the boy's right leg.

Startled, Sandy turned and looked down, seeing me sprawled there like a bum in the gutter. "*—bi Abel!*" he exclaimed.

Shlomo, the son of Binyamin, had completed his speech and bar-mitzvah rites, hallelujah.

א

——Hi, Dore. How are you?
——*Fine, Rabbi. Gee, I feel awful.*
——What's the matter?

——*I mean, about the mix-up. Here I invite you
to the house for dinner, and at the last minute
Rona remembers this long-standing date with her
sister.*

——That's all right, Dore. We'll make it another
time.

——*You must get awfully tired of eating here at
the Posh Nosh.*

——Not me. My childhood dream was to marry a
delicatessen owner's daughter.

——*That makes me luckier than you. Because my
dream came true.*

——What was it?

——*To get filthy rich. If it hadn't come true, I'd
have chased that dream all my life without realizing how empty it was.*

——You may be right, Dore. When I was dreaming
of becoming a rabbi—

——*Yes?*

——Well, it hasn't turned out as expected. My being here doesn't seem to make that much of a
difference to the congregation. If I disappeared
down an open manhole, probably nobody would
notice—not till their son's bar mitzvah or their
own funeral.

——*You just happen to be all wet, Rabbi. You've
accomplished so much here. Take the religious
school. Sandy Margolin and the rest of the kids
—they love you. And since most people join
synagogues for the sake of their children—*

——It's funny: my father's generation worships God
with the hearts of their parents, and this generation worships Him with the hearts of their children.

——*Rabbi, in my business when even ten percent*

of the audience responds, that's a fantastic success. And you've had dozens of successes here.
——I have?

——*Count me one of them. I don't know where
I'd be today without you, Rabbi.*

——Your involvement in adult education and social
action—they *have* pleased me, Dore, very much.
If only more members followed your lead—

——*I was referring to something else, Rabbi. Like—
well, what I just told you about Rona's forgotten
date with her sister—it wasn't true.*

——It wasn't?

——*No. You see, Rona still can't face you, not yet—*

——Dore! You know?

——*Ever since that night. Rona saw us together out
front and assumed you'd told me everything. So
as soon as I set foot inside the house—*

——But I didn't know till an hour afterwards that it
was Rona. Not till I found her handbag.

——*I see. But if you had known before, Rabbi,
would you have told me?*

——Well, no. What good would it have done,
Dore? I was hoping that her shock and guilt . . .
I was hoping that would help the both of you.

——*It did, Rabbi. But you know what helped most
of all?*

——What?

——*You. Your attitude—it never changed toward
Rona. From the way you treated her after that
night, nobody could have guessed that she'd—
Anyway, that's why I took her back finally. You
set me the example. We're going to make it too,
Rona and I.*

——I'm glad, Dore. You have no idea how glad—

——*So I don't want you getting discouraged. From*

*where I sit, you're the greatest rabbi in the whole
world.*

——Are you including Brooklyn and the Bronx too?

——*There are only a few areas that could stand
some improvement.*

——Oh?

——*Like maybe it wasn't such a good idea to spring
that sixth-grade exam in Jewish beliefs and practices on the board; they resented it, especially the
seven trustees who flunked. Why couldn't you at
least have marked on a curve? And proposing
a new dues system based on ability to pay in
order to eliminate fund-raising—don't you know
the only thing two Jews will ever agree on is
how much a third Jew should give to the temple?
And then—*

——What happened, Dore? From one swell rabbi,
all of a sudden I've become Public Enemy Number One.

——*See what a good educator you are? Always a
word of justifiable praise before offering criticism,
didn't you teach us that? Mind you, Rabbi, these
aren't my own criticisms. But some members have
made them, and you should take note—*

——Meaning?

——*Look, June is only a few months away. Why
don't you lay low till then? Forget about Vietnam,
for one thing—*

——Lay low? You *do* think I'm Public Enemy
Number One.

——*I only want your convictions to take a vacation, that's all. They could use the rest. You're
always giving them such workouts.*

——Oh . . . because the congregation will be voting on that four-year contract for me.

——*Rabbi, this has nothing to do with any four-year contract.*

——It doesn't?

——*No.*

——Then why do you want to muzzle me? You, my best student and social activist.

——*Rabbi, some vital things we have to take on faith. Isn't that another wise thing you taught us?*

א

SPRING

AFTER Mrs. Greenwood's wedding I *had* to see Gina again. Didn't we meet cute enough, after all, to warm the typewriter of any Hollywood screen writer? You remember: if Rock Hudson goes shopping for pajama bottoms, Kim Novak is sure to be there trying to buy only pajama tops; or they bump into each other during an electrical blackout in New York; he thinks she's a boy, and she mistakes him for a girl, so they decide to room together at the Y.

But Gina didn't share my feeling of inevitability. The first few times I tried to date her for my one free evening of the week, she was busy, then at Grossinger's or the Concord, and finally—it was almost Passover now, the time for reading Song of Songs, and there's nothing more depressing than to read that exquisite book to a synagogue full of people or to yourself alone—she hemmed and hawed.

"What's the matter? Don't you want to go out with me?"

"Well, you being a rabbi, it would be sort of like dating God—"

That accounted for the girl's reluctance: I awed her. How *about* me?

She continued, alas: "—since I'm not sure I believe in God—I mean, you think a Christian Scientist would date a doctor?"

"If they're both Jewish, why not?"

The girl laughed, and agreed to see me.

Gina's mother, a stocky grandmotherly woman who looked a lot like Sydney Greenstreet just before he discovered the Maltese Falcon in his hand was a fake, beamed when her daughter introduced me. "It's a honor to meet you, a real honor," Mrs. Sitomer said. "Now how do you like your rice pudding? With raisins or without?" The entire Marine Corps couldn't have stopped her from sitting me down at the kitchen table for a snack even though I was taking Gina out to dinner that evening. "Eugenela likes without; she's modern. Barnard girl, you know. Scholarship. Some head on her shoulders. And isn't she beautiful?"

"Eugenela?"

Gina made a face. "My legal name is Eugenie, after Eugene V. Debs. Mama was one of the early organizers of the I.L.G.W.U. Lucky she was a socialist and not an anarchist, else I'd have ended up Vanzettila."

Mrs. Sitomer served me a salad bowl full of rice pudding. "On the right is without; on the left, with. I figure you should taste both—even people who ain't crazy for raisins like my with; it's my mother's recipe from Russia, and she was some cook—so next time you should be able to make a intelligent choice."

It was no use, long experience with my own mother told me, to point out it would take all the Children of Israel who had participated in the exodus from Egypt to consume so much rice pudding in one sitting. I dug in. "Delicious."

"How can it be delicious without nothing?" Mrs. Sitomer said, and emptied a pitcher of cream into my bowl. "Now you'll taste what good is." But before I could, she pulled up the left sleeve of her dress. "You know skin?"

"Skin?"

"Here, give a look." She showed me red scales encrusting her arm. "You see? Splotches."

"Mama! He's eating."

"He's used to it, Eugenela." To me: "And on my back too, splotches. Itches something awful. If my back was my nose, I'd never sleep; the whole day I'd be sneezing."

"That's a shame," I said.

"You're a very sympathetic person for a professional, you know that? That's real nice. Well, what do you think?"

"I'm sorry, but I'm ignorant about skin."

Mrs. Sitomer patted me on the shoulder. "At least you admit it. You have any idea how many doctors I went to didn't know skin but never told me? Big men too. All they did was take twenty-five dollars— that's how big they were; twenty-five dollars used to be my month's salary in the shop—but when it came to curing my condition, there was nobody home. You ever hear such a thing? If somebody brought me a dress to make and I didn't know how, would I have the nerve to charge twenty-five dollars for making it? So where can I go for my splotches? You know?"

"No, not offhand. I don't get to see many splotches—"

"What do you specialize in?"

I smiled. "That's a good question, Mrs. Sitomer. I wish I did have a specialty, but the way things are today I'm supposed to be a jake-of-all-trades."

"Oh, a general practitioner," she said, and I chuckled. "Well, you're nice not to charge me twenty-five dollars for hocking you such a chainik. What am I talking about? House calls are double the price, and doctors don't even make them. But eat, eat, finish the pudding. I got a nice piece knubble carp I want you should try."

Sitting down to dinner afterwards, while still picking raisins out of my teeth, I finally caught on. Gina had introduced me as Dr. Abel, and Mrs. Sitomer had taken me for a physician. Why, I asked, hadn't she corrected her mother's mistake?

"Well," Gina said, "I want Mama to get to know you first as a human being."

"A human being? In contrast to what?"

"I mean, before telling her you're a rabbi. You see, Mama doesn't go for religion; she calls it the television of the masses. Synagogues to her are settlement houses for the rich, and rabbis overpriced camp counselors for adults . . ."

To accommodate Gina on subsequent dates, I acted like a human being, at least when picking her up at her mother's Brighton Beach apartment. And graciously she returned the accommodation by taking an interest in Judaism after I called her my fair shiksa.

"The first thing you can teach me is," she said, "what exactly is a shiksa?"

The week before *My Fair Sadie's* opening—did I forget to mention that I had taken over the show during its final throes of rehearsals, when it fell apart, raising the specter of having to refund five thousand dollars' worth of tickets?—I spoke to Gina about Milton Steinberg's *Basic Judaism*. And never did I enjoy adult education more, perhaps because never before had I delivered a lecture while holding hands with a beautiful greenish-blue-eyed adult.

"Since you're so intelligent, so eager to learn," I sighed after kissing the girl good night, "soon as you finish reading the Steinberg book, we'll go right into the Song of Songs."

On Tuesday evening I went to take Gina to *My Fair Sadie's* opening. About to knock on her door, which was partly ajar, I heard voices inside raised in dispute, and hesitated.

"Eugenela, I don't trust that Dr. Abel one bit. Tonight I'm going to ask him some questions."

"Questions?"

"A mother has a right to question fishy men taking out their daughters."

"What's fishy about Gideon?"

"It isn't fishy I know more medicine than him?"

"Oh, that. Just because Gideon doesn't like to talk shop—"

"You know why he doesn't like to talk shop? Because he doesn't know shop. Listen, Eugenela, I was telling him about Bertha Goldstein, how much aggravation ileitis is giving her, and her with two small children to take care of. And your Dr. Abel says Bertha Goldstein and her husband should go talk things over with their rabbi, maybe *he* can straighten out their marriage."

"So he misunderstood—"

"Misunderstood? Know something, Eugenela? Your Dr. Abel—I don't think he's a *dentist*. Know something else? He's a goy. Even Mrs. Silverberg remarked, who should know because her cousin's daughter married one. Platinum-blond hair like that shiksa Harlow, skinny and undernourished, no nose, and the same name as that Russian colonel spy, who was no Jew, thank God. Who ever heard a Jewish boy should be named Gideon? And what Jew talks about religion all the time? Your other dates, nice Jewish boys, never do. And over my dead body will I let you marry a goy, you hear me? What are you laughing about! You think it's so funny, running around with a fake-doctor goy?"

I knocked on the door.

Gina opened it at once. "Oh, hello, Gideon." She pointed to the pail in her hand. "Garbage."

"Dr. Abel," Mrs. Sitomer said, "we were just talking about you."

Gina said, "I'll be right back." She darted into the hall toward the incinerator as I entered.

Mrs. Sitomer scrutinized me like trustees interviewing rabbinical candidates. "Hmmm."

"Well, Mrs. Sitomer, how was shul this Shabbas?"

She regarded me suspiciously. "What kind question is that?"

"Nothing special. I just wanted to say something—Jewish."

"*Du redst a gazinta Yiddish?*"

"Pardon?"

"I asked if you spoke *Mamaluschen*."

"Yiddish? No, I'm afraid not."

She nodded. "Figures."

"But I'm fluent in Hebrew, the language of the Bible."

"Uh-huh."

"*V'ahavto l'rayacho komocho*. That's Hebrew. For 'Love thy neighbor as thyself.'"

"Smart fella. You know Hebrew is Greek to me."

"By the way, how is Mrs. Goldstein? Is her oleitis any better? It must be very difficult to take care of her family when she's so sick with oleitis."

"It's ileitis," Mrs. Sitomer said, "Doctor."

"Oh, is it? Well, that's wonderful. I mean, *i*leitis is less serious than *o*leitis."

Gina returned. "Did I miss something?" she asked brightly.

Mrs. Sitomer looked grim. "Not yet."

I said, "Why are you so concerned about my being Jewish?" Both women were startled. "Well, I overheard you."

"Because, Mr. Eavesdropper," Mrs. Sitomer said, "no girl marries somebody she don't date."

"Mama! Who ever said anything about marriage?"

"Figures. Marriage he's not interested in, only skin and girls."

"I am, Mrs. Sitomer. But why are you so insistent on Gina marrying within the faith?"

"Aha! Then you *aren't*. A Jew wouldn't *ask* such a question."

"A Jew should be able to give an answer, Mrs. Sitomer."

"Foolish question."

"Why is it foolish?"

"If you were a Jew, you'd know why."

"Mrs. Sitomer, when's the last time you attended a synagogue?"

"What's that got to do with anything?"

"When, Mrs. Sitomer?"

"Synagogues are for old people with nothing else to do and suburban all-rightniks."

"What Jewish practices do you observe? Which holidays? Do you read the Bible or other Jewish books?"

"Who's asking questions here—you or me? *My* intentions are honorable."

"I want to see how you differ from a non-Jew. Is it blood that makes you different?"

"No, not blood, but you're warm. Soul. There's a Jewish soul born out of the Jewish experience. But you wouldn't know about that."

"You mean, Jewish souls are holier than Brand X's?"

"I'll say one thing for you: you have chutzpah! But you wouldn't know about that either."

"Chutzpah is what a man has who murders his parents, then requests mercy from the court because he's an orphan."

"You know, because Reston in the *Times* wrote that in his column once."

"And James Reston isn't Jewish."

"Who says Reston isn't Jewish? A man with a soul like that! Don't you read his columns?"

"Okay, if Reston *weren't* Jewish, would you let your daughter marry him?"

"He's already married."

"But if he weren't married, and if he weren't Jewish—"

"If! *Ven mein buba zul huben beitzim, volt zee gevain mein zayda!*"

"What does that mean?"

"Never mind. In English it comes out—not clean."

"You know, Mrs. Sitomer, you still haven't made clear to me—"

"There, *that's* why I want my Eugenela should marry Jewish. A Jew has respect for parents, honors gray hair. Not like you, bullying me like a Cossack."

Gina intervened, laughing. "Mama, it's time to tell you the truth. You're absolutely right; Gideon isn't a doctor."

"Aha!"

"Mrs. Sitomer, I'm a rabbi."

"A what?"

"Mama, I didn't say so to begin with, because you're just as prejudiced against rabbis as you are against gentiles. How one person can be both anti-gentile and anti-rabbi at the same time I don't know, but—"

"A rabbi? I don't believe it! What kind rabbi looks like a goy?"

"It's true. As a matter of fact, Gideon is taking me to his temple tonight for the first time."

"Wait a minute, wait just a minute! He's taking you to his temple?"

"That's right, Mrs. Sitomer."

"On Tuesday night? You wait right here, I'm calling the police."

"Mama!"

"There's no services in any temple this late on Tuesday night."

"Mrs. Sitomer, it's not a service I'm taking Gina to. It's—it's—well—"

"Yes? Yes? Why are you taking my only daughter to a synagogue if not for services?"

"Mama, Gideon's taking me there to see a show he directed."

"So! A rabbi is taking a beautiful girl to a empty shul on a dark night to see a show that *he* directed. Did he also promise you a part in it? Modern girls today, they all think they're smarter than their own mothers. *Where's the phone?*"

How does one prove he's Jewish, let alone a rabbi? I took off my jacket and rolled up my left sleeve to search my biceps for tefillin imprints to show Mrs. Sitomer. Only then, after examining the rest of my arm for needle marks, would she grant me custody of her daughter.

Gina, who hadn't yet learned about phylacteries, regarded me with suspicion on our way to Hillendale when I explained they were scrolls of Biblical verses encased in small boxes, which observant Jews fastened to their heads and their left arms, every weekday morning before prayer, by means of long, thin strips of leather, as reminders to love God with all one's heart and mind. "Long, thin strips of leather? Like whips?" she asked, and I regretted having told her my nickname for the show, *My Fair de Sade* (because the three solid weeks I had given to it pained me).

Barney Singer welcomed us in a state of euphoria: "Isn't it marvelous to see the temple packed? Biggest crowd we've had here since the Yom Kippur Night Ball. Isn't it *marvelous!*"

Suddenly I felt depressed.

Sandy Margolin came running over. In addition to having grown and gained weight since his bar mitzvah, he now started conversations. "I've changed my mind about being a doctor," he said.

"How come?"

"I'm going to be a rabbi."

"Great!" I punched him in the arm. "I'll save all my sermons to sell you at half-price."

Sandy laughed, something he had also learned to do since his bar mitzvah.

I was buttonholed by Ellie Prinz, a tough cookie of a congregant, who was high on my Love Thy Neighbor Nevertheless list. "You must talk to my son," she told me. "He wants to go off to Israel for a year."

"Wonderful!"

Ellie Prinz gave me a look that would have killed anyone who hadn't been vaccinated by dozens of dirty ones. "I want you to talk him *out* of going."

Rick Adler, attired in a carnationed tuxedo, announced that the show was starting, and Gina and I took our seats on the aisle as the lights dimmed. Immediately she began squirming, pulling at the skirt of her blue-sequined green angora sweater dress, whose colors matched those glorious eyes, and yanking up its turtle neck.

"What's the matter?"

"The way my neighbor's eyeing me," she whispered, "something of mine is either too high or too low."

Leaning over, I introduced Gina to Maurine Levenson, beside her, as the curtain arose on Sadie Doolittle selling knishes in Williamsburg and crying, "Aaaooo-www *vey!*" when somebody accidentally knocks them out of her hand . . .

. . . Two hours later, the curtain fell after Hymie Higgins' singing of the show's biggest hit, which was, deservedly, Eve Greenwood's parody:

> I'm joining a shul in the morning.
> Dunning me, the building fund'll begin.
> My head starts to ache!
> Such sacrifices I make!
> But I'm doing it for my kin.

For my son's getting bar-mitzvahed in a few years.
And my in-laws vowed to pay the tab.
Pull out all the stops
For dear old grandpops!
We'll throw a reception that's fab.

Rabbi Abel says we can't duck
Confirmation;
But with a little bit of luck,
Before then he'll go to another shul in the nation!

I'm joining a shul in the morning.
Duplicate bridge I will now have to play,
Support its bazaars
And raffles for cars.
For God's sake I'm joining the temple today!

The audience gave the cast an ovation, which they had earned if only for their seven months of preparation that neither snow, rain nor adult education had kept them from. Suddenly the cast began to applaud the audience, as Russian troupes do—only, it turned out they weren't applauding the audience, but their director. Hands pulled me out of my seat and up on the stage, where I received a standing ovation. For the first time that year I had done something that all five hundred of my bosses approved.

The crowd quieted down, expecting a speech, but all I could say was "Thank you." Then I hurried back to Gina, grabbed her by the arm and propelled her out of the temple, disengaging myself from those who besieged me with offers to direct their organizations' *Goys and Dills, The Manomanischewitz from La Mama,* and the like.

Inside my car, Gina remarked, "Your congregation is certainly fond of you."

"Yes, they consider me the Gower Champion of the rabbinate." I said no more till we reached a diner, where I apologized for my long silence.

She smiled. "That's all right. My father used to say, a person who doesn't understand another's silences won't understand his words either. Me, I don't listen to words so much as to pauses and inflections. For example, Sandy isn't so much interested in the rabbinate as he is in adopting you to be his spiritual father—and you accepted him. Another for instance— one woman's voice told me her feelings for you are more than congregantly."

"Only one?" I smiled in disbelief. "If you're so smart, tell me, why couldn't I respond to the applause before?"

Gina sighed. "For the same reason I don't enjoy hearing I have eyes like stained-glass windows."

She was such a joy, this Gina, so perceptive, warm and bright. But I didn't fall in love with her till after picking up a morning paper at the cashier's stand. Next to the *Times*, I couldn't help seeing a tabloid's front-page photograph of a girl, about twenty years old, lying in the street—was she asleep?—while an older woman crouched over her. No, the girl couldn't have been sleeping, for grief contorted the woman's face; alas, the caption reported that the girl had jumped out of her apartment window to her death when the mother failed to restrain her. Horrible!

Halfway back to Brighton Beach, for no apparent reason, Gina suddenly began to cry. Startled, I pulled my car to the curb, asking what had happened. Unable to control her sobs, she couldn't speak coherently; all I heard was something about disgusting human beings. Finally, quieting down, she told me she too had seen the front page.

"Horrible tragedy," I said with a shudder.

"That horrible photographer! Can you imagine anyone taking that picture? Focusing his camera to get in every gory detail, walking around those poor people to snap them from the best angle, all the while the mother's crying her heart out—but how could any *normal* person snap such a picture to sell to newspapers? And what normal people would want to *look* at it!" Again she burst into tears.

No, this was more like a Russian movie: the girl's sensibility is what attracted me. Sliding my arm around Gina, I pulled her toward me.

"*No!* Don't—"

I pressed forward.

"No, don't *move!*" I hesitated, and she explained, shamefacedly, "My contact lenses—I've cried them out of my eyes."

We spent an hour searching for the lenses, which were so tiny they might have been clinging to any of Gina's long hairs or those of her form-fitting angora sweater, so each had to be examined, delicately, one by one. And by the time we found the lenses—in the hollow of her warm, pulsating throat—Gina's face was dry to my lips, and I no longer cared that her unique stained-glass eyes were falsies.

א

Dear Vernon,

That makes us even: I miss you and Iris and the kids too. Worse yet, next Christmas where can I put to good use all my tree-trimming experience?

Your Mission's recent "exercise" sounds kind of C.I.A.-ish—sending you to spend a week in a Chicago slum with seven dollars and no identification "to teach you about the down-and-outers and survival." Yet if that was the idea, why not have you live like that for a week in suburbia? It's far easier to learn to eat your heart out when everybody around you is eating high off the hog.

You may have started a trend hereabouts, did you know that? One of the priests at Saint Mary's up and quit too; only in his case he quit the Catholic Church as well. Some of his reasons, as reported in the press: "The Church has become an impersonal, dehumanized corporation which no longer embodies the living reality of Christian presence. . . . it's an outmoded pseudo-political structure more concerned with authority and procedures than with truth and people . . ." *Everybody*, to quote the sage James Durante, is trying to get into the act of religion! Hallelujah.

Me, I've been having some second thoughts myself. Seems what I'm doing in Hillendale is symbolizing ethnic togetherness, like a Jewish Queen Elizabeth. A master of religious ceremonies for specific occasions is what I am, the living sign that God's in His heaven—and He'd damn well better stay there. All's right so long as I sanctify, glorify and magnify, but when I specify—! God knows it isn't easy being a prophet on a payroll.

I've considered leaving the temple for work in some charity. But I'm no organization man; I still prefer people. I also thought of following my grandfather's example and going off to Israel, until I realized it's impossible for me to live there as a rabbi. The Orthodox monopoly of Israel recognizes neither

Conservative nor Reform rabbis; we are to the Israeli rabbinate what Red China is to the United States: not there. So here I stand; I can do no other.

We pause now for a happy announcement: I got me a girl! (Please ask Iris to forgive me; she'll understand.) Can't describe her in less than a dozen pages, and since I still have two sermons to complete—

Write! Soon! Sooner than that!

> My love to the mishpochah,
> Gideon

א

APRIL

S AM Warren was bemoaning to the ways-and-
means committee his failure to stimulate be-
quests—"Nobody's put the temple in their wills yet,
and all those members who fly so much won't even
name us the beneficiary in their flight-insurance pol-
icies"—when Charlie Hecht summoned me to the
phone. It was dead, however, when I got there. Who
had called?

Charlie didn't know. "She wouldn't say. She just
asked for you; even that was hard to catch because it
sounded like she was crying."

For thirty minutes I waited near the phone, but the
woman never called back. The only other call that
evening was for Jerry Greenwood, and it didn't upset
him, though he did leave the meeting at once.

Subsequently Barney Singer gave pointers on his

specialty, taxes. "The thing to stress always is the business advantage of contributing to the temple. Show people how to be religious and business-wise at the same time. Because you can deduct the full value of religious donations, regardless of their appreciation. For example, you own a stock which cost you five hundred dollars, say, and now is worth a thousand; if you sell the stock and donate the thousand dollars to the temple, that money is deductible, but you must still pay a capital-gains tax on your five hundred dollars' profit. But—now listen carefully—if you donate the *stock* to the temple, you still deduct the thousand dollars, but you avoid the capital gains entirely. See the business advantage?"

Strange! Dad never called Treasure Chest a business (to him it had always been something of a religion); yet to my president, as he was constantly reminding everyone, this house of God is a business. And while Treasure Chest's officers dwell on the product, new trends in bras and the latest theories about breasts, the trustees had spent four nights in a row with the closest thing to God my partner's imprecation when I had reneged at bridge at a men's club meeting.

"Or let's say you're a manufacturer. Well, when you contribute merchandise to our bazaar, you can deduct its retail price, which means you profit a third or more right there. And if instead of donating, say, ten thousand dollars in cash, your corporation gives us ten thousand dollars' worth of merchandise (whose real cost to you is only five thousand dollars, remember), then your contribution costs you nothing at all, because you're giving our plant the five thousand dollars you'd have had to pay in corporation taxes anyway."

Damn! Well, how would *you* feel, spending five years in divinity school only to wind up junior administrator of the Hillendale Plant? You suppose a graduate of the Harvard Business School, like Barney Singer, for example, would relish landing a job where everyone talked constantly about death, never taxes?

"Any questions?"

There were dozens, all from people impressed with his tax expertise, who asked about personal-income-tax loopholes, and by the time he answered them all— it would be unfair to refrain, because he had become president to serve people, Barney Singer said, distributing his business cards—it was midnight, and the meeting was adjourned till the following week.

Early the next morning I was awakened by a phone call from Eve Greenwood.

"How's the daughter-in-law of the bride? Where are they now—?"

"Rabbi, I have some news to tell you—"

"What—?"

"Bad news. Jerry's mother—she—she—"

"*Eve—*"

"—died last night in—"

She kept talking, but I heard nothing. Mrs. Greenwood—Mrs. Palmer—dead? God in heaven! "Then it was *you* on the phone last night."

"Yes, Rabbi. Mr. Palmer had just called and I didn't know who to turn to, what to do. So I phoned you, before realizing it would be better for me to tell Jerry myself. So I hung up—"

"I'll be right over."

"Oh, would you? I'd be so grateful."

My eyes burning with unshed tears, I sped to the Greenwood house. Perhaps if I hadn't introduced Mrs.

Greenwood to Mr. Palmer, perhaps if they had never married, perhaps if they hadn't taken that trip around the world—

"It's so good of you to come," Eve kept saying, mistakenly assuming *I* was there to comfort *her*.

"What happened?"

"I told you on the phone. A stroke. All of a sudden."

"Jerry—how's he taking it? Where is he?"

"You didn't hear me before? I drove him to the airport last night. He didn't have to go to London—Mr. Palmer was bringing her back—but you know how close they are—were." Eve wiped her red eyes. "I loved her, I really did, like my own mother."

She served coffee, and we sat without touching it as we reminisced about Mrs. Greenwood Palmer. Thank God Eve never said the stroke had been God's will; I couldn't bear that thought. Surely it's more religious to believe in a limited good God than in an omnipotent Heartbreaker.

"Jerry will be back tonight with the—" I steeled myself, but Eve never completed the sentence. "The funeral will be tomorrow, I suppose."

Returning to my office, I reread all of Mrs. Greenwood Palmer's post cards, the Book of Psalms and the thirty-first chapter of Proverbs, before starting on the eulogy for what would be my most trying task as a rabbi; never before had I officiated at the funeral of somebody close to me. By the time I finished writing —about the lovely woman who was born in a Russian shtetl, came to America as a child, grew up on New York's Lower East Side, left high school as a teenager to work and bring money into the house, married early, helped put her husband through law school, raised a family—I had twenty pages of notes which would have to be cut to four. Then I called Gina and broke the terrible news to her.

In the evening Mr. Palmer came to my office directly from the airport. He talked for two hours about his late wife, punctuating every few minutes with "Don't forget to say *that* at the funeral." Wiping his eyes, he said, "I didn't love her when we got married, you know that, Gideon. But I did by the time we got to Athens. Such a *remarkable* woman! To her everything in the world became *we*. It wasn't 'I Ruth' and 'you Ben'; from the start it was 'we.' In Israel it was 'Isn't it beautiful what we Jews have accomplished in our tiny country?' Even in Greece, it was 'we Athenians.' Because, she told me, Western civilization is the child of Jerusalem and Athens. Who knows from civilization, and who cares? But I loved how she incorporated everything around her. Gideon, say *that* at the funeral." His voice cracked. "And now I'm only an I all over again." Suddenly he burst out, "It wasn't *my* fault Ruth died. The doctor said it was an accident—a cardiovascular accident, he called it. Couldn't be helped; it would have happened in Hillendale too. Please say *that* at the funeral."

"I know, Mr. Palmer. Dr. Lipton told me the same thing." I had called him that morning to relieve my own feelings of guilt. "Nobody's blaming you."

"Jerry is. In London and all the way back on the plane he never said one word to me. Would you talk to him, Gideon, report what the doctor said? And tell him I loved his mother. She was so remarkable."

The Greenwoods weren't home when I called that evening; a neighbor directed me to the funeral chapel, which was packed with visitors (even though Jewish law forbids condolence calls prior to the funeral, while mourners are still in a state of shock, ill equipped to receive them) and the chatting—about golf, bridge, vacations, children's summer camps— gave the mortuary the sedately festive air of a cocktail party whose first guests had not yet gotten stoned. And then, chilled, I saw her: up front inside an elaborate bronze coffin atop a flower-bedecked dais, Mrs. Greenwood Palmer lay exhibited beneath a pink spotlight.

A man emerged from behind a rubber tree to greet me. "Rabbi, glad to see you." It was Goldwyn, the undertaker, who for business reasons belonged to ten times as many synagogues as Maimonides had. "Your eulogy at the Grossberg funeral was a real highlight, I want you to know. And everybody there thought you look exactly like Harry Belafonte, isn't that something?"

I asked where Jerry Greenwood was.

Goldwyn lowered his voice. "You're not going to start anything now, are you, Rabbi? About closing the casket, I mean."

This was not the time, I said, but he knew Jewish law required that the dead be treated with dignity, not displayed in coffins like store-window mannequins.

Goldwyn frowned. "It's a casket, not a coffin. And if we close it up, how can anyone see how beautiful it is inside and all the workmanship?"

According to Jewish law, I said, people were to be buried in plain pinewood boxes.

"My God, you're talking communism! A wooden crate for a beloved mother? It violates the Seventh Commandment. Besides which, Greenwood drives around in a Cadillac, and you want his only mother buried in a Volkswagen?" He proceeded to explain that the United States was a democracy, where money meant nothing when a loved one passed on, because far more important was showing respect in the proper fashion, thereby discharging guilt—

Excusing myself, I sought out Jerry Greenwood. He was sitting in a corner of the room, sunken-eyed and gray-faced, barely responding to condolences.

"Jerry? Let's go someplace quiet to talk." (I should have said something about being sorry, but could sorry cover the loss of his mother?)

I led him into the clergyman's room off the main chapel, where he turned to face me. "What do you want?"

"If there's something special you want said tomorrow—"

"Tomorrow?"

"At the funeral."

"What about it?"

"The eulogy for your mother. I talked with Eve and Mr. Palmer, but you, as her son, being so close to her—is there anything you'd like me to say tomorrow?"

"*You?* You're not burying *my* mother."

"What—?"

"I've asked Rabbi Jacobson to officiate.".

א

London

Dear Rabbi,

We think you're in the wrong profession—you should have been a matchmaker. You're better at it than Hello, Dolly! Yes, we're very happy, thank you. (In marriage, I suspect, Like triumphs far more often than Love.)

Our best regards to Gina, that lovely girl. And when are we going to dance at *your* wedding already?

See you next week—

Loads of love,
Ruth and Ben Palmer

א

MAY

THE first time I saw Caleb was at the church-and-synagogue sing, which featured the choirs of all Hillendale's houses of God—this was three moons *after* Brotherhood Month; now I ask you, isn't that progress? Happily too, not only were the hymns beautifully rendered and the public-school auditorium crowded, but here a dozen houses of worship had assembled with nobody's congratulating himself or the others once during the evening on having apprehended the most elusive of -hoods, brotherhood. It was almost enough to convince you of that other -hood, God's Father-.

After the musical program, Dr. Bidwell, chairman of the evening, invited questions from the audience about the various faiths, their practices and beliefs.

The queries were all polite, even the one inquiring how the three branches of Judaism differed. Rabbi Jacobson, answering, was also polite: "The difference between Orthodoxy and the other two is like the difference between day and night," he said, but that was all.

When a lithe young Negro up front stood to ask the next question, Reverend Hobbes, who was sitting beside me (he's the one who finally took those Thanksgiving turkeys off my conscience), exclaimed softly, "No."

The youth spoke up in a throbbing bass, so loud he seemed to be wired for stereo. "What kind of *farce* is this? So many churchmen haven't gathered under one roof since the Council of Trent, and what do you do? You sing. While my people are dying!"

Dr. Bidwell reddened. "Young man, if you don't have a question—"

"Oh, I got a question, baby, a million of 'em," he retorted, and Reverend Hobbes winced. "*Why* did the churches convert the slaves to keep them subservient? *Why* did the churches focus Negro attention on the afterlife to keep us docile? *Why* did the churches start segregation in this country? *Why* did the Southern churches unanimously endorse the Civil War? *Why* are the churches today still shot through with racism? *Why* have the churches always sinned against my people?"

Reverend Hobbes clasped and unclasped his hands as Dr. Bidwell replied sharply, "But the churches *have* supported freedom rides, sit-ins, the March on Washington, civil rights legislation—"

The Negro sneered. "They were only getting on the bandwagon, baby. Even Republican and Democratic party platforms were always more outspoken on race than the churches. And just look at them today: still more segregated than any whorehouse in the country, still not using their enormous wealth and economic power to end slums and get us jobs and a decent education. Your churches are as morally bankrupt as the rest of society, and I say the hell with them all."

Dr. Bidwell, losing his British accent along with his temper, cried, "Young man, there's such a thing as good manners. If you were a Christian, if you were anything, you would know that issues must be discussed with courtesy and a civil—"

"You want us to die politely—isn't that it?" the Negro shouted back. "Well, go screw yourself, baby!"

The audience gasped. Reverend Hobbes jumped to his feet. "Caleb!" He rushed to the podium. "You must excuse the speaker for his intemperate—"

The youth roared, "Don't you *dare* apologize for me! Not to white bastards!" And he dashed out of the auditorium.

The assembly broke up almost immediately. Nobody could think of anything to top that outburst, I suppose, unless it was to kick Dr. Bidwell in the head.

I went over to Reverend Hobbes, who remained alone at the podium. He was trembling.

"Don't let that last speaker bother you," I said. "There are people like him in every congregation."

Reverend Hobbes's voice trembled too as he said, "Caleb is my son." (The look on his face reminded me of Zayda when he discovered that his children no longer observed the Sabbath; a year later he left for Israel.)

Caleb appeared one week later in, of all places, my office. Without knocking on the door, he strode in, saying, "I'm Caleb Hobbes. *You* remember, the party pooper." He snorted. "These brotherhood binges are too much. Like some guy hitting the sack with the same chick for two thousand years, and all he does every night is declare his love for her without once scoring. Makes you suspect, to say the least, the guy's intentions."

I asked him to take a seat.

"You also disapproved of my 'intemperance,' didn't you?"

Yes, but was that fair? How did I react that Sunday in Vernon's church? Yet I had been provoked. Well, wasn't silence sometimes more provoking than words? True, but I didn't respond out of hate. But why assume Caleb Hobbes's passion was hate? Had he said anything, after all, that Vernon hadn't said before? Still— "What did you hope to accomplish, Mr. Hobbes? You think you can goscrewyourself people into aiding the freedom movement?"

The fellow stood up. "Well, that answers my question, baby."

"What question, Mr. Hobbes?"

"Don't patronize me, baby," he snapped. "Everybody calls me Caleb."

I smiled. "And what would you have said had I called you Caleb? Tell me, what's the question?"

He shifted from one foot to another, then back again, so full of nervous energy he seemed to be running on electricity. "I want you to join in picketing a slumlord who lives on Peachtree Lane. That is, baby, if you ever join things besides sings."

Funny guy. Here to make a request, nevertheless he wouldn't stop insulting me. "Suppose you give me the details—sweetheart."

Caleb told me—in the same roar he had used in

the auditorium; he was either deaf or wished to deafen—of one Ev William, who owned fourteen tenements, which he was milking dry, and Caleb had documentary proof. William's houses had scores of violations that he never remedied. It took up to eighteen months to bring him to court; even then the court treated him so leniently, fining him less than fifteen dollars per violation, that it was cheaper to pay the fines than to make repairs. For the courts never jailed more than a dozen slumlords a year, and with the housing shortage so acute, the city could not vacate William's buildings and board them up; there was no place to relocate the tenants. Caleb therefore wanted to shame the slumlord, whom he had traced through a dozen dummy corporations, into rehabilitating his buildings. Publicly identifying him as a slumlord, the youth thought, would do the trick.

Shall I tell you the truth? My first reaction was: Thank God William isn't Jewish. (His name had not appeared on the membership committee's untapped-market list.)

"Well, baby," Caleb concluded, "are you with us? Or against us?"

"Let's talk a little more, sweetheart."

He flared. "*Don't* call me sweetheart."

"Don't call me *baby*; I have a name. Besides, from the way you talk, I'd guess you're a college graduate. Aren't you?"

Caleb scowled. "Smart man. Yes, I'm a college grad—and one who'll matriculate till his thirty-sixth birthday. Whitey isn't going to turn *this* black man into mercenary cannon fodder. Well, baby—Rabbi? What's it going to be?"

"Let me see one of William's houses first. I can't be hasty."

"*Behold: one gen-u-ine slum!* Hur-ry, hur-ry, hur-ry, be the first of your race to get in on the ground floor!"

So saying, Caleb pushed open the front door of the five-story tenement at 34 Halifay Street. He played with the latch. "Behold, no lock, designed to make the premises all the more inviting for addicts and winos." And waved a hand overhead. "Behold, no light bulbs, to foster that romantic atmosphere for prosties eager to turn quick tricks in the hall." And pointed a finger upward and sideways. "Behold, ceiling and walls with matching holes." And nodded at the filthy floor. "Behold, no janitor for the last four months." And touched one of the upright uncovered iron spikes along the stairwell. "Behold, no banister, the easier for playful children to make shish kebab out of each other." A kitten brushed by my leg in the dim hallway as Caleb concluded, "Now for the denizens of the deep-pressed."

He showed me through a few apartments—introducing me as the Miseries' Inspector—and it was hard to tell whose reaction distressed me more: those tenants who bombarded me with complaints about clogged toilets, inoperable refrigerators, uncollected garbage, lack of heat and hot water, rotting walls, shattered windows, exposed electrical wiring; or those whose apartments contained the same violations but who never complained at all, accepting them as their due. To think that people lived like this in the richest, most powerful nation in the world.

I felt nauseated and ashamed.

The fifth apartment's occupant had just admitted us when her baby started to cry. Going to a half-open closet, the woman climbed up on a chair in front of it, then lifted the infant out of a basket on the top shelf.

I couldn't restrain a chuckle. "That's a funny place to keep a baby. Why put him up there?"

My question seemed to surprise the mother; she looked from me to Caleb, then back at me, before saying what evidently was common knowledge: "We got rats."

I remembered the furry animal that had brushed by my leg before, in the dark hall—then it *hadn't* been a kitten—and shuddered. Turning to Caleb, I said, "Let's go. I've seen enough. *Too* much."

"Can we pick a picketing date now?" he asked, on our way out of the building.

I delayed my reply till we reached the street, then said, "I want to be fair. Will you show me those documents?"

Caleb snickered. "What good are documents if you're blind? But okay. I'll have them sent to you."

The next day a folder marked "Willev Enterprises" arrived special delivery at the temple with a notation from Caleb: "Here's *integrated* proof—everything's in black and white." But I was in over my head as soon as I opened the folder. How could anyone whose major contact with legal documents had been his birth certificate evaluate such material?

When Caleb called me that evening, I told him I had forwarded his papers with a letter of explanation to—

He cut in. "Stalling again, baby?"

"It's necessary to check these things with a lawyer—"

"But a lawyer prepared that file, a *black* lawyer. You need whitey to tell you it's kosher, right?"

A few days later Charlie Hecht phoned. "It's true," he said. "Willev's profits are unconscionable. The corporation is making four times the normal returns by writing off building-violation fines as business expenses. Actually, the government is to blame here, for allowing slumlords full depreciation—on an accelerated basis yet!—though they never maintain their buildings. Well, Rabbi, what are you going to do?"

That's what Caleb wanted to know when he stopped by the temple the next day and learned Charlie Hecht had corroborated him.

"Why so anxious to get *me* on your picket line?" I asked.

"Because black pickets are a drug on the market today; no newspaperman covers us any more unless there's a fresh angle. Now if we got white middle-class clergymen to picket one of their own, we'd make TV and every paper in the country, maybe inspire other clergymen to follow suit and scare other slumlords into fixing up their rattraps. Dig?"

"What other clergymen will be picketing?"

Caleb looked at me with feigned surprise. "Does that matter, Mr. Minister of God?"

I flushed. "No."

"I'll tell you this much: if you join the picketing, that'll mean one hundred percent of the clergymen I invited are cooperating. Well, Rabbi?"

Sure, I was reluctant. The seminary hadn't educated me to be a vigilante. "Let me contact this William, tell him of the picketing. Maybe that will persuade him to do what he should. Your goal here is to get him to repair the buildings, not simply to picket—right?"

Caleb smiled a smile that was darker than anybody else's glower. "Okay, baby. I'll give you enough rope."

Why did I take such abuse from this guy? I felt responsible, of course, for the horrible way those people at 34 Halifay Street lived; isn't our High

Holiday confession, listing more sins than any one human being could ever commit, always said in the first person plural? Moreover, I admired Caleb's single-minded devotion to justice for his oppressed people. The fellow was embittered, sure—wasn't he entitled?—but he overacted his toughness, a certain sign he was overcompensating for a good heart too bruised for him to let it show.

I wrote William, care of Willev Corporation (his Hillendale phone and address were unlisted). He didn't reply. Registering my next letter, I called when there was no response. But his secretary had the gall to deny there *was* an Ev William!

Caleb phoned, a few days later. "I can hardly wait," he said, "to hear this month's excuse."

"Okay. Name the date."

For the first time Caleb seemed at a loss for words. "Christ!" he swore, finally. "You're really going to picket!"

What else could I do? There was no moral alternative. To justify my action, to myself as well as to others, I made my own picketing sign, printing on it the Biblical verse: "He hath oppressed and forsaken the poor; he hath taken a house and will not build it up. Because in his greed he suffered nobody to escape, therefore his prosperity shall not endure."

Gina, seeing the sign, remarked, "Why, that sounds like something Mama would say." She smiled. "Who would ever have guessed the Bible was so socialistic?"

The afternoon before picket day, Caleb stopped by the temple to hand me a big placard. I refrained from showing him mine; clearly he regarded his as a bond uniting us in our common cause, for as he presented it to me his gaze never left my face.

"Caleb, I certainly appreciate this. It's a fine—" I looked at the sign and saw:

```
YOUR NEIGHBOR

WILLIAM EVANS

IS A

SLUMLORD
```

William Evans?

"What's the trouble, Rabbi?"

I barely got the words out. "You told me *Ev William.*"

Caleb shrugged. "A mistake. I thought Evans was his first name and William his last. Sometimes it's hard to tell with Jewish names, you know?" His eyes searched my face. "Why? Does it matter?"

Only if it mattered for a rabbi to picket a member of his own temple. Dumbly I shook my head.

"See you tomorrow on the picket line. Oh, did I tell you? You're the only clergyman I invited. You should feel honored."

As soon as Caleb left, I looked up Evans' office number in the temple files—yes, it was that of Willev Enterprises—and phoned him. This time the secretary put me through immediately.

"Rabbi? You want to know about my contribution to the kitchen fund, I presume—"

Quickly I revealed the reason for my call—Evans

sucked in his breath sharply—then asked why he hadn't answered my letters.

"They sounded like practical jokes, all being addressed to a nonexistent Ev William. Besides, everyone knows I live on West Drive, not Peachtree Lane."

"Just as long as I got to you in time. Can we get together tonight to discuss—"

Evans cut in. "I have nothing to discuss with you, Rabbi."

"Your houses, the violations. I'm sure you know nothing about them, being so busy with all your other enterprises, but to the people living in tenements like 34 Halifay—"

"Rabbi, have you checked all your other congregants' enterprises to make sure they're a hundred percent pure?"

"What?"

"Well, till you do, *my* business is none of *your* business, understand? Don't think I'm going to let you spoil things now the way you spoiled my bar mitzvah. Who set you up as judge over me anyhow?" And he hung up.

The phone began to shake; no, it wasn't the phone that was shaking, because it stopped when I returned it to its cradle. My hand was shaking, and not only my hand, but my entire body. I never knew that rage could give a sober person the D.T.'s. In a cold fury— make that a hot fury; now I was sweating too—I called Western Union and sent off a telegram to Evans, telling him it was one great shame that Judaism doesn't practice excommunication. The operator read the message back to me as regretting that Judaism doesn't practice decapitation, and I let it stand.

The phone rang. When I picked it up, my hand was still trembling so much I waited before speaking, because my voice would be shaking too.

"Hello? Hello? That you—?"

I let Evans have it; for all his victims I gave it to him. How could a *Jew* be so callous to human suffering!

"Who do you think you're talking to?"

Such chutzpah! I told Evans of my tour of his filthy building with the rats and no superintendent, the broken toilets and exposed wiring, the busted refrigerators and no heat, the rotting walls and filthy—

"*Gideon!*"

I worked Evans over some more, pointing out that the cost of his son's bar-mitzvah party could easily have paid for 34 Halifay's rehabilitation—

"Gideon, this is your father."

"Dad?"

"What's going on there?"

"Well—a little disagreement—with a congregant—"

"A *little* disagreement? What do you say to members during a major one? Or do you simply fire off an H-bomb?"

I told Dad the whole story—up till Evans' last words: "Who set you up as judge over me anyhow?" —and bless his Jewish heart, he volunteered either to join the picket line or to donate money to have 34 Halifay Street repaired, or both. Yet when I began to thank him, he stopped me.

"Don't thank me, Gideon, because then I'll only have to call up Evans and thank him."

"Thank Evans? For what?"

"You'll see, Gideon, you'll see."

What did he mean? Dad wouldn't tell me.

Dore Redmont stopped by my apartment early that evening to ask, "Are you *crazy*, Rabbi?" Before I could enter a denial, he rushed on: "You can't picket Evans. Know what he's doing? Trying to oust you from the temple. He called me today to help him."

Evans' move was obvious. He hadn't called Dore for help—everyone knew we were friends—but to get him to pressure me. "I told you before, I don't care about any four-year contract."

"Rabbi, we're talking now about a *one*-year contract."

"What? Oh, but the great majority of the congregation are fine, decent people, and they're with me."

"Rabbi, fifty percent of the congregation would march on Cairo if you asked them to. Probably sixty percent. Maybe even seventy percent—"

"Well, then—"

"But according to our constitution, you need a vote of seventy-five percent—"

That shook me. "Seventy-five—?" (Now I remembered why Evans' words had sounded familiar. Who set you up as judge over me? That was the line that had impelled Moses to drop his princeship and beat it out of town after smiting an Egyptian slumlord.)

"—and that's hard to get under *normal* circumstances. Look, five to ten percent of the congregation hated you even before you set foot in Hillendale, just as the same percentage loved you then too; who can explain some people's reactions to father figures and God images? Another five to ten percent wouldn't know, much less care, if we had installed Popeye here as our rabbi. So that leaves between five to ten percent who'll be deciding your election, when it's your luck to be running against Peter Perfect. In an

ordinary election a nominee is matched against somebody who also has faults, but here people will be
voting you down now, and later start thinking about a
replacement, who will have flaws but not the same
ones as yours; if he does, he can be got rid of just as
easily. On rabbis it's always open season. Don't you
know that?"

"Dore, you're asking me not to picket Evans—"

"I'm begging you, Rabbi—"

"—not because it's wrong, but because it's impol-
itic."

"What's the difference?"

"Dore, people are always telling me I push integration so hard because I don't own a home of my own,
whose value might decline. And here you want me to
think of a paying job first?"

"I want you to think of all of us here who love you,
and yes, I want you to think of yourself too. What's
wrong with that? You think Hobbes is thinking of
you? Picket Evans tomorrow, and the majority of the
congregation will cheer, sure; they too despise these
rotten slumlords. But there's bound to be some members who'll wonder who's next. Rabbi, there's a great
big business world outside this temple, and some
of the things some members do in that world aren't
exactly kosher—that includes me—and if they start to
worry that soon you'll be indicting them too—"

"Goddamnit! Shouldn't a house of God have standards? Why allow somebody like Evans inside a
synagogue? Rotary and the Boy Scouts have qualifi-
cations for membership; why shouldn't we?"

"That sonofabitch Hobbes!"

"Dore!"

"Oh, I'm not cursing him because he's black; I'm
cursing him because he's a bastard. *That's* all right,

isn't it? Look what he's done to you; he's placed you in an impossible position."

"It isn't Caleb's fault. He even gave me the chance to back out by telling me the slumlord's Jewish. Caleb only acts tough; he's really—"

"If Hobbes tipped you off beforehand, it was for some devious reason. Look what he pulled at the sing. Was that rational? Or productive? And how did William Evans ever turn into Ev William? Or West Drive into Peachtree Lane? Hobbes knew from the start Evans belonged to this temple. And didn't you just tell me you're the only clergyman he asked to picket?"

A call from Barney Singer interrupted us; Evans had gotten to him too, of course. "Your picketing would force everyone to take sides," he exclaimed. "It would split the entire temple."

Justice, I said, comes first.

"Gideon, I'm no bigot. But this is different. How just is it for a rabbi to wash dirty linen in public by naming a prominent temple member as a slumlord?"

Everyone knows, I said, that the Jews, far more than any other group in America, have consistently supported civil rights.

"How many people you think would remember that, once a rabbi denounced a congregant for slumprofiteering? Gideon, you can't picket Evans. Haven't groups seceded from synagogues before over things as small as a skullcap? Wait there. I'm coming over to talk to you."

Dore implored me to heed Barney. But was the social-action-committee chairman being any more Jewish than the president, whose first allegiance was to an organization, or, for that matter, than Curt Langer, who was emotionally tied to one rabbi? "You're more concerned about my welfare than Caleb's because you like me and not him. Dore, didn't I teach you better?"

Was there ever a nobler speech? Yet as soon as Barney reached my place, I surrendered Caleb's phone number. Astonished? Well, don't be. Once my fury was spent, I had no stomach for picketing Evans. No, I didn't fear losing my job—the rabbinate I've never considered a mere job—just as I didn't regret sending that telegram. It's simply that denouncing evil is one thing; it's something else altogether to publicly identify it in the person of someone with a wife and four innocent children, who would suffer for sins not their own. If I could not bring myself to expose Pete Schuster's adultery or the fly in Rona Redmont's soup, how could I now shame the Evans family?

Dore got Caleb on the phone. Instead of asking about what had puzzled us, however, Dore began to holler: "Do you know what you're doing, Hobbes? Do you? You're going to get Rabbi Abel fired, that's what you're doing. And his successor would never be half as involved in civil rights—"

"That's not fair!" I grabbed the phone away from Dore to apologize to Caleb, and we both heard his throbbing voice: "Who the hell cares what happens to Rabbi Baby? No honky white devil is my concern except as a *tool*."

"Caleb!"

"That you, baby?" Hobbes said without embarrassment. "The same Rabbi Bountiful who tries to erase a lifetime of guilt with ten Thanksgiving turkeys? You want to know what happened to one quarter of one of them? I'll tell you. My father kept it for us—a man like him with three college degrees but black, so he's condemned for life by the clergy placement office to a one-room church which doesn't pay him enough to buy a decent Thanksgiving meal—but I threw it into the gutter. Nobody's gaining absolution that easy!"

"Those turkeys weren't mine. I explained to your father. Two little girls here wanted to—"

"Forget it. I'm interested in one thing now. Are you joining us tomorrow? Or do you have a previous engagement to deliver Easter bunnies to other unfortunates?"

Dore had been right: Caleb was a sonofabitch. "You," I cried in a roar to match his, "can go to *hell!*" I slammed down the receiver.

"Didn't I tell you?" Dore said, while Barney Singer shook my hand in relief. "Hobbes knew all along Evans was your congregant. That's why he hid his name from you. Understand now?"

Not at all. If Hobbes had been so eager to enlist my aid, why did he reveal Evans' name prematurely, enabling me to withdraw? And even after I had agreed to join him, why wouldn't he stop insulting me? It didn't make sense.

That night I could not sleep. Half the time I tossed in bed, excoriating Hobbes for his Machiavellian manipulations; afterwards the people at 34 Halifay Street kept me awake, complaining about busted toilets, rotting walls, no janitor, the rats. If I chose not to humiliate the Evanses, who would suffer? Not Hobbes, but the blameless tenants. That momzer! Here I had gone far out of my way, and did he give a damn? *You* heard: "Who the hell cares what happens to Rabbi Baby? No honky white devil is my concern except as a *tool.*" And such hate spewing out of him, triggered by a loving gesture of two sweet children. Hobbes wasn't embittered; he had been poisoned. Maybe God had the antidote; I certainly did not. Nobody would blame me for not picketing. (How many knew the situation, anyway? Without Hobbes's forcing it on my attention, I'd never have known about it either.) And look at Dore, who respected me; my change of mind had elated him. No, *nobody* but Hobbes would condemn me—not even that baby on the closet shelf—and Hobbes was a gen-u-ine hundred percent bastard, as callous in his own way as Evans. No, nobody but that damn *Hobbes.*

And myself.

Two blocks away from the elegant Evans estate, I heard Hobbes's blaring voice leading a chorus in: "William Evans is a slumlord." Yet when I parked near Evans' fourteen-room house, I saw that Hobbes was using no mechanical amplifier; he simply had turned up the volume on his own thundering basso profundo.

I took out my placard—the Biblical one, not Hobbes's, for his had been given to an instrument, not to a person—and joined the twenty shouting picketers, positioning myself behind the mother who had to hide her baby in a closet. She was my bond here.

Hobbes broke off his chant to exclaim, "What are you doing here, baby? I never expected *you* to show."

The expression on his face—no joy at seeing an ally alighted there, only sullenness—finally solved the mystery of Hobbes's actions. The solution was too obvious to have occurred to me. "You never *wanted* me to come. Did you? Even though you needed me—"

"What are you talking about? Baby, you're full of—"

Scowling, he stopped short, hesitated for a moment, then turned to a companion. "Phone the papers and networks again. Tell them now we have a newsworthy story: 'Rabbi Pickets His Own Congregant.' That should bring them running." Yet for the first time since we met, his voice sounded low and colorless, almost uncertain. Was it possible the mystery's solution had never occurred to him either? Did powerlessness corrupt too?

Well, at any rate Caleb Hobbes didn't tell me what to go do to myself. That, also, was progress.

א

——*Rabbi?*

——Yes?

——*Oh, did I wake you?*

——No, no I've been up for *hours*——

——*You can come clean with me, Rabbi. This is Eve Greenwood.*

——Eve. Why didn't you say so in the first place? And why wake me so early in the morning?

——*I couldn't wait to tell you the good news.*

——What is it?

——*Well, last night we held our final meeting of the sub-rosa committee*——

——Sub-rosa committee? I never heard of *that* one.

——*You weren't supposed to. Because you're its total agenda.*

——Me?

——*Yes. The last few weeks we've been polling the congregation about renewing your contract*——

——What?

——*also proselytizing borderline cases to vote for you and the Right.*

——Really? You've been doing that?

——*Not just me. There's Dore, the Margolins, Charlie Hecht, dozens of people; ours was the most popular committee ever. Because, as it turned out, you're getting eighty-one to eighty-five percent of the vote. Mazeltov!*

——No joke!

——*It's true. Know what is a joke? Your picketing of that creep Evans, it did cost you votes—five, to be exact. But it won over nine undecideds. How about that?*

——I don't know what to say. You've done all that for me?

——*No, Rabbi. We've done it for us.*

——You're sweet, Eve. I'm very grateful. Frankly, the Evans affair did have me worried. Not getting my contract renewed after my first year in the rabbinate—that would have been . . . humiliating.

——*There's one thing—*

——What is it, Eve?

——*Something crazy—a couple of families are splitting their votes, like the wife will be voting for you and the husband against—*

——You mean Jerry? That was to be expected.

——*You have no idea how ashamed I feel. The way Jerry took a dislike to you, what he did at his mother's funeral. It made me feel terrible. And now, voting to fire you—*

——Forget it, Eve. After all, I do have eighty-five percent with me.

——*You do, Rabbi, but I don't. All I have is Jerry. Oh, I suppose after fifteen years of marriage, I should have learned to accept his limitations. But when he starts arguing with me and I com-*

pare him to a man like you—Rabbi, don't you
ever get married at eighteen.

——I promise, Eve. But you have to promise me
something too.

——What is it?

——Don't ever discuss me with Jerry. If you two
must argue, let it be about something important
in your marriage.

——A rabbi is important to a marriage when the
husband always throws him up to the wife as
the other man. Not that Jerry's wrong about my
feelings for you, Gideon— Oh, I didn't mean to
say that! I never wanted you to know I— Goodbye—

א

JUNE

THINGS have a way of working out, don't they? Not only was Caleb proven right in exposing slumlords—the ensuing publicity shamed Evans into selling nearly half his slum holdings and repairing the rest—but Dore's fears for my future in Hillendale had been polled wrong. The contractual meeting held no nervous stomach for me now, since justice would be renewed for at least another year.

Even the night before the meeting ended happily, when I joined a colleague, a psychologist and a marriage counselor in a panel discussion on marriage at another synagogue. Mine was the finest presentation of the group, I admit; you could tell from the women's sighs when I proclaimed marriage a religious art

form, how they nudged their husbands and the way
husbands glared at me.

Following my talk, I answered a dozen questions
to perfection, before one lady called out, "Rabbi Abel,
your wife is *such* a lucky woman."

"Well," I said, and called for the next question.

"Is she here tonight, Rabbi?"

I twitched my head spasmodically to indicate either
a negative or that something had got stuck in my
ear which kept me from hearing the query. "Since
there are no further questions—" I said, and sat down.

The woman had to persist. "How long have you
been married, Rabbi? I mean, to have gained such
understanding about women and marriage. You look
so young."

I didn't lie; there was no time, for Rabbi Schwartz
rushed to my debacle. "Oh, Rabbi Abel is a bachelor,"
he said. "Couldn't you tell from his talk?"

The women took the news slightly better than
the fall of Adam, except for those who had nudged
their husbands before and were now being punched
back.

"*A boy!*"

"*Aha!*"

I hastened to say, "Surely you all don't think one
must always speak from experience, do you? My good
colleague, Rabbi Schwartz, for example, preaches a
great deal about sin, yet he doesn't indulge *every*
day."

They didn't buy that. I received no more questions
from the audience, only dirty or amused looks and
the impression that the psychologist on the panel who
had mentioned impotence before would soon be
called on to prove his. After the meeting (coffee and
cake were served, of course; a thousand years hence

archeologists will dig up today's synagogues and churches, and finding all our refrigerators, ovens, coffee urns, hot plates and Danish pastry, will conclude that we in the twentieth century worshiped cafeteria-style) five husbands gave me the lowdown on marriage.

"You can't learn about marriage from books," one said.

"That's right," another agreed. "It's nothing like *Fanny Hill.*"

But, as I said, things turned out deliciously. For I realized on my lonely drive home the reason for my hymeneal. Of course: I wanted to get married. After my broken engagement I had hesitated to commit myself again, but this time I was sure; Gina was the girl for me. So I called her for a date for the night after the congregational meeting.

"But that's a weekday night," she said. "Don't you have a meeting?"

"I'm skipping it. There's something I want to ask you."

The following evening, when I arrive at the meeting, after composing my spontaneous acceptance speech, I suspect at once that the sub-rosa poll contained some errors. Dore Redmont must be one; I see Rona pick up the anonymous family ballot with a sidelong averted glance at me, and I know that unless Dore himself fills out their ballot, there's .7 percent down the drain. No matter—even without the Redmonts, 84.3 percent is still with me (113.5 families versus 19.5, with the seven undecideds apportioned proportionately).

True, Bernstein, whom I haven't seen since the Thanksgiving interfaith service, comments, "Dr. Bidwell never proposed a raise in dues at his church."

Since Bernstein is doubtlessly a con voter anyway, I tell him, "Okay, so join the low-priced spread."

Barney Singer, a silver-plated *T* in his hand, calls me aside to ask me to present Pete Schuster with this year's Mr. Temple Award.

How do I get out of this? By suggesting an *A* for Pete Schuster instead? "You do it, Barney. I've already promised sisterhood to make the presentation to the raffle winner of the free weekend at Grossinger's."

The president shakes his head. "I don't understand you. It's always hardest for you to do the easy things."

After the meeting is called to order, I read from Henry Slonimsky: "The assertion of God in a godless world is the supreme act of religion. It is a continuing of the act of creation on the highest plane. . . . That is true religion: to insist on God in a God-forsaken world or rather in a world not yet dominated by God, and thus to call Him into being."

Barney Singer comments, "Thank you, Rabbi. Nobody, I'm sure, will ever accuse you of talking *down* to us." He presents the Mr. Temple Award to Pete Schuster, whose ineffable contributions to the shul this past year, he declares, manifested the greatest qualities of heart and mind, head and hands, body and soul, his inventory omitting only Schuster's kishkes and loins.

With a catch in his voice, Mr. Temple accepts the award in the name of Hillendale, the synagogue, his wife and God, whereupon a photographer snaps his picture for the Hillendale *News*, the congregation applauds and Gladys Schuster weeps—which leaves only the Lord to be heard from. Then he takes over the meeting briefly while the evening's first vote is taken, for next year's officers and trustees.

There is no discussion, only a call for a show of hands, and Pete Schuster jubilantly announces, "For president, it's Barney Singer again! By unanimous vote!"

(You'd never guess, would you, that Singer had run unopposed on a single slate. Or that he had made a deal beforehand with Pete Schuster, guaranteeing him the Mr. Temple Award provided he wouldn't challenge Barney for the presidency.)

The president, touched, thanks everyone for the heartwarming vote of confidence, adding, "I've always tried to guide myself by a proverb on this ashtray that I keep on my desk as an eternal reminder: 'Use the talents you possess, because the woods would be silent if no birds sang except the best.' Now I'm not the best singer there is (except in this congregation, of course, because that is, after all, my name; get it?), I don't know so much about Judaism, and I'm not that religious. But I assure you all of one thing in all humility: I'll do the very best job I can. Because it's a rare privilege to serve you. I therefore accept this mantle of leadership for the greater glory of the Hillendale Temple and Jewry."

If you think mixed emotions are elbowing me throughout this meeting, you're not wrong. For that's the state of communications between my congregants and me: mixed—half the time I don't know what they want from me, the other half of the time they don't care for what I want of them. A doctor exists to cure the sick, an accountant is to find tax loopholes, a dentist fixes teeth, a lawyer takes money away from one sonofabitch in order to give it to another sonofabitch, or so Vernon told me—but with rabbis everything goes. Each member has his own peculiar concept of the ideal rabbi, which makes my vocation much like playing Hamlet before an audience of English professors; have you ever met a Jew who doesn't consider himself an authority in three areas of life: his own business, show business and shul business?

How then is a rabbi to gauge his effectiveness? Effectiveness? Hell, it's hard to tell if the congregation is marking you present. All year long now I've preached essentially one sermon: that religion is a demand and God the challenger, who obliges us to set ourselves and the world aright. Yet how many got the message, when no requirements whatsoever are demanded of congregants? And so religion inevitably ends up the name people give their own biases.

No more than Vernon's church needed him, alas, does my temple need me. For there's a growing Jewish community in Hillendale, devoutly middle-class, with a sizable number of school-age children, fecund parents, lots of churches and plenty of up-coming affairs. And if you think I'm jealous of the new temple kitchen and carrying on a fierce sibling rivalry with its contemplated walk-in freezer, you're right.

"The first order of business is a proposal to add a steam room to the temple, which can be constructed at the same time as the kitchen for a few extra thousand dollars."

I assume it's a steam room for corned beef and vegetables—to complement the walk-in freezer—until somebody tacks on a request for showers and a masseur. Following the defeat of both proposals, Charlie Hecht outlines the adult-education committee's plans for next year's expanded educational program, which will include weekly Sabbath Eve lectures and discussions in place of sermons. Then Dore Redmont reports on his committee's activities in promoting no less than thirteen important social issues. ("Dore for God!" cracks Pete Schuster, patiently projecting his own ambition.)

This makes me feel, after all my misgivings, like a gold-plated ingrate; now I regret not having invited my fair Gina to the meeting to shep nachas along with me from Charlie Hecht's and Dore's reports, a rain-in-Spain sort of climax. Sure, the synagogue has weaknesses and the rabbinate limitations, but what doesn't? Where can one better invest his life than in continuing a magnificent four-thousand-year-old heritage, inculcating values in children, setting goals for adults, combating injustice, alleviating cruelty, asserting dignity, confronting people with the living God? My batting average needed improvement, but at least part of the congregation (like sisterhood, which runs the preschool kindergarten; the youth group, which tutors disadvantaged kids; Dr. Lipton, who's organizing a neighborhood health center in Harlem; Charlie Hecht, who contributes his legal services to an antipoverty agency; a college senior, who applied to rabbinical school; the nineteen regulars who never miss adult education; Dore's social-action committee, not to mention the sub-rosa committee), at least they know I'm in there swinging. Well, you know how it is: life, even for clergymen who urge the counting of one's blessings, is like sitting on a tack; you don't usually spurt to your feet, shouting "Hallelujah" over the unpunctured state of the rest of your bodily terrain.

When Barney Singer announces that next on the agenda is my contract renewal, I leave the room, as he had earlier requested, in order to make it easier on nit-pickers. "Suppose we go at this in a businesslike

fashion," the president says, and I repeat along with
him: "Suppose we list now on one side of the blackboard Rabbi Abel's debits and, on the other side, his
credits." (Yes, I pause behind the door to listen,
partly out of nostalgia; this is how I came in—at my
interview, remember?)

Pete Schuster clears his throat. "Since we owe first
consideration to our beloved temple and what's best
for it, I'll start the ball rolling. Now according to all
the letters I received, scores of members oppose retaining Rabbi Abel because: one, he's too young and
immature; two, he has a negative attitude toward
everything; three, he draws more flies than people at
Sabbath services; four, his personality is abrasive and
ungodly; five, he couldn't inspire a sardine; six, his
reputation is terrible—"

An uproar breaks out inside. (Me, all I can think is:
Forgive him not, Father, for he knows damn well
what he's doing.) Barney Singer gavels it down.
"You'll all get your turn to speak, so please . . .
Courtesy is due Mr. Temple, don't you think? I'm sure
Pete doesn't enjoy saying these things. But we must
go about this chore scientifically."

Pete the Ripper thanks the president but says no
more. He doesn't have to; there are others to pick up
the knife.

Sam Warren: "What disturbs me about Rabbi Abel
is his taking a stand on everything under the sun,
even moon shots and their cost. He's only a rabbi,
after all, not the Secretary of State or Defense. There
are lots of things people agree on; why can't Rabbi
Abel ever find the consensus in something? He's much
too controversial."

Shirl Rosenman: "Exactly. I joined the temple for
peace of mind, but all Rabbi Abel gives me is constant

headaches. I resent his trying to make me feel guilty every time some Hottentot on the North Pole stubs his toe. He never gives us the spiritual uplift a rabbi should. Only guilt and *more* guilt."

Rick Adler: "It's true. Rabbi Abel is not the least bit inspiring. And have you seen that green jalopy he rides around in?"

Some people laugh, others boo. Barney Singer raps his gavel. "Please, *please*."

?????? ?????: ". . . . Proposing to make the temple self-sustaining through graduated dues! You can bet the rabbi wouldn't be so liberal with his own money if he had to work for a living."

???? ????: "Speaking of liberal, you know why Rabbi Abel's so liberal about Negroes and integration? Because he's a bachelor. Personally, I don't think we should be led in the race thing by somebody who has no daughters."

?????? ?????: "Hy has touched on something vital here. Rabbis must be married. Else how can he counsel people with sex—I mean, marital problems? Not that I even know anyone with sex—I mean, marital problems, but it's vital to have ourselves a rabbi who's experienced."

Cheryl Wohl: "Who would want to marry Rabbi Abel? He's so cold and unfriendly—no personality. It's no wonder he has to resort to prostitutes. Yes, I said prostitutes. From what I've heard from people whose neighbors told them—"

"Objection! Objection!" It's Charlie Hecht for the defense. "Mr. Chairman, you can't allow such slander from the floor. It's entirely unfair and prejudicial to my client—I mean, Rabbi Abel."

"Really, Charlie," Barney Singer says, "This isn't a court of law, just friends trying to do what's best for our temple. But okay, no more charges; from now on let's stick only to our opinions. Go ahead."

??? ????: "Well, I believe Cheryl. All the anonymous letters the board's been getting—about the rabbi running around with Negresses and other gentile girls, his orgies after adult education (I myself have seen the light burning in his office many times after midnight), why he doesn't date any more girls from the congregation, his illegitimate child—I'm not saying they're *all* true. But where there's that much smoke, you know. Didn't the rabbi propose introducing a sex course for teen-agers?"

Charlie Hecht: "Objection! Objection!"

"Sustained," Barney Singer cries. "Let's have no innuendoes, please. Anonymous letters are not scientific. Go ahead, Doug."

Doug Bettleheim: "This is no innuendo—because I was there—laying in a tremendous bed of pain at the hospital. And did my rabbi ever come to visit me? He did not. What did he care about those stones in my bladder, and how I was passing them? For all he cared, I could have choked to death."

???????? ????????: "And he has no sense of the sacred either, Rabbi Abel. You should see him training bar-mitzvah boys. I stopped off at the temple once for a Coke, and what do I see but the rabbi busting paper bags and blowing a horn in the bar-mitzvah boy's ear while he's chanting—imagine."

"How can you say that?" Ben Margolin shouts. "If you knew what Rabbi Abel did for my son, Sandy—"

"You want to say something to the rabbi's credit?" Barney Singer asks.

"You bet!" Ben Margolin replies. "My wife and I don't have the words to tell about the change that's come over Sandy since the rabbi—"

The president interrupts. "Well, that's fine, admirable—glad to hear it. But would you hold it till we get to the other side of the blackboard? Go ahead, please."

????? ???????: "About bar mitzvah—what right does Rabbi Abel have to hold our children here for ransom, blackmailing them into continuing till confirmation in order to get bar-mitzvahed? This is America, isn't it, the land of the free choice?"

Ralph LeVine: "Speaking of America, how dare our rabbi oppose our government's policy in Vietnam? I don't want a dove for my rabbi—*or* a chicken."

????? ?????: "You're nuts. Rabbi Abel is a hawkish apologist for American imperialism. Has he called for America's immediate withdrawal of our mercenaries in Vietnam? Well, has he?"

A tumult of outcries . . .

Barney Singer gavels them down, shouting himself hoarse. "Let's have no more talk about Vietnam. It's much too complex an issue; most people feel exactly the way I do about it—confused. Remember, we're here to vote on a rabbi, not foreign policy. Yes, Mr. Steingut?"

Steingut: "Speaking objectively—I belong to so many shuls it doesn't matter to me who your rabbi is—the word of mouth about Abel at all my Mountain Tiptop affairs is something terrible. He's giving this temple such a bad name. A regular Jewish Typhoid Mary is what he is."

Goldwyn: "Exactly what I've heard at my funeral home. People would rather not die than be buried by Rabbi Abel. That's the truth. Look what happened at Jerry Greenwood's mother's funeral."

Eve Greenwood: "I want everyone to know *I'm*

voting for Rabbi Abel! Because he's an extra-
ordinary—"

"Order in the court," Barney Singer exclaims. "Let's
calm down, take matters in turn, without rebuttals.
Otherwise we'll be here all night. Please—"

Eve Greenwood: "But all this slander—"

"You'll have your turn, Eve, very shortly. Be patient," the president says. "Okay, Ellie. And let's all be
pleasant now, shall we?"

Ellie Prinz: "Pleasant? About that man? I told him
to dissuade my only son from going off to spend a
year in Israel—who knows if he'll ever come back?
Instead, Rabbi Abel tries to convince me to give
my only son my blessings. Well, if Israel is so vital to
Jews, like our Jewish champion here keeps telling us,
why doesn't *he* settle there?"

????? ?????: "Some Jewish champion. What does he
do in his spare time? Trims Christmas trees. I'm sure
it was no dog but God Himself who pushed him off
that ladder—"

?????? ??????: "Even so, that doesn't excuse him for
his shenanigans at the Episcopal church. Getting up
in the pulpit and quoting their own Bible at everyone!
My Episcopalian friends were so insulted."

Curt Langer: "Barney, I think I can sum up what
everyone's been saying. Rabbi Abel is just no Irv Terman—that's all there is to it."

Let's see, that makes twenty out of 140 against me
—sure, I'm counting. Yet even if all the undecideds
vote me down, over eighty percent still favor me, so
there's nothing to worry about.

Maurine Levenson: "He has no temple spirit, Rabbi
Abel. He gave us absolutely no cooperation in our
expansion-fund drive—no personal letters, no pep
talks, not even a contribution. And he refused even to

deliver the invocation at the kitchen's cornerstone-laying ceremony."

Edythe Loring: "I never would have joined this temple if I'd known you had a rabbi here making it *so* Jewish. Extremism in the pursuit of Judaism, I distinctly believe, is a vice."

"Anybody else?" Barney Singer asks, whereupon I begin to wonder. Wonder, not worry. Jerry Greenwood, Bill Evans and Bernstein would swell the total to 24.5 "No" votes, but what of the five whom my picketing had alienated? None of the Evans backlashers had spoken up—no doubt they were ashamed to—and maybe there were *more* than five of them; had everyone told the sub-rosa committee the truth? Now I regret that in a try for an appearance of saintliness I had refrained from asking for my opponents' names—

"Okay, that does it for Rabbi Abel's debits," Barney Singer says. "Suppose we start now on his credits."

People *applaud!* I am immodest enough to feel pleased. Relieved too, if you must know; for a while this meeting was shaping up like the prelude to a disembowelment.

"Please, please, no demonstrations. This is not a political rally," the president says. "And let's be brief. We have so many other important items on tonight's agenda. Pete? You want to speak now *for* Rabbi Abel?"

Pete Schuster: "No, not for him. For brevity. I think we can dispense with further discussion. At this late date, nobody's decision will be affected in the slightest by comments. I therefore move for an immediate vote."

Shouts and catcalls.

"Ladies! Gentlemen! Everyone!" Barney Singer

pounds away with his gavel. "Let's settle this in the parliamentary way—by a vote. My own feeling is that eliminating anything at this point would be a godsend; it's already almost midnight. Okay now, who thinks they need to hear more about Rabbi Abel before making up their minds? Raise your hands . . . Okay, those who don't need testimonials . . . Well, I guess Pete was right. Let's go ahead with the vote on retaining Rabbi Abel . . ."

While the secret ballot is tallied, I think up a new acceptance speech—on the order of "With malice toward eighteen percent . . ."—until Barney Singer announces the results. Only 30.5 voted against me! That means I won almost eighty percent of the vote, or about what the sub-rosa committee had— What's this now? Only 83.5 voted for me?

What *happened?* Some twenty-five families were absent from the meeting. I knew that, but—

"Recount! Mistake!" Dore Redmont shouts. "You didn't include the seventeen proxy votes!"

"Of course not," Pete Schuster says, then reads from the temple constitution an article that disallows proxies in rabbinical elections.

"But Sam Warren assured us," Ben Margolin cries, "proxies are valid."

"We're responsible only for what the constitution says, not Sam," Mr. Temple states and rereads the article, adding, "I guess your sub-rosa committee didn't think of everything, did they?"

Pandemonium!

The loudest yeller is Charlie Hecht: ". . . and moreover, I challenge the vote of Steingut's partner at Mountain Tiptop, Romano. How can he vote on our rabbi when he's a Catholic and belongs to Saint Mary's?"

Sam Warren shouts back, "I'll have you know Romano was our first member this year to pay his dues."

As Barney Singer calls for a discussion the door bursts open, and the sub-rosa committee skitters about me like scalded cats. Dr. Lipton runs into my office to phone the absentee members, Dore Redmont dashes into the phone booth to call his proxies. Both swiftly emerge, however; somebody has misplaced the key to the lock on the office phone, and the coin slots in the pay phone are full of chewing gum.

So the two of them, plus Eve Greenwood, Charlie Hecht, the Margolins and a dozen others, race off to make calls, but their cars conk out on the way because, according to what we learn later from mechanics who tow them away, just that night some kid had poured sugar into the gas tanks, and though some do get to phones, by then Romano's vote has been invalidated and another vote taken (in which Barney Singer again doesn't participate, because, he explains, his role is like that of the Vice-President in the United States Senate, who votes only to break ties) by then—

Now is the time to worry. Yet when I start, already it's too late. Yes, that's right; my fair laity had fired me.

ℵ

——*Hello?*
——Oh. Hello, Mrs. Sitomer. This is Gideon Abel.
——*I thought you were dead.*
——No, just—well, busy. How are you?
——*So you really were a rabbi, after all.*
——Yes. May I speak to Gina?
——*Now I believe it because I hear you got fired.*

——Is Gina home?

——*Why were you fired?*

——Mrs. Sitomer—

——*And why did you stand up Gina last month? Personally, I'm glad you did, but was that nice?*

——I had to get away—suddenly. But I sent Gina a telegram—

——*She bought a new dress yet.*

——There were reasons, Mrs. Sitomer—

——*What reasons?*

——I'll explain to Gina.

——*I got a right to know. Who's got a better right? But you don't have to tell me because I'm not letting my daughter run around with no defrocked rabbi anyway.*

——Rabbis don't get defrocked. I'm still a rabbi.

——*Where?*

——Where what?

——*Where are you still a rabbi?*

——Well, I don't have a congregation, if that's what you mean.

——*What do you have?*

——All rabbis don't have congregations. Some write, some teach, some work for charities or other worthwhile organizations—

——*So what do you do?*

——I—well—I'm in business.

——*Business? What kind of business?*

——Well, it's my father's business.

——*And what business is that?*

——What difference does it make?

——*I'm curious what kind of business defrocked rabbis go into.*

——I'm not defrocked. I was just—

——*Yes?*

——Unsuited. That's it: I was unsuited.

——*If your business was a legitimate business, you'd have told me by now.*

——Goodbye, Mrs. Sitomer. I'll write Gina.

——*You don't have to go to all that trouble. I see the mail first.*

——Why are you so prejudiced against me!

——*A rabbi was bad enough, but a rabbi drop-out . . . Anyway, my Eugenela is going with somebody now, and I don't want you should spoil anything. He's a labor-union lawyer, and not disbarred.*

⌇

SUMMER

T HERE's more to brassieres than meets the eye;
the average woman, all she's interested in is
putting one on, and the average man cares only for
tearing one off; people just don't appreciate what
goes *into* brassieres. No, these witticisms aren't mine;
they belong to Treasure Chest's sales manager, who's
teaching me one phase of the business while em-
ploying much of temple vocabulary: institution, service, long-range growth, promotion, plant expansion,
inspiration, make an impression. The biggest switch
here is the four-letter-word explosion, from Love and
Laws to: hold, mold, slim, skim, pare, bare, push,
tush, et cetera. Yes, I left Hillendale the morning
after the annual meeting, because I guessed, after
being fired, the congregation didn't want me.

Good old Barney Singer stayed in character to the end—out of focus as the president of a house of God and in the saddle as an accountant. When I called to tell him where to pick up my keys and two hundred dollars some members had given me for the Cadillac raffle, he said, "But if you leave before August first, we'll have to prorate your month's vacation and deduct five days' salary."

The day after my return home, Dad gave me—without one I-told-you-so, for which I blessed him—a business card reading: "Gideon Abel, Vice-President, Treasure Chest." I accepted it despite the salary's being almost four times my temple honorarium, or enough to endow any kitchen. Not to be outdone, my mother put a catalogue from Columbia University's medical school under my pillow for me to sleep on, along with a feature article from the *New York Times* about Joseph Coleman, the president of Maidenform Bras, who, it turns out, is also a *doctor*.

"Wouldn't you consider it a sign," Mom asked me, "that Maimonides, a rabbi, and Coleman, who's Maidenform, both got medical degrees?"

Engaging in ladies' undergarments full-time, I felt at first like a paid fetishist. To overcome my manly embarrassment, I forced myself to spend a week going from department store to department store, stepping up to counters and asking strange saleswomen for an assortment of brassieres, not an easy thing to do when half of them reminded me of my mother and the other half of old girl friends, and all of them wondering aloud over my purchasing, then returning so many bras of diverse sizes. (One lady wanted to know if my memory was that bad, another asked if my wife was on a diet or out of town, a third inquired just how much I dated, a fourth re-

ported me to the store detective.) But after a week
of wallowing in brassieres, I could finally look upon
them dispassionately, as if they were nothing more
than pairs of skullcaps sewn together.

That accomplished, there were no further adjust-
ments to make. A year at the temple had accustomed
me to business meetings, and Treasure Chest's were
briefer, always to the point, exclusively about the
product, and best of all, nobody felt impelled to
testify what brassieres and breasts meant to him personally and how grateful he was for the honor of
bringing them together for the greater glory of mankind. Add to that a forty-hour week, a four-room
apartment with three terraces and a view of six
bridges, Fifth Avenue's New York Public Library's
excellent Jewish Room close by, plenty of time for
myself, no bitching by customers, no factions in the
office, no gripes from executives that any time spent
on my studies was taken out of their mouths—and
who could ask for anything more?

Yesterday, for example, my father told me what my
congregation voted down. "Gideon," he said, "I'm
proud of you."

"What for?"

"That name of yours for our new false-bottomed
girdle and your slogan—they're the talk of the industry. The results of the Chicago test run just came
in. We got eight percent of the market. The Philadelphia test with a different name and slogan never did
better than four percent. So it must be you who made
all the difference. This means already you've earned
your entire year's salary."

I was incredulous. "With just seven words?"

"You of all people, Gideon, should appreciate the
power of the word. 'Fanny Hills'! That doctorate of

yours in English finally paid off. And that slogan—'There's *bold* in them thar Fanny Hills'—brilliant!"

My rabbinical training made me confess, "Actually, Dad, I think both the name and the slogan are a little on the vulgar side. No, a lot."

"You don't like it?" Dad was taken aback. "Why suggest it then?"

"Well, I was joking at the time. How should I know your sales manager would take it seriously?"

"Joking?" Dad's face turned as pink as Pete Schuster's tongue. "Gideon, one thing you got to understand: business is serious business. Yet creative too, just like art or literature. Only difference is, instead of with words and pictures, we create with dollars and cents and underwear, utilizing the same imagination, style, innovation. It's creative to manufacture a false derrière, it's creative to promote it with a good name and a catchy slogan, it's creative to capture eight percent of the market at the very start. You see that, Gideon?"

I sighed. "Frankly, no."

Dad smiled indulgently. "Well, you're young yet. You'll learn."

That made me feel right at temple. Congregants used to tell me that all the time, and it will probably end up carved on my tombstone:

Here lies
GIDEON ABEL
He'll learn

Otherwise, my job has only one annoyance: people at work are constantly asking about my switch from the rabbinate to Treasure Chest, as if I were Norman Vincent Peale taking a vow of poverty. I could answer them all with "Well, I'm still in the uplift busi-

ness, aren't I?"—but that's too flip. So I try for dignity-
cum-pathos by presenting nosey bodies with a copy of
a recent resolution of the Central Conference of
American Rabbis:

> We are deeply disturbed by the fact that an in-
> creasing number of rabbis have suffered improper
> and unjust dismissal from their pulpits. These all too
> frequent actions reflect a growing spirit of aliena-
> tion between the laity and the rabbinate, which
> eventuates in great personal tragedy to rabbis, se-
> rious injury to the morals of the community, and
> harm to the growth of the movement.
>
> We therefore recommend that a special com-
> mittee be appointed to study and to report in de-
> tail to the next convention on the cause of this
> situation and to recommend appropriate action.

Coincidentally, the *New York Times* has broken
out into a rash of articles—one even made the front
page—about dozens of Christian clergymen being
fired by their churches. Happily, the Hillendale Temple's interfaith-lovers had kept in smart ecumenical
step.

8

——*Gideon!*
——Hello, Gina.
——*What are you doing here at the hospital?*
——Your mother has you guarded tighter than
   Rapunzel. She won't let me write you or phone.
   I waited outside your apartment house half of
   August—
——*But I was away in Europe.*

——Mrs. Goldstein with the ileitis finally told me.

——*That's too bad. I mean, that she told you.*

——Gina, I'm sorry about canceling our date on such short notice.

——*It wasn't the canceling that bothered me or even the new dress I bought; it was the way you did it. In a telegram—so cryptic it sounded like the FBI was after you. Why couldn't you have seen me, called me? I thought there was something between us, Gideon.*

——There was—is.

——*Is there? Then why didn't you come to me?*

——I was—well, you see—

——*I know what happened, Gideon. I called the temple, and whoever it was who answered the phone told me. But why didn't you tell me?*

——All year long people have been coming to me for help, comfort—

——*And you were too proud to come to me.*

——Proud? Gina, I was ashamed. I couldn't talk about it then.

——*Gideon—*

——And I don't want to talk about it now. I want to forget the whole thing—and concentrate on us.

——*Us?*

——You know what I mean, Gina.

——*I used to. Gideon, my father often said a good marriage is when a man can come home and say to his wife, "They beat me today," and she says, "It's all right," and then it is all right. Gideon, when a woman doesn't feel needed—*

——Yes, I know, Gina. I know now all about needed; Hillendale gave me a diploma in it. It was wrong of me to withdraw—

——*Where are you now?*

——Where?

——*Your new congregation.*

——Congregation? Well, I don't have one. All rabbis don't have congregations. Some teach, some write, some work for organizations——

——*Where are you teaching?*

——I don't. Well, Sunday School.

——*What do you do the other six days of the week?*

——Your mother didn't tell you? I told her when I phoned——

——*No. Mama doesn't even speak against you any more, not since she fell in love with this labor lawyer I've been dating.*

——Oh? Who is he?

——*Somebody who says my eyes remind him of the color of the lines on a legal-size yellow pad. The horizontal lines, I presume.*

——Is that why you cut your hair? He likes it short? I like it long.

——*Short hair is cooler in the summer.*

——How often have you been seeing him?

——*When did you disappear?*

——That many weeks?

——*Oh, let's not play games, Gideon. Mama loves my labor lawyer; I don't. Tell me about you. What are you doing now?*

——Well——

——*Why so hesitant?*

——I've gone into my father's business.

——*Business? You? And isn't you father in——*

——Gina——

——*——ladies' underwear? Oh, wait till Mama finds out you're a boss now!*

——Gina, there's a rabbinical-association resolution I want you to——

——*What?*

——Skip it.

——*Gideon?*

——Yes?

——*Are you happy?*

——I'm successful. I'm a vice-president already, with only one boss, and he's on *my* side. What's more—

——*I seem to recall someone telling me that the great use of a life is to spend it for something which outlasts it, that what man is he ultimately becomes through the cause he's made his own.*

——You didn't give me a chance to finish, Gina. I was saying that last month I read more than I did the whole year at Hillendale; I can study, now that I no longer lead a congregation. I work on different causes, teach Sunday School and—

——*Gideon, I know brassieres will outlast us all, but are they what you want to* become?

——That's not fair.

——*Fair? Is it fair what you did to me? Stuffing me with all your religious books, turning me into My Jewish Lady. You know why I don't go for that labor lawyer now, when I liked him well enough four months ago? Because since meeting you I can't approve of somebody who works for this union that's as rapacious as any of Mama's old-time bosses. And then this doctor I was seeing, when I saw his feeling for medicine was a mechanic's—talking about organs and cases and never persons—Gideon, you've spoiled me for everyone else.*

——Great! Gina, you don't want anyone else now. I'm here.

——*You're here, Gideon, but is it you? In bras-*

*sieres? Know something? I think you've spoiled
me also for you ...*

א

"Are you free for lunch today?"

It was Dean Tchernichovsky on the phone, and before I could stop myself I had told the truth. "Yes."

I met the dean at his office—he had been in Israel
most of the summer—and we walked downstairs to
the cafeteria, a long way to fidget. After the dean
thanked me for Dad's sending his wife three dozen
brassieres of the wrong size and I promised to ex-
change them, I resorted to chattering about the rumor
that *Time* magazine had chosen God its Man of the
Year, despite His reputed death.

"It's significant," the dean commented, "that belief
in God is nowhere listed as one of the Bible's six
hundred thirteen commandments; actions, our tradition teaches, prove one's belief. When man appears
before the Throne of Judgment, the ancient rabbis
said, the first question asked of him is not 'Do you
believe in God?' or 'Did you pray to Him and perform
ritual commandments?' but 'Did you deal honorably
and faithfully with your fellow man?' "

We went through the cafeteria line, then seated
ourselves at a table, as I wondered how to explain
myself. But before I could begin, the dean said, "The
placement commission told me you were taking a
sabbatical. Usually sabbaticals come every seventh
year, but since everything else is so speeded up in
this modern world, why not sabbaticals too?" I relaxed, and the dean, whipping his fingers through
his tousled white hair, continued throughout lunch to
speak about God and not me, thank Him.

"Perhaps during the childhood of the human race, people could not face the truth about God's imperfection. But today they must be told: God is now only *growing* toward omnipotence, just as people have only just *begun* to be religious. Therefore, when God's justice and love are in eclipse and, impotent, He can do nothing but weep, it is up to us to take over for Him, offering the Lord our faith and strength in return for His continuing light and support . . .

"All this is the merest guesswork, of course, for faith has never been more than a working hypothesis. Yet the believer stakes his entire life on this glorious hunch about God—that He indeed lives and needs us —and what is heroism but acting as *if* something were true in order to *make* it true!"

א

—— . . . *Gideon will be here later. He always spends Shabbas with us . . . Oh . . . Who is she? . . . no, I'm not interested in what her father's worth . . . But who is she? . . . Well, I can't promise. Give me her name and number . . . All right . . . Goodbye.*

——Hi, Mom.

——*Gideon. I didn't hear you come in.*

——Who was that? On the phone.

——*Just some mah-jongg player.*

——You must have an awfully good memory.

——*Why?*

——You didn't write down that girl's number. I never thought I'd live to see the day my own mother would stop force-feeding me prospective daughters-in-law.

——*To tell the truth, Gideon, I'd just as soon you*

didn't date right now. It's liable to end up badly.

——What do you mean, badly?

——*Marriage. Oh, I want you to get married, of course, but not while you're with Treasure Chest. The daughter of Fetching Stretchpants who'd marry a brassiere vice-president might not make such a good wife for—say, a medical student.*

——You never give up.

——*Look, even if you never practice, the education is a good thing. What can it hurt, a medical education? The worst thing is, you'll have six degrees instead of five. Gideon, if you ask me, it's a pity.*

——I'm not asking you. What's a pity?

——*A person like you, who works so lovingly with people, burying himself in bras—its.*

——That's the trouble, Mom. I can't work with people. I don't get along with even seventy-five percent of them.

——*Gideon, I remember your weekly visits to Chronic Diseases. The patients still talk about you, they loved you so.*

——That was different; nobody paid me to visit Chronic Diseases. Dad was right: the only good rabbi is a self-employed rabbi—the way it used to be centuries ago, when rabbis supported themselves at trades. But suppose we change the subject for a change. Who was the woman who called? Maybe I'll try her stretch-pants girl.

——*I thought you were going with that Gina.*

——No more.

——*What happened?*

——Nothing.

——*Nothing?*

——Everybody in the world knows what I should

do! Like you love medicine, Gina wants to see me crucified on still another congregation.

——*Well, anything is better than its. Take your father and me. The money we don't need, the vacations he doesn't take, the fancy style I don't care to live in. All I can say for Treasure Chest is, it keeps your father busy; it's like his being president of a temple. But you, Gideon, with your feeling for* people—

——For crying out loud!

——*I'll say one thing more, and that'll be the end of it, Gideon, for now. Did you ever look at medicine this way? A doctor, when his patients disagree with him, they leave.*

א

Since the dean never questioned me about leaving the congregational rabbinate, when we met for lunch the third time I told him of my Hillendale experience, relating it dispassionately, as if it were another man of God altogether who had got bushwhacked, because I didn't want pity, no pity at all, just a comforting word maybe, like "Those bastards."

Dr. Tchernichovsky listened attentively, and when I had finished he commented, "Well, you know what the great nineteenth-century scholar Malbim said when people asked why he went from pulpit to pulpit: 'Tell the truth and see the world.'" He added, "But the Midrash reminds us, Abel, that oil is improved only by beating."

"My story doesn't disturb you?"

The dean sighed. "Only because it isn't new. It's a serious problem today in all houses of worship— minister-congregation relations. And it's not always

the congregation's fault. Last week, for example, when
Fleisher died in Philadelphia, Axelrob left his shul to
replace him—at twice the salary of his Connecticut
synagogue—and here it's September, and all available
rabbis were hired by last June."

"Good. Now a temple will know how it feels to be
fired. You know what kills me, Dean? All those people
who voted me down—not one of them was even religious."

"What about those who voted for you?"

"Well, most of them weren't religious either. But
who is nowadays? You know what houses of worship
are today: parent-teachers associations of the Sunday
School."

"That's the way it is, Abel: man's religion is of his
life a thing apart; 'tis a clergyman's whole existence.
Do you think, however, theatergoers care passionately
for the drama? Still, there is this saving grace: in a
house of God, congregants are there for the minister
to get at."

"You mean, before they get him?"

"Really, Abel, when you think about it, it's amazing
a rabbi accomplishes as much as he does. Remember,
a rabbi doesn't mediate between man and God, nor
can he promise anyone heaven or threaten him with
hell. His authority derives from his personal virtues,
which are taught only through example. Yet a teacher
influences all eternity, I believe that; he never knows
where his teaching will end. Just because a rabbi
deals in nothing so tangible as diseases cured, law
cases won, sales made—"

"Dean, you know how congregants think? The rabbi
is hired to be religious—their vicarious Jew—and that
lets them off the hook."

"You think you had a worse time of it than our

first rabbi? Moses, you recall, started out so disgusted with his people he smashed the Tablets of the Law. Yet he ended up blessing them before his death."

"Yes, but nobody voted to fire Moses because his ass was sixteen years old and green. Dean, you want to know my greatest success at the temple? I directed a show there, *My Fair Sadie*, which netted four thousand dollars, and everybody called me a champion rabbi. For directing a play. I used to do the same thing in college every month, and all they called me there was a drama major."

"Is it total victory you were after, Abel? In one year?"

"What?"

"Abel, in our vocation, success is measured more by dedication than achievement. There is such a thing as the *success* of failure. God Himself gains strength from our failures, I devoutly believe, so long as they are undertaken for His sake. So long as man struggles, so long as God struggles, so long as man and God both grow through their shared struggling—well, that's as much as we can hope for in this world. Yet that should be enough to see us through to the next battle, and beyond."

"Dean, are you telling me I was a bad rabbi?"

"Not at all. In my desk are over one hundred letters from your congregants, which came to the seminary— apparently you left no forwarding address—and I don't imagine all of them wrote to express delight with your departure. There's also a scroll petitioning your return, which, according to a notation, every child signed, including one who promised not to write on any more walls, whatever that means. No, Abel, you weren't a bad rabbi. You were an illusioned rabbi—*that's* bad. Because illusions go before despair, and despair is the cardinal sin; hope, you see, half creates its own objectives. But do you know what's worse even than despair?"

I was afraid to ask.

"Self-pity is worse, Abel. Self-pity is a nice place to visit; it's like a warm, wet diaper. But who would want to live there? After a while it begins to stink."

Always a word of praise before that damned crusher.

The dean reached out and touched my hand. "By no means is that my last word to you, Abel. This is, the Talmud's: 'If a rabbi is popular, it is not because the people love him, but rather because he does not reprove them.' Doris Day is popular, also well-mannered, soft-spoken, innocuous, relentlessly cheerful. But I would never want Doris Day for my rabbi. Abel, I prefer *you*." His hand gripped mine. "Have you forgotten? I am seventy-seven years old now, and you are my rainbow."

א

——That rabbi of yours ought to be shot!

——*Gideon!*

——Today's Rosh Hashanah sermon of his, Mom— it was immoral.

——*What was the matter with it?*

——Didn't you hear him, Dad? Talking about the importance of law, and then, in passing, taking a slap at Negroes for rioting, without explaining any of the underlying causes.

——*When did he do that, Gideon?*

——*While you were dozing, Sol.*

——*The new air-conditioning system in the temple —it's wonderful, Lena.*

——That sermon was a disgrace.

——*Then I'm glad I was dozing. If it was such a lousy sermon*—

——It wasn't lousy. It was harmful, vicious—

——*Gideon, I've never heard you talk like this. I wish you'd stop*—

——Mom, that rabbi was distorting Judaism. Law is important, certainly it is, but he should have been teaching congregants *Pirke Avos:* "The sword comes into the world because of justice being delayed, because of justice being perverted and because of those who render wrong decisions." That's what he should have preached, your miserable rabbi.

——*Gideon, it's time you got married.*

——My God, you too, Dad?

——*I notice it's always the bachelors who are such firebrands. If you were a family man with a wife and children, you wouldn't constantly be running a temperature about everything—and you'd probably accomplish more good too.*

——My father has become a Marxist of love, an erotic determinist!

——*Who? What?*

——It's because of those brassieres of yours.

——*Ours, Gideon. Treasure Chest is ours now. Oh, yes, speaking of ours—the shul has asked me to read the Book of Jonah at services on Yom Kippur. Would you like to read instead of me?*

——Oh? Usually the board gives the Jonah reading to its president, the shul's greatest scholar, if it has one, or the congregation's biggest giver. Which one are you, Dad?

——*Well, I contribute some.*

——But so much? Why? After all your own criticism of the temple's shortcomings—

——*Well, when somebody invents something better than the synagogue, I'll give to that instead. Gideon, what about it? Want to read in my place?*

——I'd love to. Jonah is a favorite of mine; too bad most people think it was written by Walt Disney. But that sermon today. If a doctor operated the way your rabbi preached, the congregation could sue him for malpractice, and collect.

——*No question about it, Gideon. You'd be far superior.*

——You mean, up there in the pulpit, Mom?

——*As a surgeon.*

——You're pushing again.

——*Yes, but did you notice, Gideon? You've stopped overreacting.*

——*Now, Lena, you cut that out. Leave my vice-president alone!*

——For crying out loud, will you both stop!

——*We're sorry, Gideon. You know what we want for you. Only one thing. We want our only son to be happy, that's all. If you're happy we're happy. What else do parents live for?*

§

She was standing at the door, awaiting my return from the office, as I now constantly fantasied, for my apartment was too big to live in all by myself, and my new color television set made me lonelier still, its commercials insinuating that I was a sex-for-nothing, while the programs reminded me that I didn't have anyone even to beat up . . .

"*Gideon—*"

No fantasy this time! It was Gina, forlorn in her clipped hair, inside the lobby of my apartment house. Braiding her fingers together, she stammered, "I came to ask forgiveness before Yom Kippur—isn't that required?—for my sin."

"Sin?"

"Losing faith in you . . . Forgive me." She began to cry. "Oh, Gideon, I've been so unhappy—"

I pulled her close, my soft benediction. "Me, I've felt like a dybbuk with nobody to inhabit."

"—and even if you do stay with Treasure Chest, knowing you, I'm sure you'll be manufacturing the most . . . *humane* bra in the world."

Intoning her name like an invocation, I squeezed her to me.

"My contact lens, it's in your ear—"

"—Gina Gina Gina Gina—"

"Oh, yesyesyesyes!"

"You'll marry me?" I kissed her.

She pulled away and gulped for air. "Gideon," she gasped, "you certainly don't *kiss* like a rabbi . . ."

8

. . . And God saw the works of the people of Nineveh, that they turned from their evil way; and God repented of the evil which He said He would do unto them; and He did it not. But it displeased Jonah exceedingly, and he was angry.

And he prayed unto the Lord, and said: "I pray Thee, O Lord, was not this my saying, when I was yet in mine own country? Therefore I fled beforehand unto Tarshish; for I knew that Thou art a gracious God, and compassionate, long-suffering, and abundant in mercy, and repentest Thee of the evil. Therefore now, O Lord, take, I beseech Thee, my life from me; for it is better for me to die than to live."

And the Lord said, "Art thou greatly angry?"

Then Jonah went out of Nineveh, and sat on the east side of the city, and there made him a booth, and sat under it in the shadow, till he might see what would become of the city. And the Lord God prepared a gourd, and made it to come up over Jonah, that it might be a shadow over his head, to deliver him from his evil. So Jonah was exceedingly glad because of the gourd.

But God prepared a worm when the morning rose the next day, and it smote the gourd, that it withered. And it came to pass, when the sun arose, that God prepared a vehement east wind; and the sun beat upon the head of Jonah, that he fainted, and requested for himself that he might die, and said: "It is better for me to die than to live."

And God said to Jonah, "Art thou greatly angry for the gourd?"

And he said: "I am greatly angry, even unto death."

And the Lord said, "Thou hast had pity on the gourd, for which thou hast not labored, neither madest it grow, which came up in a night, and perished in a night; and should I not have pity on Nineveh, that great city, wherein are more than sixscore thousand persons that cannot discern between their right hand and their left hand . . .?"

ח

——Dr. Tchernichovsky? This is Gideon Abel. Am I interrupting your supper?

——*No, no. On Yom Kippur night I wolf everything down. How was your fast?*

——Fine, fine. Dean?

——*Yes?*

——I read Jonah in shul today—

——*Oh? And "Art thou greatly angry"—still?*

——That's why I'm calling. About that congregation in Connecticut, the one whose rabbi left them in the lurch—how hard up are they? I mean, is the congregation desperate for a rabbi?

——*Desperate enough. There are no rabbis to be had at this late date.*

——So desperate they'd accept certain conditions in order to get a rabbi?

——*What kind of conditions?*

——Oh, I don't mean a big salary—

——*That condition I feel certain they'll accept.*

——Conditions like: required attendance at adult education, no fund-raising, a cause for every congregant, seventy-five percent of the cost of each bar mitzvah and wedding reception and funeral must be donated to charity, bar mitzvah at eighteen, ethics in business, the rabbi not be required to attend every cat-hanging—things like that, Dean.

——*Abel, Abel. I'm beginning to wonder if you're not too idealistic for the rabbinate. You left out the most important condition of all.*

——What's that?

——*The first condition to lay down is that only fifty-five percent of the voters need approve the rabbi's contract. Eisenhower was elected to the Presidency of the United States by fifty-seven percent, and that was considered a landslide.*

Anyway, ask for fifty-five percent—and settle for sixty-five percent.

——Oh. I see what you mean. Maybe I ought to follow Maimonides' example and become a doctor, after all; doctors don't have to play the percentages.

——*Medicine is one of the noblest of professions, that's true.*

——Dean? What do you advise me to do?

——*What do you think you should do, Abel?*

——Well—

——*Bearing in mind that a rabbi's obligation is to learn, and to teach, so as to bring about what he affirms—*

——I could take some med courses, I suppose, on the side—

——*Nu, Rabbi? What shall I tell the placement commission tomorrow about that Connecticut temple? "Whom shall I send, and who shall go for Me?"*

——Okay, Dean—for the sake of heaven. "Here am I; send me."

א